with lots of love

W. Gail Langley

DIVINE

INTERVENTION

by

W. Gail Langley

PublishAmerica
Baltimore

Hardcover 978-1-4489-3044-9
Softcover 978-1-4489-4217-6
PUBLISHED BY PUBLISHAMERICA, LLLP
www.publishamerica.com
Baltimore

Printed in the United States of America

CHAPTER 1

Jenna's words of agony pierced the air. "What did I do to deserve this? Why are you putting me through this torture?"

Debbie stepped into the house at that moment and heard her mother's words of pain. She grabbed a vase and ran toward the bedroom door. The carpet muffled her footsteps. Just as she reached for the knob Jenna cried out again, "Please help me, God, I can't carry this burden alone."

Debbie released the doorknob. Her mother was praying, not trying to stop an intruder or rapist. She went into her bedroom and held to the tall bedpost. Looking at the ceiling, she whispered, "God, please do help Mom. She's the best mother in the world. She didn't deserve to have a rotten husband. Help me to bring joy back into her life."

Jenna Wilson seldom cried. She rarely let anything get her down, because her husband had taken care of everything. He paid the bills and kept track of her appointments. Jenna realized too late that she should have taken more control of her life. By now she should have known how to do all the things she let her husband do for her.

After Stuart's death, Jenna unsuccessfully tried to keep track of appointments. She failed to get to most meetings on time, and always had to make a mad dash to the post office with envelopes stuffed with payments. Stuart managed the important matters like making sure there was enough money to pay insurance bills or have food on the table. Now it was her chore to handle such matters and she was doing a bad job of it.

A couple months after Stuart's funeral Jenna got so many calls not of sympathy but from businesses wanting to know when she would pay her bills that she quit answering the phone. She just covered her ears until the answer machine clicked on and took the messages. "I can't stand to tell anyone else that I'll look into the matter and get back to them," she told Debbie. "I have no idea why the bank drafts aren't covering the bills."

"Mother, I'm afraid it's time you went to the bank and found out. I know you don't want to face it, but maybe Daddy had something to do with the payments. Apparently those women at the cemetery were right when they said he wasn't the nice, caring man he wanted everyone to believe him to be."

Jenna gave Debbie a hard look and said through tight lips, "Gossipers don't know everything. They often make mistakes and hurt people by their nasty remarks." The more she talked the higher her voice rose. "Why did they say that Stuart's girlfriend was in the crowd? Who were they talking about?"

Debbie shook her and said softly, "I don't know."

But they soon found out.

When Jenna realized that she could not afford the upkeep on their big, beautiful home she sold it and bought a smaller three-bedroom house. Debbie complained about living close to town. "The noise keeps me awake. I can't stand all that traffic. I believe a hundred cars zoomed by every hour. Horns of every description honked about as often. And those tree limbs outside my window made me jump out of my skin when they brushed against the house."

Jenna sighed heavily and said, "I'm sorry that we had to move from the country club where it was peaceful day and night, but what else could I do?"

Debbie picked up her gym bag and headed toward the door

mumbling as she went, "I just wish your heart wasn't broken. I hate to hear you crying at night. Your pain and grief are mine."

Their problems rose mountain high when Stuart died. He had robbed them of their heritage. There was not enough money to cover household expenses, college fees, or even a new coat. Jenna did not know she was almost penniless until she went to the bank to see why several checks were returned due to inadequate funds.

The meeting that she and Debbie had with a lawyer made her problems more pronounced with his news, "The only money going into your checking account now is interest on the stock from your father's herb business and the money you deposit from craft sales and speaking engagements. Stuart spent money like there was no tomorrow."

Jenna popped up from the chair and paced the room. "He didn't have many tomorrows, but hopefully Debbie and I still do. Unfortunately because of big time spender the rest of our lives will be faced with very little money. Our future looks more depressing by the minute."

The freckles on Debbie's face stood out more than usual. With a fierce look she said, "He got what he deserved. If he hadn't died on his own, if he were alive now I'd kill him myself."

"Debbie!" Jenna exclaimed. "I can't believe you would talk about killing anyone, not even your father."

Debbie gave a look of remorse. To the lawyer she said, "Forgive me. But I'm so mad."

He patted her shoulder. "I understand. I'll leave now. If either of you need me, just call."

After their house was sold, it took a lot of shuffling around to make room for the furniture in their smaller home. Once she and Debbie settled in, both of them began looking for work. Jenna did not want to go back to teaching. She was afraid she would not be able to hold her emotions in check. She and Stuart had not taught at the same college but had attended various meetings at both institutions. They knew many of the teachers and staff members at Montreat College and UNC Asheville.

"I can't make myself face the office staff and teachers at Montreat," she told Debbie, "but I've got to work."

At each business where Jenna filled out an application, the personnel managers refused her employment because she was overqualified for their vacant positions. When she complained to her daughter, Debbie said, "Perhaps one of them later will decide to hire you, if not, try a temporary service. The income won't be what you're used to, but some money is better than nothing. And when the job ends, if you're any good they'll place you somewhere else."

"At this stage, beggars can't be choosy," Jenna responded.

The first job placement was ideal for her. She looked forward to going to work every day at the doctor's office. As a receptionist she met lots of people. Fortunately for Jenna, none of the patients were close friends of hers. Several of the women were mere acquaintances, and their words of sympathy did not threaten her emotions. She managed to get through each conversation without breaking down.

Debbie also got a job as a gymnastic instructor. Added together, their salaries were still not enough to live comfortably. Jenna had to come up with more income. While looking at some paintings, trying to decide where to hang them an idea came to her.

"I don't have room to keep everything I paint," she told Debbie, "I think I'll try to sell some of them."

"That's an idea," Debbie answered thoughtfully, "but where?"

"I'm going to let my fingers do the walking through the yellow pages. I guess I'll approach some galleries and art supply stores. Perhaps I can hang a painting in some of the businesses."

Debbie looked excited. "I'll also ask at the recreation center about possible locations."

The next day, Jenna loaded her van with paintings. Some of them were done years earlier.

"They are not my best," she told Debbie, "but I'm hoping they'll bring in a few dollars."

At an art store in a strip mall, the owner did agree to display one painting and then told Jenna about a consignment shop. "Most any item that you could want is found there, including antiques and paintings."

"It can't hurt to check it out," Jenna responded. She walked down the street a couple of blocks and then stopped outside a consignment shop. For several minutes she stood and observed the display in the window. She thought, *my paintings are that good.* With a determined look she shuffled the paintings under her arm and pushed open the door.

The owner introduced herself and then took a look at Jenna's paintings. Mary Wiggins smiled and said, "I love your work. I won't have any trouble selling it. But have you ever painted pictures or designs on anything else?"

"Like what?" Jenna asked.

Mrs. Wiggins showed her several displays of china and picture frames that some local artists had decorated with their specialty pictures. "People paint nearly everything from pottery to wood to metal. If you decide to try something different, bring it in."

Jenna rushed home. She was eager to see what objects she could paint. Within a short time she found several old picture frames in a storage box. She completed one frame and then started working on a jewelry box made from oak wood. Every once in a while her face broke into a smile as she examined the lid she was covering with magnolia flowers.

After looking at the clock ten times, Jenna wondered what was keeping Debbie. When she finally heard the front door open, Jenna called out to her. "Debbie, come see what I've been working on. Tell me what you think."

Debbie admired the new look given to the jewelry box and picture frame. "I like the box, but I love this," she said picking up the rectangular frame.

"Be careful," Jenna said. "The paint's not dry."

Debbie eyed the entire piece of work, admiring the cluster of pink roses in one corner and the buds that trailed across the top and down one side. "I want this."

"Sorry, love. I'm taking it to market with everything else I can find to paint." Jenna picked up a metal tray and applied a coat of base paint. She told Debbie about her visit to the consignment shop. "The owner advised me to paint as many items as I could. What I don't leave there, she suggested that I should then set up a table at Asheville's Spring Fling. Do you think my work would sell at a place like that?"

"Is it the same festival where I performed with the school gymnastics team years ago?"

"That's it, the one that's held up-town on Montford Street."

"I bet you'd do great there!" Debbie said, looking enthusiastic. "Lots more people attend it now. Rich people from Florida who have come to the area for the snow are preparing for their trip back home. They come here to ski but they also buy local crafts to show their friends what they missed by not going north for the winter. They'll probably check out the festival for some crafts."

Jenna gave Debbie a questionable look mixed with a grin and asked, "Where did you get that information?"

"At work. When I stand off to the side of the gym floor, watching my students practice handsprings and back flips, I often hear the mothers talk. Just the other day their main conversation covered the festival. Most of them attend it every year. A couple of them even set up tables and sell their crafts."

"What do they have?"

"Two women make jewelry. They have their own store in nearby Canton, but they make extra money at the festivals." Debbie explained. "I believe another woman said something about hats."

Jenna's eyes widened with interest. "What style?"

Debbie shrugged and said, "I don't know. I didn't hear everything. I was trying to concentrate on my students. Guess you'll have to go find out."

"The festival idea sounds more inviting by the minute," Jenna said with a grin. "Guess I better buckle down and get to work." The last few words reminded her of Stuart. He used to tell her, 'Guess you better buckle down and get busy with your newspaper article, if you want it finished in time for the Wednesday edition.' With Stuart no longer around to keep her motivated, Jenna had to come up with a solution to remind herself of dates and meeting times. She considered sticking notes everywhere, because she surely couldn't count on Debbie to keep her on track of everything.

Debbie laid in a fetal position with a pillow pulled up close to her chest, still awake when Jenna came in to say good night. "Mom, I'm glad that you're trying out new craft ideas. I hope you do plan to go to the Spring Fling."

"I'm getting excited at the idea. That just means a lot of hard work on projects so I'll have enough to display."

Jenna painted all the time, except when she was at the doctor's office or with the women at church or studying her Sunday school lesson or repotting plants or writing for the newspaper or...

"She has too many responsibilities that she doesn't need right now," Debbie grumbled to one of the mother's at the gym. "I know why she's so busy, running here and there; she's trying to keep busy so she'll fall to sleep quickly. But it's not good for her to be too busy. I've got to do something before she drops dead."

Once she got home, sitting alone in her room, Debbie got out a pad and pen to make a list of ways to help her mother. She first wrote: quit college, but Mom would cook burgers and wash cars before she'd let that happen; get Mom interested in an exercise or dance class, but she'd complain that she doesn't have time for either; hook her up with a man, but who?

Debbie's eyes left the notepad and settled on the desk calendar. Marked in red was the date she was to return to college. When she turned her attention back to the notepad she wrote: Before I leave I want to see Mom looking a whole lot better. A man could do that but what man would want a woman who people pity? Where can I even find a man who can let gossip roll off his back? Who is the ideal man that could fall in love with my mother?

Debbie sat up straight and murmured, "I know who can help me. Lynn Story has helped me solve many problems in the past; she can do it again. God knows she's gotten me into enough trouble with her mischief; she owes me something."

She got out her diary and read about a most embarrassing prank that Lynn had organized.

"She knew I had a crush on her brother Chuck McAdams, and that I was getting nowhere with him. It appeared that our relationship was not going to go beyond friendship.

"Chuck was the only one of us three who had a driving license. Still Lynn had to sweet talk him into taking us to the movies or skating, especially shopping. She always managed to reach his good natured side but with reluctance. With a resigned twist of the lips he would agree and took us wherever we wanted to go. Lynn, too, wanted Chuck to take me on a date, so she schemed to set the ball in motion. For Chuck's seventeenth birthday she ordered a sing-a-gram for his present. She called the agency where I was working and requested my services. When speaking to the owner of the establishment she was firm with her request. "I don't want anyone but Debbie Wilson.

"With anticipation and dread, I headed for the McAdams home. For part of Debbie's present, I was to sing to Chuck…that I could handle okay until I reached the last line. I was afraid that Chuck would laugh when I did the second part: kiss him. Each step I took from the curb to the front door got slower and slower. I wished with all my heart that the job had been given to another employee. But it was a no go. Lynn insisted that I do it or send no one.

"After standing at the front door of the McAdams home for what seemed like an hour, trying to get up my nerve to ring the bell, Lynn opened the door. Knowing why I was there, she hollered for Chuck. Soon as Lynn disappeared, I sang Happy Birthday, loving Chuck's bright smile. Before I ran off, I stood on tiptoe and aimed for Chuck's cheek. He jerked his face around and I hit his mouth. When **we** broke contact, I stared at him, waiting for a teasing remark. He stared back at me, never saying a word.

"Lynn came around from behind the door and said, 'What a way to go, guys!'

"I wanted to go all right, out of sight. I wished the porch would split open and swallow me. I could have strangled Lynn instead I turned and ran to the car, never looking back."

With a smile Debbie stuck the diary back into the desk drawer and murmured to the room at large, "Yep. That woman owes me a favor. A major one! And I'm taking care of it in the morning."

Debbie was eating a bowl of cereal when Jenna entered the kitchen. "Morning, Mom."

Jenna bent over and kissed the top of Debbie's head. "Good morning to you, too."

"You look beautiful, Mom," Debbie said with a bright smile, "perhaps too beautiful to be having breakfast with a bunch of old women."

"Thanks, Deb. I'm one of those old women."

Debbie apologized. "You know what I mean. You look gorgeous enough to be going out with a man."

Jenna's smile stiffened. While putting on her "happy" hat, as she called the red beret, she said, "I can do without a man, but I need the women in my Sunday school class. They are fun."

Debbie carried her bowl and spoon to the sink, gave Jenna a hug, and said, "So I've heard. Hope you have a good time."

Jenna adjusted her beret and said, "Those women are entertaining. All through the meal they will try to see who can outdo the other with a funny experience at someone's expense, usually their own. They always give me a lift." Jenna reached up to readjust her hat and murmured, "When I'm alone is when memories plague me."

Debbie gave her mother a confident look and said, "I believe God's going to do something about those memories, and soon."

"What a blessing that would be," Jenna responded and left.

Debbie immediately went to the telephone and dialed Lynn Story's phone number. When Lynn answered Debbie put her on the speakerphone and continued to work on her hair. While using a curling iron to control the red hair about her face she said, "Hi, Lynn. Got a minute?"

"Hi, girlfriend. I've always got time for you. Since I'm feeling big as a well-fed bear, I'm not going anywhere anytime soon. I've got more than a minute to chat."

"Are you hibernating now?"

Lynn chuckled. "You might say that. But it won't be long before I'll get all the action I want and then some. The way this little fellow kicks around, I have a feeling he's going to be a very energetic kid. I'll run my weight off, chasing after him."

Debbie pulled the rest of her hair back and plaited one braid to hang down her back. "Has the due date been settled? I know the last time you were pregnant, you were in and out of the hospital with false labor, and we were wondering if you'd ever have the baby."

A giggle burst from Lynn when she said, "It kept my hubby on his toes. During the last month, Kenneth wouldn't work on any investigative cases that would take him out of town. I think the doctor is still guessing this time, but he says Little Nathan is due in two months. Kenneth has a little more time this go around to plan his comings and goings."

Debbie chuckled and said, "By being a detective and married to a meddlesome wife with an active daughter, Kenneth can't say his life is dull."

"True. Nobody's life around here is dull, not even yours. I'm asking you for the umpteenth time, when are you coming to spend more than two minutes with me? I know you're busy, working and trying to help your mom get over the death of your father, but Deb I enjoy being with my best friend. We always have so much to catch up on."

Debbie sighed. "You don't know how much I miss our girl talks. That's why I'm calling, other than checking on you, to find out if we can get together today. I need your help with something concerning Mom."

"Can we ever? Deb, if you'll come for lunch, I'll shuffle to the kitchen and have something ready for us to chow down when you get here."

"Only if you make it simple. A salad will do."

"I can handle that," Lynn said. Before hanging up she asked, "Is Jenna all right?"

"Mom's...okay." Debbie cut short their conversation. "Hate to hang up, Lynn, but I've got to get to work, really. See you for lunch."

As Lynn struggled to get her heavy weight pushed up from the recliner, questions about Jenna tumbled from her full lips. "Will the rumors about Stuart's affair ever die? Will poor Jenna ever be able to trust another man?" She shook her head in disgust. Jenna was too good a woman to be dumped on. While checking to see if she had enough fixings for a salad, she continued to talk to herself. "I know Stuart wasn't Mr. Goody-Two-Shoes like everyone assumed, because Deb told me tales about him. I just wish Jenna hadn't been so trusting and had seen the real Stuart much earlier."

At twelve-fifteen Debbie raised her hand to ring the doorbell at Lynn's house. The door was open before she could punch the button. Grinning from the threshold was a big, beautiful woman, her dear friend Lynn.

"I half expected the door to be open by Shelley," Debbie said, hugging Lynn.

In an oversized pink knit pant suit, Lynn looked adorable. She reached for Debbie, pulling her into the house. "I'm so glad to see you. When I don't see you for two weeks or more I get depressed."

Debbie chuckled. "You depressed? You don't have time. By the way, where is that inquisitive daughter of yours?"

"My wonderful mother-in-law took her to see some movie that Shelley's been dying to see. Shelley won't be here to bombard you with 101 questions?"

Debbie grinned and then took a second glance around the room, looking surprised by the disorder. Newspapers were spread out on the coffee table and a stack of detective journals were in a haphazard pile beside the couch. She also saw a doll sticking out from under the coffee table. With her hands on her hips she grinned at Lynn and said, "I'm surprised at the clutter, but I admit it makes the room look more comfortable, more lived in."

Lynn tried to retrieve a mystery thriller paperback from the floor beside the recliner. "Live in is right." After a second attempt at the book, she kicked it toward Debbie. "Do me the honor."

Debbie laughed. "I would have done it anyway," she said, picking it up along with some other stray objects. "I just wanted to see you in action."

Lynn's lips twisted into a rueful grin. "Never thought you'd see my house in a mess, did you?"

"Honestly no."

"Guess what? Right now orderliness is no longer a priority."

Debbie stacked all the papers and journals in a neat pile on the coffee table and said, "I have a feeling that Detective Lynn will get back in the groove of keeping everything and everyone in tip-top shape once Little Nathan is born."

After Lynn set a bowl of salad and a bottle of dressing on the table next to a wide bay window she said, "Its news I'm after now. What's wrong with Jenna?"

Debbie got two bottles of water from the refrigerator and sat them on the table. Instead of answering right away she said, "I used to enjoy looking out the bay window in our other house until I saw something that led to the destruction of my parents' marriage." She continued to stare outside as she explained. "One night I went into the kitchen for some water. The moon made it easy to move around without having to turn on the light. I took my bottle of water into the den and stopped to look out the bay window. It was then that I noticed a movement just beyond the house." She looked over her shoulder at her friend and with a sneer she added, "It was my beloved father. He was walking quickly across the yard and looking back every few steps. His actions plainly showed that he was guilty about something.

"Later when I told him I saw him, he got so mad. His eyes bulged, his nostrils flared, and his face turned blood red. If looks could kill, I'd be dead. He said, 'For your information Mavis…Mrs. Witherspoon asked if I'd come over and repair a lamp. She wanted it available in case she had to get up during the night.' I mumbled something about using a flashlight and walked off. At the door I looked over my shoulder and saw him glaring at me."

Lynn raised an eyebrow. "Convenient wasn't it? A broken lamp beside her bed. They didn't have far to go for a roll in the sheets."

Debbie's lips tightened together. "A lot of things or should I say women were a bit too convenient for Stuart Wilson. He's the reason I'm here asking for help with Mom."

Lynn popped a crouton into her mouth. "You can count on me. How can I help?"

"Mom needs a man in her life and a good one! A man that will let her know she really matters to him."

Lynn poured nearly half a bottle of Ranch dressing onto her salad and said, "I agree. Daddy needs a good woman in his life, too. He's been a widower much too long." Her eyes lit up. "Wouldn't it be great if our parents got together? It would make us sisters."

"We are already closer than blood relatives," Debbie said. "Don't get me wrong, but it would never work between our parents."

"Why not?" Lynn asked with a touch of disbelief. "They are Christians, enjoy similar activities, and both have great personalities."

"That's just it: their personalities. Mom likes to be with people who have a wonderful sense of humor and isn't tongue-tied. But she doesn't like a man who pours on the charm with every woman he meets. You know Charles McAdams' womanizing reputation better than I do. Tell me the truth. Do you think they could hit it off?"

With a sigh, Lynn said, "Daddy does flirt a lot, but actually I don't think he means anything by it. Using his charm started out as a way to get women to talk to him, especially when a case he was working on needed pertinent information."

Debbie's lips twisted into a wry grim. "Charles is the only detective around here who doesn't take his work seriously."

"Oh but you're wrong. His devil-may-care attitude is a ploy. Wouldn't you rather talk to a handsome, friendly officer than a serious, sour-looking one?'

Debbie laughed. "You're right. Your father probably would be good for Mom. Even if she didn't believe a word he said she would smile."

Lynn shook her fork at Debbie, saying, "I know Jenna, too. She's not above making men take a second look at her."

"I know, but that was before she got shafted."

"Jenna may not get as animated when she talks now, but she has never been boring. One of these days she'll be back in the groove."

"I can't sit back and wait for the day to eventually come. She needs to perk up now."

Lynn looked sympathetic and said, "I know how you feel. I want the same for Jenna, too. She's been like a mother to me." With a reminiscent look she added, "I remember the first time I heard Jenna teach; it was at your church. She was perky then. I had never heard anyone like her. She held everybody's attention, even the boys. During the story of when Joseph's brothers put him in a pit, I could feel his discomfort. I thought I'd smother then and there. I wanted someone to find him quickly. When Jenna finally got him rescued by some Midianite businessmen, I actually inhaled all the air I could get into my lungs. I was so happy for Joseph. He was alive! Safe! I went home that evening and told Daddy that I wanted to go to your church all the time. He said I could go once in a while, but it was too far for him to take me there and then race back across town to his church every Sunday. That's when I asked if I could spend Saturday nights with you."

Debbie nodded and smiled appreciatively. "I'm glad you did. We had some great times, talking all hours of the night. I agree with you about Mom; she can tell a good story. She makes you feel as if you're part of it. Remember those ghost stories? At times I could actually see a ghost standing in front of me."

Lynn chuckled. "I know what you mean until I found out those ghosts were Chuck. But it all seemed so real. What's so fascinating is that Jenna's paintings also tell stories."

Debbie shivered and said, "For some reason, some of them haunt me, like the one of an old woman sitting in a rocking chair, holding a baby. Seated on the porch is a child playing with a doll. Standing beside the rocker is an older girl with a tray of lemonade. To the side is another girl washing windows, and at the edge of the porch is a boy scraping paint off a post. In the yard is another boy trimming shrubbery. I get the feeling that I should be more helpful to others. Know what I mean?"

Lynn nodded. "Yeah I know. You're talking about "Ma's Caring Grandchildren. It makes me wish I had a grandmother."

"Me, too. At least a live caring one," Debbie said with a catch in her throat. I think about Grandma Frazier every time I look at that painting. I used to sit for what seems like hours and look at each person in that picture and wish I was one of those girls. I even wished that the woman was my Grandma. I didn't get to spend much time with Grandma Frazier since she lived so far away, but when we did go see her, she was so good to me. Although I made more of a mess than anything worth eating, she let me help bake cookies. Once they were done, Grandma said they were the best she had ever eaten."

Debbie wiped tears from her eyes and added, "Now that she's dead, I'll never get to show her how much I care for her."

"I guess Stuart's parents never showed any love," Lynn said.

"You can say that again. His mother would not allow me to call her Grandma, Grandmother, or Nana, not any loving name. It had to be Shirley. Also, instead of Grandfather Wilson, it was George. But it didn't matter what I called them. They never came around much. When Daddy died, they just popped in and out."

"Where was it they went?" Lynn asked.

"I don't know. Somewhere out of the country. It could have been Iraq for all it mattered to me." Debbie smiled a brief lift of the lips and said, "No more depressing talk. I'm here to get help for Mom. I want to see more smiles on her face and hear livelier conversations coming from her."

Lynn drank a big swallow of water while eyeing Debbie over the end of the bottle. "What do you say, do we try to get our parents together? If it works out...great. If not, well, at least we will have tried something."

"Suits me but how?"

Lynn took the fork from her mouth and said, "I can invite them over for supper."

Debbie's eyes lit up. "I'll help cook of course...and wash dishes. Oh, I know, what about Asheville's Heritage Celebration that's coming up in a few weeks. Mom's almost ready. She's been painting flowers, especially magnolias on practically everything she can her hands on. How about Charles? Is he going? I understand he had a great time last year?"

Lynn nodded and finished chewing a mouthful of lettuce and tomato before answering, "He is. Said he wouldn't miss it." She gave Debbie a lopsided grin and added, "You do realize that Daddy goes to these things mostly for business purposes?"

Debbie raised her eyebrows. "Doesn't he do anything just for the fun of it?"

"He uses the crowd scene as a place for his contacts to leave information," Lynn explained. "While they are talking about his toys, the person slips him a note between the money he or she hands Daddy in payment for a car or airplane."

"Is that why he started making toys again?"

"Actually Tina was the reason. She wanted him to make her son Joe a train for Christmas. We all still have the toys he made for us when we were kids."

"I love that doll bed of yours. It's the one Shelly plays with now, isn't it?"

Lynn nodded. "Daddy decided to use the toys as ice breakers at craft shows and festivals. He didn't realize how well they would sell. Last year, he barely had enough toys to last throughout the day. This year he made twice as many and a bigger variety of items. He's hoping to use them as conversation pieces before bringing in politics."

Debbie looked puzzled. "I didn't know he was involved in politics."

"He's not yet. Some friends want him to run for mayor of Asheville. He plans to use opportunities at the festival to get the attendees' views on certain points. If he feels he can make a difference, he'll probably decide to run. But his main objective this year is to see long time friends. Last year, several people he hadn't seen in years stopped at his table. Their conversations were short but welcoming. He hopes to see some others this year."

"Has he already confirmed a spot?"

"Oh sure. Months ago. He then said he wished he had someone to help with the customers while he talked. I suggested Chuck."

Debbie's eyes perked up. "Is Chuck going?"

Lynn's hand stopped before her fork reached her mouth. "How do you feel about seeing my big brother?"

While looking toward the window Debbie said, "I'd like to see him."

Lynn quickly responded. "Good. Let's see if we can't make it possible for romance to progress."

With a wide-eyed look Debbie asked, "What do you mean by that?"

"Calm down, Deb." Lynn crossed her fingers behind her back and added, "I'm not hoping that you and Chuck get together again. I know you two have unresolved problems. I was referring to Daddy's and Jenna's tables being close together."

Debbie relaxed. "Good idea. But how? They probably have assigned spots by now."

"Things can be changed," Lynn said with an excited look. "Chuck knows the festival director. I'll ask him to see about getting them put close as possible."

Debbie rose and carried their dishes to the sink and began running the water.

Lynn heaved herself up from the table saying, "You don't have to do that. I'll get them washed before Kenneth comes home. He tells me not to worry about the house, but I can wash a few dishes. I don't have to do any bending with that job. It's when I have to put the pots and pans in the lower cabinet that I holler for help. Most of the time I just leave them in the drainer."

Debbie kept working. "It's no problem for me. I'll put these things away and then I'll go. I've got to get back to the recreation center. My new students will be arriving soon to start their gymnastic training."

Lynn looked Debbie over. "I admire your slim body. Still tumbling yourself?"

"But of course," Debbie responded, looking down at her sloppy shirt and sweat pants. "No one can tell it by the way I look that I'm little, but this form of exercise is the best way for me to keep in shape."

"You ought to be able to do all the stretches, runs, and flips with your eyes closed. When we were kids, I wished I could do it as easily as you. I had this hang up—fear that I'd fall on my head."

Debbie tapped Lynn's forehead and said, "You did fall on your head."

In a deadpan voice, Lynn asked, "Which time are you referring to?"

Debbie grinned, "The time a girl in a department store tried to get away from you. With you hot on her trail she dropped a pair of jeans in front of you. You stumbled, skidded, and then fell, hitting on your head."

Lynn smiled. "I still caught her. At that time, I had some get and go about me." She then rubbed her forehead and added, "Chuck says all the falls and bumps on my head gives me a good excuse for the crazy way I think and act. I reminded him of all the times he made me fall on my head as a kid. It's a wonder I'm not loony."

Debbie's smiling face grew serious. "How is Chuck? What happened between him and Peggy Sue or Tammy Lou or whatever that pretty little brunette's name is?"

Lynn shrugged. "Who knows? Girls come and go in his life. I truly think he's carrying a torch for you."

"Yeah right." Debbie said with disbelief. She flipped around and started walking across the porch. "Let me know what happens about the festival set up."

"Will do." Lynn shut the door and immediately dialed her brother's number. In a serious voice she said, "Chuck, I've got a problem. You're the only one I can talk to about it. Will you be able to come by here on your way to work in the morning?"

"Thanks. I appreciate it. And don't say, 'Since When?' I've always appreciated you."

Chuck's loud laugh made Lynn hold the receiver out from head. She got in the last word before the phone went dead. "You better be here tomorrow or you'll be sorry."

CHAPTER 2

Chuck stood at the kitchen doorway and looked in amusement at the woman seated at the table with a bowl and spoon. She appeared to be unaware of his presence as she mixed mashed avocado with chocolate syrup and marshmallow ice cream. Dressed in an extra large powder blue T-shirt over navy Capri, her pale ankles revealed a little swelling. Her bare feet showed fire engine red toenails that were in need of repair.

He liked the picture she made: at age twenty, the youngest McAdams sibling was delightful. Her blond curls were in a tight array and tended to curl more when the weather was damp. His, got wavier. The best part of this wonderful woman was her constant joy, and she was thrilled to be pregnant again. He smiled as he walked on into the room. "You'd be great for a Pillsbury commercial. I can just see someone poking a finger at your tummy."

Chuck was almost excited as Lynn and Kenneth as they await the arrival of a playmate for their three-year-old daughter. He hoped that she does not have trouble with this delivery. He hated it when his sister was hurting in anyway. And childbirth had to be awful. He shivered at the thought.

In order for Lynn to not complain about him looking uptight Chuck undid the top three buttons of his red knit shirt. With a smile he stepped into the room, saying, "I see you're at it again, always eating. Got any more ice cream?"

Lynn's head jerked around and a smile lit up her round face. "Chuck!" She stretched up her arms for a hug. She kissed his cheek and then added. "No. It's all I've got." She gave him a cheeky grin and added, "But there's some banana pudding in the fridge. Grab a bowl and join me. How did you get in?"

"Climbed in through the basement window."

Lynn gasped. "No! Did I leave it open again?"

"Hold it. Don't get upset and disturb the baby. I was just teasing. Kenneth let me in as he was leaving for work." He licked banana pudding from the dipping spoon and straddled a bar stool. "How are you, little Mama?"

Lynn chuckled, patting her tummy. "Little? Besides looking like a bowling ball I'm fine. She jumped back from Chuck. "Hey, keep your dirty fingers out of my eyes and mouth."

"Since you haven't returned my bowling ball, I thought I'd use you to practice with for my next tournament."

A puzzled frown drew Lynn's thick eyebrows together. "You can have it back as soon as I find it, along with your basketball and baseball glove."

"It's about time you bought your own equipment," he said.

With an endearing look she said, "Why don't I just keep yours for Little Nathan?"

"Oh all right. You can keep my bowling ball and the other equipment, too. You'll need them to help exercise your beautiful body back into shape."

She wiped ice cream from her mouth and said, "Like father like son. You've got Dad's charm even if it's a backhanded compliment. True or not, it's good for my ego. I need all the encouragement I can get right now."

"That's enough chit-chat," Chuck said. "Tell me the reason you called. It couldn't have been just for a pep talk; you were too serious." When she grinned, he added, "Or were you just pulling my leg to get me over for a visit?"

Lynn's smile faded. "I really need your help with something. Are you still going with Daddy to Asheville's Heritage Celebration?"

Chuck nodded. "I'm not crazy about it but yes. He bribed me. Said he'd give me a raise. I think he only promised that because it's about time for my yearly evaluation at the office."

"And you can't turn down a nickel much less some green backs."

"You know it."

"You bet I know it," Lynn said with a twinkle in her eye. "When we were kids and I offered you a quarter, or even a dime to do something for me, you jumped at it."

"To my grief. Why were you so mean?"

Lynn gave him an affronted look. "I wasn't mean. If I was, so were you...and Tina. She was the best at pulling pranks."

Chuck grinned. "She was good. I'll never forget my first secret mission. You had told her about the old woman across the road throwing wrapped packages into her trashcan."

Lynn giggled. "We both had to know why she threw away unopened presents. 'What nut wouldn't want to see what was in a package before throwing it away?' Tina asked. So she offered to pay you a quarter to find out, which also was to be your initiation into becoming a family detective."

"Daddy should have taken away those binoculars of yours or cut down the apple tree. Hidden behind tree limbs, you watched everything that moved."

Lynn burst into laughter. "I even watched you rummage through Mrs. Cook's trashcan. Was it gross?"

"Not until I opened the "presents". They were soured leftovers! Hey, I never got paid for that dirty job."

"Because you didn't finish it. You were supposed to have found out why she gift wrapped her garbage."

"I didn't care. I figured all the heaving and gagging earned me that quarter. But no-o-o. Tina said I didn't deserve it."

"It taught you lesson, though, didn't it?"

He nodded and said, "To never again do business with you two."

"Daddy always said to leave no stone unturned, because the last stone could be the one concealing the answer. Since I had to finish snooping myself, Tina suggested that I take some of Rosie's cookies to Mrs. Cook." She closed her eyes and licked her lips. "Daddy's housekeeper is the best cook."

Chuck clicked his fingers in front of her face. "Come on. Finish your story. I forgot what did happen."

"Oh. Sorry. I was thinking about our dear sister. Sometimes I miss Tina so badly. I wish she'd move back here so we could pull another prank on you." When she noticed Chuck's antsy look she rushed on. "About our creative neighbor: she wasn't a nut. She was practicing her gift wrapping for an upcoming job in a department store. Boy was she fast. She pulled forward a box, wrapped it, and whipped up a bow in nothing flat and had the package ready and slung aside in record time, ready to do another one. She looked like someone working on an assembly line."

Lynn giggled as she continued her story. "Mrs. Cook presented a coy smile before explaining her behavior. 'I've been wrapping everything I could get my hands on,' she said, 'even my garbage. If anyone had seen me they would have thought I was crazy.' I almost told her I thought she was, but I hid my guilty-looking eyes and changed the subject."

Chuck swallowed a spoon full of banana pudding and said, "You could hide your guilty looks from everyone but me. I soon learned that you twisted hair around your finger to draw attention from your face when you were about to be found out. Like now. What are you up to?"

Lynn quickly released her hair and said, "Uh, so you're going to the festival, right?"

Chuck nodded. "Actually I'm kind of looking forward to it. It's one of the biggest street scenes in this area. People come from everywhere. Last year, it was estimated that 40,000 people attended. With more activities planned this year, a bigger crowd is expected."

"Having America's Idol, Karen Underwood, is a great drawing card," Lynn added.

"She'll draw my attention," Chuck said, making his eyebrows

waggle, and then he frowned. "But I probably won't get to see her at all since she'll be on stage at the other end of town. Why are you so concerned about the festival?"

She kept her eyes on his face. "I was talking to Debbie…Wilson yesterday."

Chuck shrugged. "So what. That's nothing new. At least she'll talk to you."

"Maybe she'll talk to you Saturday," Lynn responded with a gentle smile.

Chuck's brown eyes opened wide. "Why?" he asked through a mouthful of banana pudding.

"Since Stuart's death, Deb's been staying with Jenna as much as possible. I wish I could do more to help Jenna, too."

Chuck looked confused. "I'd like to help Jenna, too, but what are you driving at?"

"The festival. Jenna has planned to set up a display of her arts and crafts."

"Okay. Maybe I'll see them both."

Lynn perked up. "I certainly hope so. That's where you come in."

"Uh-oh. That look means trouble for me. Your eyes twinkle and turn chocolate brown when you're scheming."

"Chucky boy, it's not trouble for you this time, but it does require a little conniving on your part." She twisted her head sideways to cast him a look out of the corner of her eye, the way she used to do to get her way. "I'm simply asking for your help."

"What kind of help?" he grumbled.

"You know the president of the festival. I want you to see if he'll assign Jenna's space next to Daddy's."

Chuck rolled his eyes heavenward. "You're matchmaking again."

"What's wrong with that? Daddy needs a companion. He's been living by himself now for…oh, about twenty years. Even though you're still at home sometimes, you're not the kind of companion he needs to keep him company on a cold winter's night"

"Come on, sis, it's only early spring."

"Right and it may take until winter to get Daddy and Jenna to see they need each other."

"How do you know Jenna wants a man in her life? I like Jenna as much as you do, but her and Daddy together? It will never happen. Stuart was such a jerk that I'm guessing she'll stay clear of all men now."

"Maybe not. Debbie and I are hoping that something will gel between our parents. She feels that Jenna needs someone to keep her on track. Having to return to college soon, Debbie can't remind her of every appointment on her calendar or when to pay bills. Because Stuart was a spend thrift, he didn't leave Jenna financially secure. She writes checks on money she doesn't have. With Daddy being a whiz with numbers and record keeping, he's the ideal person to help her."

Chuck's face was filled with doubt when he said, "That's not enough reason to set up our parents."

Lynn gave her brother a frustrated look and continued, "Jenna takes on too many engagements. When someone asks her to speak at a meeting, before she checks her calendar she says, 'I'd love to come. Tell me when.' She overlaps her appointments, doesn't schedule enough arrival time. And above all, she doesn't have a proper social life. Daddy doesn't either. I've always wished Jenna was my mom. I know you have felt the same way. Think about it. Don't you think they would be good for each other?"

"Sure I do. But if Jenna became our mother, that would make Debbie my sister. I don't want her to be my sister."

With a mischievous smile Lynn said, "Chuck, she wouldn't be blood kin."

"I know. And I do agree with you about Daddy and Jenna. He always had good things to say about her. Remember the first Christmas that Stuart, Jenna, and Debbie came to the house for a party. Daddy couldn't take his eyes off Jenna. At first I thought it was admiration, but then it seemed to be envy. At times he looked so sad. I guess he was missing Mama."

"I don't remember her much, but I do know Dad loved her," Lynn said softly with a far away look in her eye. "They both looked so happy in their wedding pictures. I wish she hadn't died."

"Before you have me in tears, let's get back to the festival. What am I to do about Daddy and Jenna? Should I tie them up until they agree to date?"

"What a good idea. But I think with them having crafts in common, they will get together eventually and talk about them if nothing else. Perhaps Daddy will ask her for a date."

"What if Jenna is off men so much that she won't even speak to Daddy?"

"No way. She's not rude. No matter how she feels, she talks. Debbie isn't called Jenna-the-second for nothing. Those women are people-persons."

"So maybe Debbie will talk to me, too," Chuck said with a wistful sound in his voice.

Lynn pretended not to notice. "You know Daddy's still handsome, charming and intelligent, all attractive stuff we women fall for. I've been praying about this, and I believe that this is a step in having my prayers answered."

Chuck hesitated. "Lynn, I don't know…"

"Please," she begged. "If not for Daddy's sake think of Jenna's. Ever since Stuart died, she's been depressed. She talks to people but not with as much spirit. She seems more reserved. And she doesn't smile much. It's as if her flame has gone out. If she and Daddy see more of each other maybe he'll brighten her life. He's due for a change in his own life."

"Okay, okay," Chuck said, raising both hands. "I'll do what I can to get them side-by-side. I'll call Don Apple today about putting their spaces together. I'll even encourage them to talk, but I can't promise anything more." He shook his head. "I'm twenty-two years old. I know your ideas mean trouble for me, but I can't resist helping with your schemes. I just hope Daddy doesn't get mad when he finds out what we're doing."

"It's for his own good, and for Jenna's, too," she assured him. "Also, you will help Debbie get them together because you're so wonderful and I love you. You're the best brother I've got."

Chuck rolled his eyes. "I'm the only brother you've got. If this scheme of yours backfires on us Tina is going to be my only sister. For her sake, it was a good thing she moved out west far away from you."

"You mean yourself, don't you? She was the one who told me to make you believe there was a body buried in the yard." Lynn laughed at his surprised expression. "I'll never forget the Mystery of the Bone. It was time for you to come home from a ballgame. While helping Rosie dig in a flowerbed, Tina found a bone about a foot long. Her imagination took over. She saw your coach's car coming down the road and told me to run out and meet you."

Chuck took over. "I hit my first homerun that day. I was on cloud nine. You came running up to me, looking scared to death. You took all my glory away, especially when you held out an old bone toward me. 'There's a body buried in the backyard,' you said. Wanting to follow in Daddy's footsteps, I jumped on the case, thinking it would prove to him that I could be a good detective."

Lynn laughed so hard, barely able to talk but managed to say, "All it proved was that you could tear up a yard."

"Well, I had to find the rest of the remains," Chuck said in defense. With a reluctant grin he added, "The bone belonged to none other than somebody's old cow."

Lynn sobered and wiped her eyes. "That farm was a great place to live and make up mysteries to solve."

Chuck rose, leaned over and kissed her cheek. "You know, I'm beginning to look forward to Saturday. I hope we can get Daddy and Jenna interested in each other. I've got to go. I know it's hard for you, but try to be good."

Just as he stepped out onto the porch of the Colonial style home Lynn hollered, "Bye Chuck. Don't be digging up anymore yards unnecessarily!"

Once the door was shut Lynn reached for the telephone. She pushed buttons in rapid succession.

"Deb? Chuck's going to see about the table setup. Don't forget to leave Jenna floundering for help."

"I know you don't want to. I'd like to be there to help her myself. But it's just for part of the time. If I know Daddy, he'll be right there to help Jenna unload her van. Remember, it's for her own good to leave her alone for a little while."

CHAPTER 3

Jenna stared at the piece of paper in her hand. She could not believe what she saw. The words *you have overdrawn your checking account and are in the red one hundred dollars* were not actually written on the bank notice, but they may as well have been. To her, the notice meant trouble. She was short of funds.

She took both hands and combed them through her hair and then dragged them down across her face. How could she be short? When she called the bank about her balance, there was enough money in her checking account to buy a new washing machine. She had to have it. The endless trips across town to the Laundromat would have been more costly in the long run. "But the bank notice shows that I couldn't afford anything," she grumbled. "I don't understand!"

The more Jenna looked at her checkbook the more aggravated she became. Why did simple addition, subtraction, and entries have to be so complicated? "I'm not stupid," she said, wadding the paper into a ball, "so why can't I keep an accurate record of expenditures?"

Nearly all of her life, Jenna had trouble with numbers. Other subjects had been a whiz. She made straight A's in everything except Math. She was lucky to have scraped by without a failing grade in algebra. In college, her father sent her money to get a tutor. The smart upper classman did help Jenna do better in math, but it didn't seem to stick. For some reason, maybe because of plain old carelessness, regular math failed to help with balancing a check book.

When her husband was around, she did not have to think about credits and debits; he handled all her financial affairs. Jenna gladly let him do it. By letting Professor Stuart Wilson take control, she never worried about expenditures or much of anything else. She took great solace in knowing that money was always there when she wanted something. Also, she was comfortable in knowing that she would get to her appointments on time, because he took care of that matter, too. He took care of everything where Jenna was concerned. Actually he took care of too much to suit her.

Before Stuart took control, her clothes and attitudes were predictable. Her clothes consisted of long skirts and loose blouses and she kept her hair pulled up in a bun. "I'm comfortable," she argued when Stuart suggested she wear pants and a sweater.

The truth was she really did want to dress better, like she did while living on the island. Growing up, most of the time she ran around in shorts and tee shirts, but church and social events required dressy clothes. It was after she moved to Florida that her style changed completely. The family she stayed with went to church every time the doors opened and very strict in their beliefs.

"Young ladies don't show their bodies," Reverend Shaffer said, and refused to let her wear shorts or jeans. He instructed his wife to give Jenna some of her clothes until they could go shopping. "Mrs. Shaffer will advise you on what to buy, Jenna. She dresses in a way that is becoming to a Christian."

At first Jenna hated the loose fitting dresses and complained in the letters she sent to her parents. Her mother wrote back, suggesting that she try to live as they do. Mrs. Frazier ended the letter with "It won't be forever. You'll see that it's for the best."

To Jenna, that first week dragged by; it seemed to go on forever. Also she realized that the Reverend Shaffer was not going to give an inch, so she forced herself to try doing things his way. My day will come, she thought, when I'll be able to dress in whatever style clothes that I want.

For a month or so, as soon as she got away from the Shaffer house, she put on a belt or a scarf to brighten up her attire. She absolutely was not going to let complete strangers take full control of her life. It was when she saw other students dressed in loose fitting clothes that she willingly dropped the belt and scarf. After a time, when she did not concentrate solely on her appearance, the long skirts and long sleeve blouses became second nature.

Once she moved out into an apartment, she reverted somewhat to her old nature. She did not have to live under anyone's thumb, she thought. *I can come and go as I please and wear whatever I like.* Unfortunately by this time, sports wear were no longer part of her wardrobe.

Regrettably her boyfriend wanted her appearance to change, to be more like the youth of the day. He did not pressure her to wear jeans and fitted button up shirts, but he hinted at how nice the girls looked who did wear them. When Jenna kept wearing her Amish-looking wardrobe he quit saying anything about her dressing differently until they were married.

Again he mentioned how he would love to see her in more up-to-date clothes. Jenna adored Stuart, but she was not going to be a wimpy wife and do his bidding at every turn. She recalled their confrontations over her appearance. A big social affair was coming up at the college where he taught. Stuart became adamant that she would dress to fit his status in front of his peers and in the community. "It's time for a change, Jenna, whether you like it not."

One evening he came home with some packages for her. "There's something here that will be appropriate for the chancellor's party. All the people I work with will be there. I want to show you off, be proud of my wife."

She gave in for that special occasion. It was like pulling teeth to get her to dress prettier on a day to day basis. "I prefer to wear clothes that are comfortable," she argued.

"You mean slouchy, don't you," Stuart said. "You can find comfortable fitting clothes in dress slacks and more upscale dresses."

Reluctantly she gave in to make him happy. She even agreed to go shopping with Stuart for more clothes. She admitted that she liked his choices but balked at being told what to wear every day.

Debbie heard them arguing and asked, "Mommy, don't you like pretty clothes?"

"Of course I do," Jenna said, picking the child up in her arms. "Your father wants me to wear a red dress to one of his parties and I prefer to wear a dark suit with a blouse. He also wants me to wear my hair hanging down."

"I like it down, too," Debbie said, sticking her finger through a long red curl that hung across her shoulder.

"But Mommy's tired of it swishing around her face," Jenna said, nuzzling Debbie's neck until she laughed. "I want to wear it up on the back of my head."

"So you'll look like a princess?" Debbie asked.

For a moment Jenna was stunned. "I didn't know I ever looked like a princess," she murmured.

Debbie ran got a story book and opened it to the page of a princess who had her hair in a twist and it was topped with a tiara. "That's how you look sometimes, but without the crown," she told Jenna. Pointing to a soft knit green dress hanging in her mother's closet, Debbie added, "I like that."

Jenna kissed Debbie's cheek and took out the dress. Heading toward the bathroom she said, "I'll wear it just for you."

Over her shoulder, Jenna presented Stuart with a half smile and received a glare from him in return. She knew that she handled many situations all wrong. When she balked at the way he tried to make every decision for her, it made her angry and then he got mad.

"Sometimes I wish I'd never married you. You're an embarrassment to me," he said. "If it wasn't a valentine banquet I'd leave you at home, but seating arrangements have already been made for us."

Jenna was getting afraid of Stuart, not knowing when or if he would do her physical harm. She shivered when she recalled another time when she complained about having to wear her hair down around her shoulders, he had grabbed up a pair of scissors and started toward her.

"If you don't like the way your hair looks, I'll take care of it," he said. "I'll cut off the whole nasty mess."

Jenna had cringed away from him but struggled to find the right words to stop him. "Go ahead and cut it off," she said. "See how I'll look then." She looked him in the eye and asked, "Tell me, if you never liked my looks, why did you date me, much less marry me."

"Through those sloppy clothes, I could tell you had a good figure. I knew with some sprucing up you would look great. And you do, when you dress as I suggest."

"You never suggest. You tell. I don't like to be told to do anything."

He threw down the scissors and muttered, "So I've learned. But you will be getting that mop fixed by a professional hairdresser. I can't have you embarrassing me anymore in front of my friends."

Stuart also managed Jenna's personal life. To some extent, this she did not mind. She needed a personal secretary, but instead of hiring one, she let Stuart take over the responsibility. What she never realized until it was too late was that he had an ulterior motive in looking after her affairs. "I would feel better knowing of your comings and goings first hand," he said, pulling forward a large desk calendar. "Let me have the dates of all upcoming engagements."

Since Stuart's death, Jenna found herself having to deal with every situation in her life now. She knew how to dress and put on makeup and wear her hair in ways that were becoming, but there was still the problem of her financial matters. After her phone and electricity were disconnected, she learned that bills had to be paid on time or you lost service. Then knowing if there was enough money for paint supplies, food, clothes, or perhaps a water heater was instrumental in her staying sane. She just had to figure out how to stretch her money.

Again Jenna looked at the bank statement, along with her check book. Frustration pleated her eyebrows together. She wadded the statement into a ball and threw it across the room.

"Stuart, it's your entire fault that I'm in this mess! Why did you spend all our money? My money? Why did you have to leave me penniless? I hate you, Stuart Wilson."

Sometimes she missed her husband beyond belief. At those times, it did not matter that he had been a louse. She missed having someone to take care of her problems. Tears filled her green eyes, making them glisten like emeralds. With trembling hands she covered her face and cried, sobbing the first time in weeks. Once she managed to dry her tears, her heart felt lighter.

She looked across at the ball of paper in front of the couch. With thin fingers she picked it up and began to unroll it. Pressed flat as possible, she took it and her checkbook to the bank. She hoped and prayed that someone there would help straighten out her mess.

The accounting assistant began pointing out her problems. "Mrs. Wilson, you didn't enter several written checks and you left off a deposit. It's nothing that I can't help straighten out."

Within an hour Jenna was back home. With a smile she flipped the beret from her head and slung it toward an entranceway table. It slid across the slick surface and fell to the floor. Her smile disappeared. It was just like her life; it had passed swiftly and smoothly under Stuart's supervision, and then it fell into the pits.

She picked up the cap, saying, "But this and my life are going to be reinstated where they should be." She then laid the cap on the table. *Some way some how I'm going to learn about bookkeeping, not only for my personal use but for Daddy's herb business.*

Fred Williams was left in charge of the company after her parents died. He had worked for Mr. Frazier ever since he was a young boy, running errands after school. Jenna had complete trust in the man's abilities.

"He has proven his worth in more ways than one," she told Debbie. "When he discovered that inventory was missing and money had been embezzled from the company, he contacted me right away."

Fred assured Jenna then that he could handle things. "Unless you absolutely need to come here, why not wait until I have some concrete evidence. I'll stay in contact with you about every fact I uncover."

He stayed true to his word. About two weeks later he called her. "Jenna, I'm sorry to have to tell you, but it was my secretary who took the money and the shipping supervisor took the inventory. If it's all right with you, I've got a friend and a cousin who are willing to help in those positions until I find the right applicants."

"Do what you have to do, Fred. I trust your judgment."

Later she told Debbie about Fred's call. "He is the most capable man I know to have running the business, but something could happen to him, and then what would I do? I need to learn the financial side of the business."

Jenna prayed, "God, don't let anything happen to Fred, certainly not anytime soon. If I have to run the office, another secretary would certainly steal me blind."

Sleep did not come easily for Jenna that night. Numbers kept dancing in her head, big ones, little ones, right ones and wrong ones. She cried out, "Debbie, can't you help me?" The sound of her own voice awakened her.

Through reddened eyes Jenna barely managed to see the clock. She squinted at the dial and saw that it was late. She jumped up, ran into Debbie's room, and jerked back the covers. "Up, girl. We've got to go."

It was 8:00, past time to have her crafts and paintings on display for early shoppers.

Jenna slid to a stop in front of the only place in downtown Montford that was not occupied by a vendor, crafter or entertainer. Stages for guest speakers, musicians, dancers, and singers were placed strategically at four locations. In years past, Debbie had been a performer here. She and the gymnastics class of which she had been a member for five years won awards in competition around the state. Each year they came to the festival to show the community how they had won.

Everything imaginable lined the long Main Street and many of the side streets. Along with the sweet aroma of elephant ears and cotton candy, a multitude of people munched on huge pretzels and corn dogs as they looked at T-shirts, flowers, dolls, ceramic figurines and numerous other items that were on display.

One section in particular had wooden toys. They looked familiar to Jenna, but she did not have time to dwell on it. She had to hustle and get her own stuff out for others to see.

Jenna swung from the driver's side of her mini van while Debbie, dress in khaki slacks and a matching jacket, jumped from the passenger side. Debbie ran to the back and jerked open the door and began pulling out a long folding table. It took both of them to carry it to Jenna's ten feet long spot. As soon as its legs were straightened and the table stood level, Jenna went back to the van and pulled forward several boxes and sat them on the ground.

Since Debbie knew about her physical problem, Jenna hoped that she would automatically say, "Don't touch those boxes, Mom, I'll get them," but she did no such thing. Over her own mumbling and grumbling about not being ready for the crowd she vaguely heard Debbie say, "I'll be back shortly."

Jenna went back to the van and pulled out two large plastic containers. She dragged them over to her table while looking around for Debbie. She eventually saw the girl talking to some guys. She did not have time to analyze everything going on around her but wished that Debbie had not chosen this moment to be sociable. *Couldn't she at least help me unload before doing her visiting?* While moving around the supplies her back began to feel the strain. Also her patience began to wear thin. What was the use of Debbie coming with her if she was going to run off and leave all the work for her to do?

Jenna did not have time to run down the street to where Debbie had ventured and bring her back to work. To get everything set up by 9:30, she had to keep moving, even if it meant doing the work alone. She pulled more crafts and paintings from the van. After seeing that everything was out on the ground, she moved the van. All transporting vehicles had to be off the street, now! After parking in a lot behind the stores she was then able to cut through between buildings to get back to her area more quickly. The whiff of coffee coming from a nearby food wagon made her sniff appreciatively. She was digging into her coat pocket for some change to purchase a cup of coffee when she saw a white haired man picking up one of her boxes. He was stealing from her, right there in broad daylight. How could he? She raised the edge of her black cowboy hat, grabbed the bottom of her red denim jacket and jerked it down. The toe of her black boots barely showed from the hem of her black jeans, but the sound of stomping on the paved road drew the attention of those around her, except for the man stealing her merchandise.

Jenna did not back down. She marched right up behind the man and spoke in a harsh voice. "What do you think you're doing? That's my stuff!" She reached around him to grab back as much as she could handle. When he let go and the pressure from their tugging eased, she had to drop her end of the box to grab hold of a nearby table to keep from falling. The thief dropped his end, too and reached for Jenna.

While holding the pretty red-head in his arms, Charles McAdams smiled down at her. "Hello, Jenna," he said in a low voice.

To Jenna's ears it sounded sexy. She stared into his dark brown eyes, liking what she saw. At the age of fifty-two, Charles still looked great. His nice build showed to an advantage in jeans and denim shirt. Those items plus a pair of burgundy boots and matching Stetson were appropriate apparel for the cool mountain air. He was too good looking for her right now; she had to get away from him before she started swooning.

Stepping a couple feet backward she asked, "Charles McAdams, how long have you been watching me struggle with these boxes?"

With apparent difficulty, Charles seemed to be repressing a laugh and answered her as if she were a child. "I had to finish laying out my toys before I felt free to help a pint size woman with her heavy work. But evidently you don't want my help at all." He held up his hands in defense. "I can take a hint." He turned and left.

Jenna stood gaping at his departing figure. He had a lot of nerve. She was still staring at him, partly with admiration and partly with annoyance, when Debbie finally returned.

"Why were you so rude to Charles?" Debbie asked. With an amused look she added, "Why didn't you let him help? He's the only man that I see who looks willing to lift a finger for you." Debbie turned aside grumbling, "Still acting like an independent lady."

Jenna watched her daughter place several large vases of artificial flowers about their area. She did her own arranging, shaking her head. The movement made the pigtail hanging down the center of her neck swing sideways. No way could she be called independent, not physically anyway. With every bone in her body she wanted to be the strong, competent type in all areas of her life.

It was not happening to her, though. During the times when she over exerted her body she needed someone to lean on, to carry heavy loads. Someone except the man in the next booth, she thought, looking at him through squinting eyes. She finally answered Debbie, "Charles took me by surprise. With his back to me, I couldn't tell who he was. I thought he was a thief."

Debbie grinned. "I know it's been a while since you've seen him, but he hasn't changed that much. I thought you'd recognize him anywhere."

"Well I didn't," Jenna mumbled. She looked at her watch and saw that they had ten minutes to finish. She hung the last painting on a standing rack and then sent Debbie for a cup of coffee.

"Want a sausage biscuit, too?" Debbie asked.

"No. Make it a hot apple pie. I need the sugar to give me an energy boost," Jenna said, cautiously lowering herself into a lounge chair.

CHAPTER 4

Two ladies came into Jenna's area and immediately began admiring her work.

"Everything is so pretty," one of them said. "I could stay here for hours, looking at all these beautiful things."

Jenna's heart swelled with pride. "Welcome, ladies. If you see anything you like, I'll be glad to help you." She hoped they would buy something. She needed to make another deposit before another overdrawn statement arrived in the mail.

It was not long before her wish came true. She was raking in the money. "There you are," she said to one lady, handing her a bagged white mailbox with pansies painted all over the top.

The large lady gave a hearty laugh and said, "I'm taking this out of the bag. I want everyone to see it."

Jenna quickly attached a "sold" tag to it. She smiled and turned to assist another customer. For the short, thin lady, who looked as if a puff of wind would send her soaring down the street, she bagged up a metal tray that had a picture of children running through a field of wild flowers. She was so glad to have sold it. Knowing for sure that practically anything she paints will sell restored her confidence. Many of her picture frames, jewelry boxes, and canvass paintings have been purchased. As she looked at the wad in her money bag she smiled smugly. If only she could sell as much stuff during the rest of the day, she would certainly have enough money for a new water heater.

Jenna glanced toward the table beside her. Charles was watching her; she was certain of it. A lot of activity also went on at his table filled with wooden toys. Although she could not see his eyes, she felt sure that he knew every move she made.

But she could not understand his actions. He never waved, nodded or smiled, even when she was the target of his scrutiny. She kept wondering why he was acting so weird.

At one slack interval, Jenna decided to go over and speak to the disturbing man. But, at that same instant, a teenage boy came to her table, wanting to buy a birthday present for his mother. After waiting on him, Jenna's attention returned to Charles. They had not been in each other's company in a long time, but she had seen him. His television appearances, whether in Florida, New York or North Carolina, often blazed across her screen, capturing her attention. Also, his handsome face and detective stories stood out on the front page of newspapers across Buncombe and surrounding counties.

Jenna looked at Charles and wondered how she could have not known what he looked like, especially from the backside. Maybe she had subconsciously wanted him to see that not every woman knows every little thing about him. He had too much ego for his own good.

She again considered his looks. Like herself, Charles McAdams had changed, but he was still handsome, just in a different way. His once wavy blond hair was now thin and white. Jenna figured he got his dark tan while in Florida. During his frequent trips there, he had ample opportunity during poolside meetings to bask in the sun. With his natural dark skin tones, it did not take much sun and wind to make him browner.

Goodness, what's on his neck? She was tempted to rub her own neck but resisted. It's an awful looking scar. Wonder if it's from a fight that Debbie mentioned?

No matter how the man got marred, it did not take away from his looks. Jenna's heart began to pound. His six-foot-tall, strong profile stood out against the gray stone building behind him, helping to make him the most fascinating man in town.

Jenna's musings were interrupted by Debbie. "Mom, a new pot of coffee is being made and the pies aren't ready. Look what I did get: bright eye tea."

With eager hands, Jenna reached for it. "Great. It's a better pick-me-up than coffee with caffeine and a sugar filled pie." She sipped slowly, savoring every drop. While looking at her twenty-year-old daughter with gratitude she asked, "Didn't you want anything?"

"I drank a coke while waiting for your tea."

"You're so thoughtful."

"I know," Debbie answered with a mischievous grin, but don't tell anyone else. They may not agree."

Jenna continued to study her daughter. They were so much alike in looks: short, slender, and coppery-colored hair which was usually worn in a similar way. This time, though, where Jenna's was plaited, Debbie's was pulled up into a pony tail. A few sprigs that were left to hang along her heart-shaped face clearly showed a dusting of freckles across the bridge of Debbie's nose.

Freckles make her look cute, Jenna thought, but I don't like them on me. She could tolerate a few on her arms but hated those that the sun brought to her face. In the past, she used bleaching cream to get rid of them but gave up when they never completely left. Sunscreen did not always work wonders either. Jenna shrugged and considered the better features of her face: her green eyes.

Like Debbie, their eyes were wide spaced, clear emerald green, and fringed with thick lashes. Both women were told they made them look like troublemakers. With an endearing smile spread across her lips, Jenna recalled Debbie's mischievousness, but she was never real naughty. Jenna herself was taught that it was not nice to pull pranks on people, so she "tried" to behave.

There was one time when she wanted to grab up her brother's toys and let him look everywhere for them. She resisted the urge, afraid that she would get punished for aggravating him. "It's not nice to upset anyone unnecessarily," her father had said.

But Debbie was a regular little imp. She was forever hiding things that belonged to Jenna. When Jenna went to put on a certain hat and it was gone, she would get frustrated. After a time or two, she realized it was useless to get upset over a hat when she had others to wear. She decided to play along with the child, especially when she saw how much enjoyment Debbie got out of wearing the hats and imitating the grownups who wore them.

For instance, one day she caught Debbie prancing in front of the mirror with one hand on a hip, the child raised the hat brim of a large white straw hat covered with flowers and smiled at her reflection. "Hi," she said in a low-sounding voice. "My name is Mae West. Would you like to see my etchings?"

Jenna nearly swallowed her teeth and they were not false. "Where did you learn to do that?"

Debbie grinned and said, "On a black and white movie. Did I do it right?"

A hearty laugh escaped Jenna. "Honey, you are a bit too little in size and age to be like that movie star, but you did do a pretty good imitation."

Jenna thanked God for her daughter. No matter what she looked like or how mischievous she acted, Jenna wished she could have had a dozen children just like her.

She and Stuart wanted a large family. It had not been God's will or she would not have had three miscarriages. A familiar knot swelled in her chest and tears threatened to spill over. Jenna still saw the condemning look in Stuart's eyes. Each time she lost a child, no matter how far along in the pregnancy she was, he blamed her for losing it.

"I did my part so you could get pregnant," he said, "the least you could do is produce a living child."

When Deborah Leigh, a bouncing healthy baby, came along, they stopped trying to have more children. The doctor advised her it would be best for her health. Even though Stuart wanted at least one more child, she agreed with the doctor and had her tubes tied.

She had no idea that Stuart would get so mad over her decision. "You could have at least tried to give me a son," he said. "You think only about yourself. I didn't know how selfish you could be." He stormed out of the room and did not return until the next day when it was time to check her out of the hospital.

Jenna slept little that night. She cried most of the time. She wanted more children, but she also wanted to have the health to care for the one she did have. About three o'clock in the morning, she got on her knees and prayed. "Dear Lord, I am so grateful to you for blessing us with a precious little baby. Take her life and mold it to fit your image. I want Little Debbie to grow up to be a Christian, willing to serve you."

Tears of joy now filled Jenna's eyes when she recalled the night she dedicated Debbie back to the Lord. Several years ago at a crusade for teenagers, Debbie accepted Christ into her heart and life. Since then the light of God has shown through her. She has been so generous, loving, and caring toward others, a lot like Stuart was during the first years of their marriage. The comparison almost caused a knot to block the airflow in her throat. Jenna swallowed with difficulty. She forced herself to relax before anyone noticed she was having a problem and continued to recall certain phases of her life.

Debbie had taken a year's leave from college to be with her mother. Her presence helped Jenna to cope with the loss of Stewart, not only his physical death but the spiritual and mental separation that she and Debbie were having. Holding back the rush of tears that threatened to spill from her eyes, Jenna thought, I am so glad that Debbie has not turned out like Stuart.

For quite a while, Stuart had been the other half of Jenna. During college, when she missed the island, her home, and most of all her parents, he helped her deal with loneliness. He planned some off campus picnics where he sketched her portrait or she painted him. He also made each occasion romantic.

They did not get much done on the pictures because Stuart usually wanted to dance. He had taken ballroom dancing and was adept with the waltz and tango. Jenna had never tried either dance, but the beautiful music soaring from his CD player made her want to try. She picked up on the steps quickly. After several lessons they were dancing beautifully together. Soon they were drawing an audience into the park.

When they married and their careers were established, picnics were out. Stuart preferred to do things on a grander scale, like flying to New York, Las Vegas and New Orleans to dine and dance. At the time, they did not have Debbie and could take off and go whenever they pleased. The trips were wonderful, but Jenna preferred the simple meals beside a river or in a park. Recalling those times made her sad.

When Debbie was born, Jenna began to see a more noticeable change in Stuart. She noticed it first when he began to brag about his parents, how different they were from hers.

"My parents are successful: Mother is a lawyer and my father's a judge. I would never do anything to bring shame to my family," he said while standing at attention. "My parents would not allow me to do or act in anyway that would cause people to talk about me or them."

Stuart's acts of superiority hurt Jenna and made her defensive. "And you think I would? My family may not be wealthy as yours, but they are just as respectable. But they would never dictate to me or my brother every move we should or should not make. They felt that children should have a free spirit in them. Therefore we were allowed to feel that freedom."

Stuart's chin rose into the air and he spoke in a determined voice. "Our daughter will not be allowed to roam here and there. Neither will she be left alone with a nanny. There will be times when I'll take some French students abroad, but you will stay home with the child."

Trying to keep her anger from exploding, Jenna chose her words carefully. "I agree that it's not fair for both parents to leave a little child behind with someone it may not know, but Debbie is use to the people that I hire to baby sit."

With a distant look Stuart said, "I knew my nanny, too, but I missed my parents. Occasionally they took me on trips, but the nanny went, too. I was always with her. I don't know why they didn't just leave me and Ms. Lewis at home."

Jenna learned much more about Stuart from that conversation. He had no real family life. While he objected to being deserted by his parents, their standards of living were embedded in him. He lived by certain rules, that of being seen only when his parents wanted to show him off. If he stayed out of trouble and never whined for them he was rewarded with a new toy.

"Debbie will be trained this way, too," he told Jenna. "You will not buck me on this."

With someone having such a strict upbringing, being an adulterer was out of the question, so Jenna thought. "I certainly wouldn't have believed it. But perhaps there is certain logic to his behavior. With his domineering attitude he could do anything and no one would think badly of him."

These diverse traits explained why the man who was a pillar of the community ended up with a scandalous reputation.

Jenna was so glad that something good came out of her marriage: Debbie. This year could have been much worse for her without her daughter's company. They helped each other cope with the disaster caused by Stuart's life and death.

A clicking of Debbie's fingers and her words, "Let's get with it, Mom," reminded Jenna that they were at the festival, the morning was passing, and she had sales to make.

"I'm with it," Jenna answered and proceeded to wait on a customer about Debbie's age. The young lady bought a canvas painted picture of magnolia blooms, and then held it out for her friend to observe. "It reminds me of a painting that Grandmother has hanging in her dining room."

The tall folding rack behind the table contained several canvases filled with different flowers. As Jenna made sure they hung in the best light to catch immediate attention from passersby, she stopped to look at her favorite piece of art. It was an oil painting of a young lady resting beneath a white delicately stitched quilt on a chaise lounge in a garden filled with blooming rhododendrons. She titled it Peaceful Existence because it calmed her to paint it.

"I sort of hope it doesn't sell," she told Debbie.

"Put a high price on it," Debbie said, so Jenna did.

Nearly everyone who came by stopped to look at the painting; their eyes were filled with interest. Some of them returned to look at it a second time, but no one offered to buy it. Their comments usually consisted of phrases like, "I'd love to have it, but it's too expensive." Or "The artist is so talented." Or "The woman in the picture looks familiar."

A young boy about thirteen years old returned to look at the picture, too. Jenna observed him with a thoughtful expression and wondered if the picture reminded him of some place or someone special or if he just wished it were hanging in his house. *The poor thing looks like his family couldn't afford it at a give away price.*

She edged her way through a dozen or so people to get to him. He backed up as if he were getting ready to run off so Jenna spoke fast. "Do you like to paint?"

He shook his head and strands of brown hair fell across his eyes. With a sweep of the hand, he brushed it to the side and said, "My mama likes pictures. She used to come here every year. Now she's sick. She sent me here. 'Sammy, you go for me,' she said." With both hands jammed into the pockets of his well-worn jacket, he glanced at Jenna and mumbled, "Wish she could see this."

Tears rushed into Jenna's eyes. She blinked them away and picked up the biggest and prettiest stem of blooms from a vase. She handed the artificial pink flowers to the boy. "Take this to your mother. Maybe it will cheer her up."

He reached for it and then dropped his hand. "I don't have any money."

"It's free. It's a gift for your mother."

"Can you put it in a sack so I won't get it dirty?"

"Sammy, you're a very thoughtful boy," Jenna said and handed him the bagged up flower.

He started to run off but turned back. "Thanks. You're a nice lady."

Jenna was oblivious to the eyes watching the incident because hers were following the boy's progress as he tried to hasten down the street. The packed crowd hampered his maneuvers. People who were talking or looking at items refused to move out of his way. The last she saw of Sammy he was pushing past a group of teenagers.

Jenna turned around and bumped into someone. Bouncing back from a strong body, Chuck McAdams apologized, "Sorry. Are you okay?"

"I will be when I get my wind back," she said and breathed deeply. While letting the air flow out of her lungs she felt of his arm. "You must have been working out for a long time. I thought I'd hit a stone wall."

Chuck laughed. "I have been exercising on a regular basis. I figured I'd better be fit to chase down criminals."

"I guess detectives do have to be prepared for anything."

"It helps."

Jenna looked Chuck over from the blond wavy hair and dark velvety eyes to his shiny gray cowboy boots. "You're prepared all right, but it looks like you're ready to catch the eye of a beautiful girl instead of a bad guy."

Chuck winked. "Thanks, but I'm really trying to keep up with my old man."

Jenna glanced over at Charles. "I gather from all the publicity he's been getting that he pulls his weight."

Chuck smiled proudly and said, "You can say that again. Daddy works harder than anybody I know." He then bent down and twisted his head to get a better look at her face. "Why are you hiding under this big hat?"

Jenna pulled the brim down a little further over one eye and cocked her head sideways and grinned. "That's a story that will have to wait." She started toward a customer. "Come by the house sometime. I'll tell you about it."

"You're on," he said and went back to help his father.

His father had made a name for himself in this North Carolina area and around Jacksonville, Florida where he and his children lived for a while. Charles became popular for solving cases where the police had failed. Before his wife's death, he worked on a case at the house next to Jenna's. Her neighbor, Mavis Witherspoon had disappeared and later was found murdered.

Anger rekindled anew each time Jenna was reminded of that

woman. She did not like Mavis very much, because Stuart did, a little too much, but she did not believe the woman deserved to be murdered and buried in a shallow grave.

Stuart had been out of town for a week and returned late in the afternoon. When he drove up he saw Mavis' sons wandering around outside her house. He went over to see if there was a problem.

"We can't get into the house to see if Mama is all right," John said. "She hasn't been answering her house or cell phone. Have you got a ladder we can use to climb up to her bedroom window?"

"Sure. I'll be right back," Stuart answered and ran to the shed behind his house.

Jenna was on the deck and called down to him. "What's wrong?"

"The boys can't get into the house. Have you seen Mavis lately?"

Jenna shook her head. "No. But I seldom see her for days at a time."

After searching the house, they did not find Mavis nor a written note or a phone message as to where she might be. The police were called. Charles and Chuck arrived with the police. The sons wanted the detectives there. They were friends. Charles patted the boys on the back. "John. Richard. I'm sorry. We'll do all we can to find your mother."

The neighbors were questioned, Jenna in particular since she lived the closest. Every officer on the case came to her house at least one time, some even more. She was beginning to feel like a suspect for the woman's disappearance. When she complained to Chuck, he assured her that was not the case. "Since a driveway separates your homes, we thought you might have seen or heard something out of the ordinary."

Before this incident, Jenna had seen more than she wanted to reveal to anyone. Her husband's nightly visits to Mavis' house could put him under suspicion. At times she wanted to tell someone about them, but then she did not want to get in a fight with Stuart if she did. Jenna was not positive that her husband was having an affair with Mavis, but the numerous trips he made to her house at night to fix broken objects looked questionable. He seldom repaired anything at his own home, saying it was easier to call a repairman. Each time he came home from helping Mavis he avoided direct eye contact with Jenna, and it made her more suspicious.

The beautiful woman drew the eye of many men and the envious looks of most women. The divorcee had several male callers until fairly recently. They were narrowed down to one or two and a nephew.

Jenna had no idea that she had taken any pictures of the men coming and going in the woman's life until she had a couple rolls of film developed. For a long time she had thought of painting the Witherspoon house. She liked the old world design of the house and hoped to get in on canvass. Before she started sketching, though, she took pictures of it to have handy for the detail work.

When she picked up the pictures, she took them out to the patio where she could study the photos in the sunlight. She was deeply engrossed and did not see or hear Charles McAdams until he spoke. "What are you looking at?" he asked, sitting in the chair across from her.

"Mavis Witherspoon's house. I've wanted to paint it. I'm looking at these pictures to see what angle to give it. What's most interesting, I've gotten more than the house. I have pictures of several different men in them."

"Do you know any of them?"

"A couple of them: her nephew and sons but not the others. I've seen them getting out of their cars, but I've never met them."

While studying one picture in particular, Jenna picked up a magnifying glass to examine it more closely. "Look at this, Charles."

"It's a nice shot," he said, handing it back to her. "It would look good in a picture."

Jenna's voice was more intense when she said, "Take a closer look. Do you see a man?"

He took the magnifying glass and scanned the whole picture. Near a big bush was a man in a stooped position. "Do you know him?"

Jenna shook her head. "No. He's one that's been visiting Mavis more regularly than some of the other men. One day while Mavis and I were talking in the driveway, a big black Lincoln turned in. The driver didn't get out of the car but motioned for Mavis to come over. She excused herself, 'Guess I'll have to go see what Howard wants.' I said goodbye and came into the house."

"Did you notice anything else, maybe something about the car or their voices?" Stuart asked, looking at the other pictures for unusual markings.

"It was a warm day. I opened my windows to air out the house while I cleaned. I heard raised voices, like they were arguing, but I didn't listen closely to hear what they were saying. All of a sudden I did hear Mavis shout, 'I don't have it and I can't make it. I'll get it to you when I can. Just leave me a lone.' I looked out the window as the car took off up the road. The license plate caught my eye."

Charles sat up straight. "What was on it?"

"BOOKMAN. Wonder what it means? Perhaps his last name?"

"Possibly. Or it could stand for his profession. He could take bets. Or he could just be a man who likes to read."

As it turned out he was a bookie and Mavis owed him money. But he wanted more from her: her absolute attention. He did not want her seeing another man. When she refused to go out with him anymore, he killed her with a car jack. He then put Mavis in the trunk of her own car and buried her in a wooded area down the road. At the trial, he vowed to get even with Charles.

"What are you thinking about, Mom?" Debbie asked. "You look so serious."

Jenna kept looking at the people next to their table. "I've been watching Charles. He's quite the operator," she said softly. "His smooth sales pitch got that pretty brunette to buy a model jet airplane after she told him she didn't have any children. That man can spread his charm like maple syrup, leaving a sweet, lasting thought in the heart of his victims."

Debbie laughed out loud, drawing the attention of Charles and Chuck. With an innocent look she said, "Isn't it interesting that we're right beside the McAdams men."

Jenna knew Debbie's looks. She always opened her eyes wide and smiled brightly when she was trying to be secretive.

"Don't give me that look," Jenna said. "What are you up to?"

"What look?" Debbie asked and added, not letting Jenna answer, "Don't you think they're fab?"

Jenna squinted at Debbie. That girl has something going on that she doesn't want me know about? "I don't know about fab-ulous," she finally said, "but they are interesting."

CHAPTER 5

Charles overheard the last remarks made by Jenna and Debbie. As he watched them rearrange some paintings he thought that they were interesting, too and very pretty: Jenna in particular. She was an intriguing person, someone he would like to know better. He knew a lot of women, but none of them had the vitality of this lady. She loved to make crafts, paint, and meet the public. At social gatherings, she easily engaged in conversation with any age person. Today, he learned more about Jenna, that she was tenderhearted and loved a cup of tea.

Now ***she's*** *my cup of tea.*

A noise caused Charles to look down at the red farm tractor in his hand. It was upside down. Before Chuck could notice and question what was on his mind, he quickly put the toy in the empty space where a blue truck sat before a grandmother bought it. He liked for grandparents to examine his toys, because they usually bought something where as parents only looked at them. Sometimes they would go so far as to say, "They're so pretty. You do good work."

Charles rammed his hands into the back pockets of his jeans, inhaling and exhaling heavily. He reminded himself that he must be more conscious of the people at his table. He did not want anyone walking off with his toys. Sure Chuck helped with the crowd, but his son could not watch everyone, especially when his attention was devoted to Debbie. That boy could not take his eyes off of her.

Charles thought it was a shame that things did not work out between those two. They worked well together on whatever project they did, whether it was at school, church, or for some community activity. But they broke up after they went to separate colleges.

Chuck was not the only one who could not stay focused because of a woman. Charles blamed Jenna for his inability to pay close attention to the people around him. He was glad, though, that he could watch her now and not feel guilty for desiring another man's woman. He recalled the times that Stuart, Jenna, and Debbie came to his house for parties. He thought she was the prettiest woman in the room. He knew it was a sin to envy another man's wife, but he wished that God had given her to him instead of Stuart. The man did not deserve the loving, caring woman if he was not prepared to cherish her until death parted them, because he certainly did not do that by obeying their wedding vows. He cheated on Jenna and he robbed her and Debbie of ever having good lasting memories of their lives together.

Charles smiled as his thoughts took a turn for the better. Maybe there was a chance for him and Jenna to now have a closer relationship. He certainly hoped that her experience with Stuart will not turn her off men forever, correction, just himself.

Chuck observed the way his father kept watching Jenna. A secret smile played around his mouth. He eventually said, "Stuart's death has been traumatic for Jenna, but she doesn't want anyone to know how much. Debbie said she has too much anger bottled up to welcome sympathy. "

"I can imagine," Charles said, looking at her with awe. "She must have been devastated when she learned about Stuart's affairs. I don't see how she can manage to smile much less greet people like nothing out of the ordinary has happened."

He wondered how Jenna actually did handle the situation. He knew she was fifty, an age where most women hated the idea of knowing they may be alone the rest of their lives. In her case, she probably would rather be alone than be with someone she could not trust.

A look of pity filled his eyes as he continued to observe her. Jenna did not look physically strong. She appeared so fragile as if she would snap like a brittle twig. She looked like the type that would need lots of care and protection, not anything like his strong, confident Francine.

Francine, his wife had a lot of determination. No matter how she felt, many times she cleaned the house, mowed the yard, worked her vegetable garden, cooked a full meal, and then put three children to bed. Not once did she complain to him about having to do too much around the house.

Charles' head dropped as he recalled that it had been 20 years since Francine's death. He still missed her. When he came home from work, he expected to see her sitting in front of the television, waiting for him. At times he still wished for a chance to put his hands around Howard Bookman's neck and watch him beg for mercy. The man had no right to take anyone's life, especially Francine's.

True to his words, Bookman vowed to get back at Charles. He was angry at Charles for bringing him to justice for killing Mavis Witherspoon.

During the time Bookman was being transported from the courthouse to prison, he managed to escape. In a nearby strip mall, he forced a woman from her car and then drove off in it. He knew where Charles McAdams lived and went there. As he was arriving, Francine began backing out of their driveway. Bookman later told the judge that he had nothing to lose but everything to gain by hurting Charles, so he drove straight toward his wife's car. Before the impact, he slid around and hit the driver's side with his rear end.

Francine did not die right away. For weeks, Charles watched her suffer from broken bones and brain damage. During the times she went in and out of consciousness, he wished he would have stayed at home more, spent more time with her and the children. But it was impossible, and Francine knew it. She understood that it took a lot of work to get his detective agency going.

"Don't worry about me and the kids," she told him. "We'll be just fine. You do what you have to do."

Someone spoke to Chuck and Charles was reminded of his

surroundings. He jumped up from his lounge chair. "Chuck, can you handle things for a minute. I'm going for a walk."

"Sure. No problem."

A look of pain filled Charles' face as he walked and remembered. Many times he had done what he felt he must do, and that was helping to put criminals behind bars. Only one of them had threatened to get back at him and that had been Bookman. His children then had to suffer because they no longer had the love and care of their mother.

It was an ordeal that he hoped to never go through again. Losing someone you love is like losing part of yourself.

Charles had built a wall around his heart so he could stay immune to another woman's love and affection. It had worked until his children formed an attachment to Jenna Wilson. He had overheard a conversation where all three said they wished Jenna was their mother. It hurt but he had understood; they had not known their own mother well. The more he learned about Jenna, the more he was able to accept their affection for her. And little by little the wall around his heart was chipped away. Charles began to feel that perhaps someday he would have the desire to fall in love again. That day came.

By this time, he had ended his walk and was back at his table. He looked at Jenna and saw the gentle smile on her face as she swept a loving hand over a little girl's curly hair. He grunted and mumbled, "My children should have had a mother's touch like that."

Chuck turned from assisting a young woman with a purchase and said, "What's that, Dad? Were you speaking to me?"

He shook his head and put some more stock on the table. He knew that he should not let Jenna get to him because it would be asking for trouble, but he could not seem to help himself. He prayed, "God, help me with my growing attraction toward Jenna. I don't want to take the chance of another criminal taking his anger out on someone I love."

Running a top notch agency kept Charles on his toes and from dwelling on the past. He felt that if the rotten life he was given as a child had not made him a bitter person, he owed it to his children to not let anger toward Howard Bookman continue to grow in his heart. His life was rushing along; he needed to be in a good frame of mind should he ever want to get involved with another woman.

Charles eventually did release his anger toward Howard Bookman, and he handled it by finding something worthwhile to occupy his time. He enjoyed working with machines and tools, so he got some wood and began making toys for his children. When their friends' parents saw his cars and doll swings, they ordered similar toys for Christmas. Word spread about his craftsmanship. When he was not trying to solve a crime, help the kids with homework and take them for an outing, he made toys. For Tina and Lynn he made doll beds and kitchen furniture. Chuck got airplanes and a train set.

Charles once told his children about his youth, hoping they would then appreciate the homemade toys even more. He skipped over the really rough patches.

"I was born into a poor farming family. My mother was sick with cancer and died when I was about six years old. My father drank white lightning, a homemade brew of alcohol. He had been drinking the day of mother's funeral. As she was being lowered into the ground, he staggered up and nearly fell on top of the casket."

Tina crawled into the crook of her daddy's arm and murmured, "That's awful."

Charles nodded. "It was. I didn't want to go home with him. I knew he would beat me."

"Why?" all three of them asked at once.

"For no particular reason," Charles answered. "When he was upset, he took his anger out on me. My mother's brother wanted to take me to his home. When Daddy objected, Uncle Richard reported our living conditions to social services. I was soon placed in a home with a really nice woman, Mamie Timberlake. She was rich, but the best thing about her was that she was good to me. I learned to respect others and value what I had."

"Did you have lots of toys," Chuck asked, his eyes lighting up with interest.

Charles nodded. "I did, more than I needed. I had certain ones that I played with the most."

"Like what?" Lynn asked.

"Wooden cars and a train set. That's where I got the idea to make them for you," he said, looking at Chuck. "Mrs. Timberlake bought me a bicycle and a pedal car, but they didn't interest me as much as the wooden toys." He smiled and added, "The thing I liked best of all was the way Mrs. Timberlake treated me. I finally had someone to love me."

"Why haven't we met her?" Tina asked.

Sadness crept into Charles' face. "I had just graduated from high school when she had a heart attack and died. After the funeral I was told that she had left me enough money to go to college."

"That's why you're so smart," Lynn said.

Charles turned and grabbed her in a tight squeeze and said, "Smart enough to know you kids are keeping me talking so you won't have to go to bed, but you are and right now." He stood and ushered them to their rooms. As he listened to their prayers, he was reminded of the times that Mrs. Timberlake listened to his. She had taken him to church every week. Even though he stopped going after her death, lessons that Charles had learned at church remained with him.

The word church now made him smile and sigh with relief. Nothing had helped Charles gain peace and tranquility like the spiritual guidance he got from hearing God's word through the singing and pastor's messages.

During one particular sermon, the pastor said that no one had to continually be in despair and feel nothing but loneliness, that God could help overcome such terrible feelings. That was when Charles bowed and prayed, "God, I'm sorry that I have not been serving you as I should. I promise to read the Bible and talk to you more often. I need you and want you in my life all the time."

From then on, Charles attended church on a regular basis. When he was out of town he visited some local church and made sure that someone took his children to Sunday school. Most often Jenna took them. They loved going to the Wilson home because Jenna spent time with them, by taking them skating or to the movies. She treated them as if they were her own children. Stuart seldom paid them any attention. If he knew they were coming, he went out of town on business or to the college to work on lessons, so he said. As Charles recalled those occasions, he wondered if the visits by his children provided him with opportunities to meet some woman behind Jenna's back.

If Charles had any inkling that it had happened, he may not have taken so many trips himself. But his trips, being separated from his children, made him more eager to get home. Each time, he counted the minutes until he could hug each one and spend time with them, solving mysteries that they or Rosie, the housekeeper, had made up. Rosie's mysteries were genuine; the children's were more like pranks where someone would be fooled by the outcome. For instance, The Mystery of the Hot Cookies involved all three little imps.

Rosie had given each child a responsible job. Tina learned to cook, Chuck did the gardening and yard work, and Lynn became an avid housekeeper. Tina had just made up a batch of chocolate chip cookie dough and went to the bathroom. While she was out of the room, Chuck and Lynn put hot sauce in the batter. The cookies were awful. Once that mystery was solved, Tina put rubber snakes in their beds and in her own, giving them The Mystery of the Black Snakes.

Charles smiled and thought, *with all their mischievous ways, I adore my children.* His musings were interrupted by Debbie's voice. "Mom, can you believe this crowd? I never thought this many people could be interested in crafts, food and entertainment." Her eyes sparkled with excitement as she stepped forward to help a newly wed couple pick out a painting for their bedroom. "I really like this picture with the woman resting in the garden," the bride said. "It has the colors I like."

Debbie looked at her mother and saw the horrified expression on her face but relaxed when the young woman picked up another painting. "But this scene of downtown Montford is the one I want."

Jenna exhaled. "I thought Peaceful Existence was gone."

Debbie giggled. "I know. I thought you were going to have a stroke or heart attack. I know how easy it is for you to procrastinate. Aren't you glad you buckled down and did a lot of painting for today?"

"I am, and I didn't even need Stuart to push me," Jenna responded with a proud look.

"You've every right to be proud," Debbie said and went to help another customer. Over the chatter and laughter coming from the McAdams men, Jenna heard Debbie bragging about her work. She appreciated the way her daughter felt about her artistic abilities. Until she told Debbie about her fifth grade experience, she never said much about her paintings, except for Peaceful Existence.

One day while sorting through a stack of pictures, Debbie wanted to know about the pieces with blue ribbons attached. "They're some of my earlier pictures," Jenna told her. "I realized I was doing pretty good work after my mother received a phone call from my fifth-grade teacher, Patsy Byerly. Miss Byerly asked Mom to come to school some afternoon as soon as possible. She wanted to talk about me. I had no idea what the call was about. I thought, Uh-oh. This can't be good."

"Were your grades bad?" Debbie asked.

Jenna presented a wry twist of the lips and said in a deadpan voice, "Only in math of course, so I thought."

"Well. What had you done?"

"Painted," Jenna answered with a grin.

"What? The blackboard?"

"No, the teacher."

Debbie gasped. "You didn't?"

"No, of course I didn't," Jenna answered. "I had painted several canvasses. Miss Byerly wanted Mom to see the artwork hanging around the room. She said, 'Mrs. Frazier, pick out the ones Jenna did.'

"That's easy," Mom said. "She's always been fascinated with Mrs. Hanks' rose garden.' I was determined to paint it during the different growth periods. It was quite a challenge, but I did a pretty good job with it, so Miss Byerly said anyway."

The teacher told Mrs. Frazier that Jenna's paintings always stand out. The brush strokes defy her age. "Most adults could never produce the artwork Jenna is already doing at the age of fourteen. Don't let her talent go to waste."

"What do you suggest we do now?" Mrs. Frazier asked.

Miss Byerly smiled and said, "If you don't mind, and Jenna wants to, I'm going to enter them in a contest representing our art department."

"So she did," Jenna told Debbie, "and I won the blue ribbons that you see. Also, one of my pen-and ink designs of a scene on our island appeared on the front of our tenth-grade school annual. I was so proud of that accomplishment."

"I'd be, too," Debbie said. "I love that picture." She ran to the small bookcase in the corner of her mother's bedroom and pulled out that annual. "I like the picture of you on the last page, too."

Jenna smiled. "Thank you. I'm quite fond of it. I never dreamed that I'd get that kind of recognition for anything that I had done."

The shot of her sitting on the island dock, painting was another way for the school to honor her contribution to the annual.

With a look of awe, Debbie said, "I don't understand how you can remain silent and not brag about your talent."

Jenna shrugged. "I don't want to get the big head."

Jenna may not have bragged on her work, but Debbie did. To everyone she waited on at the festival she sang her mother's praises. "My mother has a wonderful touch with a paintbrush. When I stare at the scenes, I feel like I'm going to step right into them." She wrapped up a painting of a girl riding a horse across the meadow and handed it to her customer. "I hope you get a lot of enjoyment out of this."

When the woman walked off, Debbie flopped onto the nearest chair. Jenna dropped onto the lawn chair and reached for her daughter's hand and squeezed it. "Thanks for helping me today. I don't know what I would have done without you."

Debbie glanced toward Charles. "Oh, I think you would have managed." With a smile she added, "Your work sells itself. The paintings show what's in your heart, and you've got the biggest heart in the world."

Jenna smiled. "I've told you a thousand times to not exaggerate." She got up, still smiling and went to help an elderly man. He wanted a cup and saucer decorated with small geraniums. A twinkle came into his eyes when he said, "My wife collects cup and saucer sets. Since your signature is on this one, she'll be getting two treats in one."

Jenna's face glowed. "Thank you. Tell her I'll be at Black

Mountain's Spring Fling. If she's in the area and can come by, I'd like to see her."

"We live at Black Mountain," he responded. "If nothing happens, we'll be there.

CHAPTER 6

Jenna looked about her and saw only a few people left in the street. Everyone appeared to be heading toward the parking lots while some vendors were starting to pack up. Relief swept over her, and fatigue took over where excitement fizzled out. She looked at Debbie as she dropped onto a chair. "Are you as tired as I am?"

Debbie moved from the table were she was leaning. Remembering Lynn's words to keep Jenna floundering, she avoided looking directly at her mother. "I am a little tired," she said hesitantly, "but not so worn out that I want to stay home tonight." As pulled her pocketbook from a box under the table she added, "Chuck has invited me to supper. I'd really like to go. We have some catching up to do. Since there's not a lot to pack up, you can handle it by yourself, can't you?"

Jenna swallowed a pill to relieve the pain in her back. She needed help with the table and folding panels because it hurt too much to lift and shove them into the van. "Deb, I need…"

"Are you ready, Debbie?" Chuck asked, taking her by the hand. "If we hurry, maybe we can get a booth at the Pizza Hut before the crowd beats us there."

As they started walking up the street, Debbie stopped and looked back. "Mom?"

Jenna needed Debbie's help desperately and could use Chuck's strong arms, too, but Debbie's eager expression had her giving in. "Go," she said, shooing them on. "I can handle things by myself."

When they were out of sight, Jenna dropped her head into her hand that was propped on the chair arm. How was she going to pack up everything? She wondered. Her back felt like it would break if she tried to lift even an empty box.

She rested a moment longer before attempting to gather up her stock. By the time the boxes were packed, Charles had put the last of his equipment in his vehicle and shut the door. He was ready to leave.

Jenna watched him out of the corner of her eye. What she wouldn't give for his help, but she dared not ask for it. But on her way to get her van she prayed, "Lord, help me to get loaded up quickly so I can go home."

She was folding a tablecloth when she noticed Charles coming in her direction. She stuffed the cloth into a box with crafts. While closing the lid she asked, "Did you have a good day?"

He took her box from the table and stacked it with the others she had nearby. "I'm very pleased with the sales I made. I enjoy doing this, but I get more fun out of meeting people and visiting with old friends who drop by. How about you?"

With a smile she answered, "I sold a lot which I'm grateful for, and like you, I've really enjoyed visiting with the public." As she struggled with a heavy box she frowned. Charles stepped forward. "Let me put that in the van for you."

With a sigh of relief she said, "Thank you so much. I'll take any help I can get."

After he made a third trip to the van, she apologized for her earlier behavior. "I'm sorry I thought you were a thief this morning."

With a straight face he asked, "You don't think I'm one now? I may be planning to take off with your van once it's loaded."

"But I know now who you really are," she said. "Besides, who would drive your Suburban?"

Charles frowned. "That's a thought."

Jenna presented a crooked smile and said, "Right now you can have my van and anything else you want. The way I feel, I could lie on the ground and forget I even have a vehicle full of supplies to empty when I get home."

Charles' expression grew grave. "Are you not well?"

"It's my back. When I do too much work or stand on my feet a lot, it gives me a fit."

He placed a lounge chair at the back of her legs. "Here, sit down and let me handle the packing. It won't take a minute to finish."

Jenna was about to object but thought better of it. She needed his help.

When he came back for he chair she asked, "Will you please forgive me for being so rude to you this morning?"

His dark eyes glittered with humor. "Of course. If you'll let me take you out for supper."

"I'd love to go, but not tonight," Jenna responded, genuinely disappointed. "I would be terrible company. Can I have a rain check?"

"Sure. I'll give you a call next week," Charles said, grinning at her skeptical look. "I promise. I will call you. Have no doubt about that. By the way, where are you going next?"

"Home, where I can take a long soaking bath and I hope a good night's rest."

Charles chuckled. "A leisure bath sounds wonderful, but I meant which festival will you be attending next?"

Jenna blushed, something she seldom did. "I'm sorry. See, I'm so tired I can't think straight. If we went to eat, I'd probably fall asleep half way through the meal." She put both hands on her back and added, "Earlier today, some woman came by, trying to get vendors to commit to Black Mountain's Spring Fling. This festival was my first. Since I'd sold a lot of things by that time, I went out on a limb and paid my entry fee for it. Now, I'll have to work like crazy to have enough inventory by then. How about you? Are you going there?"

He looked directly into Jenna's eyes and smiled. "I am. Perhaps we'll be beside each other again."

A fluttery sensation churned in her stomach. What a handsome man, she thought. Charles' warm brown eyes held her immobile unable to think clearly, hardly able to breathe, she responded softly, "That would be nice."

She could not look away and wondered what is this man doing to me? Not a thing, she tried to tell herself, but he was and she had to put a stop to it. She overreacted to him because of her exhaustion. She refused to allow physical reactions to another man erupt within her. It would be disloyal, like being unfaithful to the man whom God had joined with her, even though the rat was dead.

Bad feelings of unfaithfulness to someone else kept cropping into Jenna's head. Her mind drifted back through the years. She could easily see her parents, Jeremiah and Jessica Frazier on the small island off the coast of Florida where she grew up, and then went off and left them. It was not that she had eagerly left them; they had sent her away to finish her education. She could have returned there after college, though, and helped them in their latter years, but she had stayed on the mainland. Now feelings of unfaithfulness to her father bothered her.

Jeremiah Frazier's business had been to harvest and export herbs. A number one choice with most of his customers was peppermint leaf used for a soothing relief. When Jenna was at home, she helped her father. As a teenager she worked in the fields and the docks, learning all she could about the business. She hoped to one day become her father's partner. The older she got the less time she had to work with him, though. Not only did school and social activities keep her busy, circumstances made her leave the island. She hated the thoughts of leaving home and had cried over it, a lot. "Mama, I can't go away. I won't survive."

If she were to complete her education, it meant leaving home. The island school only went as far as the eleventh grade. Higher education had to be achieved in the states.

To travel back and forth each day to Florida on the ferry was impossible. The ferry's timetable did not coincide with the school's schedule, so the Fraziers made arrangements for Jenna to live with strangers. Before they talked to her about the housing situation, Jeremiah contacted close business associates in Florida and asked advice as to where Jenna should stay.

"I suggest you put her up with a reputable family who has kept college kids before," was the advice from different individuals. They all agreed to send him some names and phone numbers of people to contact. After many extensive conversations and reference calls, Jeremiah and Jessica went to Florida to meet with a middle-aged couple. Before leaving, they told Jenna about the situation and asked her to go with them to meet the people. She refused. "No. I'm not going now or later."

"If you want to go to college, you will go sometime," her mother said.

"Why can't I take a correspondence course? Some of my friends are going to take writing courses at home," Jenna said, hoping that this would be the answer for her, too.

"I'm sorry," Jenna, her mother said. "We've checked out that avenue, but it wasn't the best one for an artist. You need the one on one lesson with a professional teacher. If you're not going to the mainland with us to meet the family, then for heaven's sake, please behave and try not to worry so much."

All the time that her parents were gone, Jenna worried and a lot. With each passing minute she grew more anxious. She hated the idea of leaving home and not being able to see her parents and friends everyday. Above all, she did not want to live with strangers. Some of her friends bubbled over with joy about getting off the island. They did not worry where or with whom they would live, but Jenna dreaded it with ever fiber of her being. And she was not going to leave the island. She went looking for somewhere to hide.

She wandered down to the docks. The closer she got to them the faster she walked. Her old friend, Mr. Cope, was loading up his boat. She tried to spend a few minutes with him each time he came to shore. He had great stories to tell and captured her attention from the first sentence. She picked up many pointers from him and hoped one day to be able to tell stories as well as he.

She ran up to the aging gentleman and hugged him. "Mr. Cope, I've got a request to ask."

"What's that child?"

"Can I live with you?"

He laughed and asked, "Do you think Jeremiah and Jessica would let you?"

With all the confidence she could muster, Jenna answered, "Oh sure. They're looking for a place to send me now. See, I'm supposed to finish school on the mainland and then go on to college. I'll be gone a long time. I don't want to live with strangers. You live in Florida, couldn't I live with you?"

"Jenna darling, if I had a wife or a sister or a daughter living with me to take care of you, I'd take you in a heartbeat." His expression was as sad as Jenna's when he added, "I'm sorry, love, but it wouldn't be good for you to live with a crusty old man who's not home half the time."

Jenna blinked back the tears that were gathering in her eyes. She gave him another hug and said, "I know. I was just hoping."

When she strolled back up the street, heading home, she veered off track and wandered around the island, trying to find a place to hide. Every idea was rotten. She could not stay in a cave long and she wouldn't want to. She could not stay with anyone on the island because her parents would soon find her. She could not just drop out of sight.

She was in the backyard, sketching her house when her parents came home and told her about the family she would be living with. "You mean I still have to go live with strangers?" she asked.

Jeremiah wrapped a big arm around her shoulders and said, "You don't have to worry about this couple; I've checked them out. People think highly of them. They are Christians. You'll be in good hands."

"But I don't know them," Jenna cried. "What if they don't like me? I'm scared, Daddy."

"You'll be fine," he said, hugging her close. In a soft voice he said into her ear, "They will love you almost as much as I do."

The night before she was due to leave, Jenna could not sleep. She lay awake in the dark room and prayed something would happen to prevent her from having to go. When Jessica came into the room, she begged, "Please, Mama, let me stay here."

Jessica gave her a cup of peppermint tea and stood over her until she drank some of it. She sat on the bed beside her daughter and brushed strands of hair back from Jenna's face. "Remember, my dear, your father and I love you and want only the best for you."

Jenna clung to her mother and cried, her tears flowing. With great gulping sobs she said, "Mama. Don't make me go."

Jessica hesitated and then said softly, "I don't like the decision we've had to make, but it's been made. If you intend to finish your education, you must go. Don't you want the art degree you've always talked about?"

"Yes, but…"

"Jenna, we're not sending you away alone. Remember, the Bible tells you to trust in the Lord with all your heart and don't depend on your own understanding. Honey, talk to Jesus everyday. Tell him your problems, thoughts and wishes, he will comfort you." Distress was evident in Jessica's voice when she said, "I'll do the next best thing: I'll write and call you often."

Jenna drank the rest of her tea and listened while her mother talked about all the things she could see and do in Florida. Sleep overcame Jenna and she fell back against the pillow.

Jessica kissed her forehead and walked out of the room wiping tears.

Art classes helped Jenna cope with loneliness. For her first assignment, she drew scenes she remembered about the island. Coconut trees, fishermen and jewelry makers filled nearly every picture. She vowed to keep part of her past alive in her heart, mind, and vision. Each time she took a different painting to class, the teacher and students liked them a lot.

One of those students who paid her the most compliments was Stuart Wilson. They quickly became friends. At Florida State University, they took some of the same classes. During their second semester they decided to go steady.

Two weeks after graduation, they married and moved to Asheville, North Carolina, where Stuart taught at UNC (University of North Carolina) Asheville and Jenna taught at Montreat College. When Debbie was born, Jenna quit work and stayed home with her. Her artwork at that time was no longer a career but a hobby. As soon as Debbie became of school age, Jenna returned to teaching.

Jenna's visits back home to the island grew fewer and far between. Yet, every summer and Christmas holidays, she and Stuart took Debbie to visit her grandparents. Each time the boat left the pier, taking them back to the mainland, Jenna felt it could be the last time she would see her parents alive. Nature soon took its course. Jessica died when Debbie was five; a year later Jeremiah passed away.

Stuart found excuses to not go to either funeral. He claimed work kept him from going. One time he said that he could not find anyone to take over his classes; another time he could not leave because it was exam time.

Jenna ached for his company. "I need your support," she said. "There may be some problems to arise that you could advise me with."

He kept his head turned away, flipping back and forth through some papers on his desk. "You'll do fine," he mumbled. In a stronger voice he said, "Just be sure to tell that supervisor that you'll be the new boss of Jeremiah's company. He's to contact you before making any major decisions."

The next area of unfaithfulness came from Stuart. For years Jenna gradually learned the real reason for his growing lack of attentiveness. The knowledge was much worse than his lack of concern for her grief over her parents, and it nearly destroyed her. His verbal abuse and adultery affected her worse than the deaths of both parents.

A weary sigh escaped Jenna. She was glad that Stuart had not suffered a lot with his heart attack but she wished that before he died he had been made to feel some grief for the sin he committed. Over and over she prayed about their experience. This time she begged for God to remove her bitterness. "I can't keep it from rising up. Please help me to overcome my hatred."

The man Jenna thought as a loving and devoted husband had not been thoughtful of her at all, at least for not very long, she corrected. Because of his behavior she was forced to sell their lovely Tudor-style home and purchase a cottage in the small community of Fletcher. The little yellow house with white trim would have been ideal if she really wanted it. The thing was if it had not been for Stuart's squandering, she and Debbie could have stayed in the house they both loved.

Despite her feelings for Stuart and the way he had treated her, she could not stop recalling his charming smile and the way his eyes twinkled when she saw the same look on the face of Charles McAdams. Was there a meaningful difference to be found in the men? She wondered if Charles pretended to feel compassion and understanding of others' faults. Did he also get frustrated and call women stupid for not being able to manage their own affairs?

Charles' muscular hand grasped her arm, catching Jenna off guard. She quivered in response, but she let him help her to stand. She apologized for not helping him load up her crafts. "My mind's on other things."

While walking with her to the mini van, Charles said, "Jenna, I know you're tired and should be getting home. Do you think you can drive? If not, I'll take you and get my neighbor who is standing up the street to drive my Suburban and follow us."

She gave him an appreciative look but said, "I am tired, but I'm well enough to drive."

"Okay. I'll follow you up the road to make sure you get home safely."

When his vehicle gunned to life, Jenna shut her gaping mouth and climbed into her van. Leading the way, she kept glancing to see that Charles was still behind her. His presence filled her with a calmness that surprised her. As she turned into her driveway, she stuck her arm out of the window and waved good-bye. He tooted the horn and drove on by. She murmured, "Now, there goes a considerate man."

CHAPTER 7

The Pizza Hut was filling up fast. Pop music and loud voices made it impossible to have a private conversation. As Chuck and Debbie waited in line to be seated, they watched in dismay as more people entered the restaurant. When a bunch of teenagers and a large family with three small children tried to be heard over each other, Chuck rolled his eyes. Just as he was about to speak to Debbie, she said, "I can't hear myself think."

"Me neither," he said and took her arm. "Let's go somewhere else."

They passed several well-known restaurants, but as always, they looked crowded. Finally he turned into a parking lot. "What's the saying about good places to eat?"

Debbie's face was filled with question but said, "Unless it's packed out, the food can't be too good? Something on that order I think. Anyway, I'm game to try this place if you are."

"Maybe we can get a BLT. I don't think you can do a lot of damage to a bacon, lettuce, and tomato sandwich. The main thing right now is a quiet place to talk. Agree?"

Debbie smiled tentatively and nodded.

As they stepped just inside the door, the aroma of steak and onions escaped the kitchen. Both of them sniffed appreciatively. "Might change my mind about that BLT," Chuck said.

Upon their request, a cheerful young lady led them to a table away from the other diners. When she handed them the menu, Chuck saw the owner's name at the bottom: Steve Randall Bailey. He looked at Debbie to see her reaction. She was looking around the room. "Do you see him?" Chuck asked in a tense voice.

"Who?" Debbie asked, looking puzzled.

"Steve Bailey."

"Why? Is he here?"

He pointed to the name on the menu and said, "I expect so since he's the owner."

Debbie began gathering up her jacket and pocketbook. "Do you want to leave?"

"Not yet unless, you do," he answered, looking toward the kitchen door.

The waitress came back. "Are you ready to order?"

Instead of ordering, Debbie asked, "Is the owner here?"

The young brunette smiled and said, "Not now. He's not here much, except when there's a meeting. Every Monday morning, Mr. Bailey and some business men have breakfast here. We're closed to the public during that time."

Debbie relaxed and ordered a BLT. Chuck did the same. When the girl left, he said, "Bet the meeting's about drugs: who made the best deals over the weekend."

Chuck threw an arm over the back of his chair and with a hard look said, "Just think, you were almost Mrs. Bailey, wife of a drug dealer."

Debbie spoke through tight lips. "I was never going to marry him."

"He said you were. He had the word out all over town."

"But you never saw an announcement in the newspaper did you?"

"No. Why wasn't it?"

"When he asked me to marry him, I said no, because I was in love with someone else. But he wasn't going to take no for an answer. At a party we attended, he took the microphone from a singer and made the announcement. I was shocked. It made me furious. I didn't want to cause a scene there so I laughed and told the people that it was all a joke. You know how people like to take something and run with it. Someone had taken the announcement and ran to a newspaper office and radio station; it was even on the television. The next day the news was all over town. Daddy heard about it and called me bright and early one morning. He was livid, not at Steve but me for being in a position where the rumor could start. He said I was a disgrace to him, not him and Mama, just him. He would have to come up with a good story for his friends and business associates."

"What did he say?"

Debbie presented a wry twist of the lips and said, "The truth, although he didn't believe it. I had been writing a paper on drug dealers and got close to Steve in order to get some information. He said in order for him to help me I would have to claim to be his girl. He made the announcement, hoping that the police would think he had changed and would leave him alone."

"So it was true," Chuck murmured. "I owe you an apology. Lynn told me the same thing, but I wouldn't accept it. Since we were no longer together, I figured you had fallen for Steve."

Debbie shook her head. Tears were in her eyes. "I cared a lot about you. I hated it when you went off to college. I was afraid you'd forget me once you were around all those pretty, preppy girls there. And I was right. You hadn't been there a month before you took one of them to a dance."

Chuck looked shocked. "How'd you know about Penny Hornbuckle? Lynn didn't tell you. She promised me that she wouldn't."

"You do remember Kenneth, your brother-in-law?"

"Duh. What's he got to do with anything? Don't tell me he told you?"

"Dawn Sparks, his cousin or some sort of relative, and her friends from Western University came into the coffee shop on Montford Street where I usually go after classes with my friends. She was telling the girls about the hunk who was going with Penny. You could have knocked me over with a feather."

"What difference did it make to you? You were with Steve?"

"Yes, I was seeing Steve, for the story and to ride his motorcycle."

When Chuck grinned, she added, "Our relationship was not serious. He did keep after me to make it serious. What about you and Penny. How serious are you two?"

"It's only friendship. Have you ever seen the girl?" At the shake of her head he added, "Penny's not very pretty but she's nice." Chuck's face filled with his most mischievous look and he laughed. On a serious note he added, "I honestly wish you could have been there. Some girls were teasing Penny because she didn't have a date for the dance. I thought she was going to burst into tears. We had a class together, but I didn't know her well. Still, I couldn't let that bunch of snobs insult the poor girl anymore. I went up, took her hand, and said, "There you are, Penny. I've been looking everywhere for you. Are you or are you not going to the dance with me? To the other girls I said, 'Excuse us, please' and took Penny away. Like a poor little lap dog, she obediently followed. She hadn't so much as grunted, but boy she was giving me a wary look until we were out of hearing distance of the girls."

Debbie giggled. "You didn't really do that?"

Chuck crossed his heart. "If I'm lying I'm dying."

"Once you were alone, what happened?"

"I told her about you. I said at first I hadn't planned to go because I had a lot of studying to do. It was too late to invite you since the dance was in two days."

"I could have made it," Debbie said, looking disappointed.

"I'm sorry, Debbie, but I hadn't planned to go. I had loads of studying to get done for my law class, but I felt sorry for Penny. After I said you were the forgiving kind I asked her to go."

In a deadpan voice Debbie said, "Oh, aren't you Mr. Wonderful."

"I hope you will think so after I tell you about Penny. She had just gotten a call from her boyfriend in West Virginia. He couldn't work it out to go to the dance. When she saw that I was serious the second time I asked her, she said she would be honored to go with me."

Debbie reached across the table and squeezed his hand. "That really was nice of you."

He grinned. "I thought so. We had a good time, laughing and talking about our sweethearts."

Not feeling too jealous at this point, Debbie asked, "How did she look?"

Chuck waggled his eyebrows and said, "Actually, pretty good. Her roommate had fixed her up."

"Evidently you were seen together more than once, since Dawn said you were an item."

Chuck looked her in the eye, his look adoring. "You are the only one for me. I thought I'd die when I heard you were engaged. Lynn tried to convince me to ask you about it, but I couldn't. Pride wouldn't let me, especially when I'd see you on the back of his motorcycle."

"We have been two dummies. Lynn tried to convince me that nothing was going on between you and Penny, but since I seldom saw you, I knew she was wrong."

Noises nearby made them look up. A group of men and women, including Steve Bailey, dressed in party clothes arrived and went into a closed off room.

Debbie whispered, "Let's go. I don't want to run into Steve."

Chuck tossed a tip on the table and added, "Me neither. I might bust his nose."

Debbie took his arm, hugging it close. "I'm so glad we've gotten things straightened out between us."

"You and me both. Now you'll soon be the one leaving me. When are you going back to college?"

"When I feel that Mom is okay. I hope she and Charles get together. How do you feel about it? I know Lynn talked you into getting their tables together. Would you be okay with them dating?"

By this time Chuck was turning into the driveway at Debbie's house. "I think it's great. You know I've always thought Jenna was a special lady, she's almost as wonderful as her daughter." He then took her in his arms and kissed her. It was a long one.

The rumble of thunder broke them apart. In a breathless voice, Debbie said, "I better go in."

He walked her to the door. "I'll have to thank my sister. She said she wanted to get Daddy and Jenna together, but she probably had other intentions, like getting us together, too. Whatever, it was a good plan. I'll call you tomorrow."

Debbie floated into the house. When the sounds were coming from her mother's room caught her attention her feet touched the floor. She slowed down at her door. In a sleepy voice, Jenna was mumbling about crafts and rain. Debbie smiled and went on to bed.

Sometime later, Jenna aroused from sleep. She looked toward the window and saw rain pelting against the glass. After a bit of rolling and tumbling she finally buried her head beneath the covers. She hated thunderstorms. A shiver shook her to the bones.

Sleep eventually came around four o'clock.

Where was she, in a dream or the real world? Everywhere Jenna went she looked for something; for what she had no idea. She felt when it surfaced she would know immediately what it was that disturbed her so much.

Sweat made her clothes stick to her body, or was it the rain? Jenna pushed her way through bushes, not looking where she walked and she stumbled. On her way down, a limb snatched the ball cap from her head and a branch pulled at her braided hair.

Rumbling thunder grew louder as it moved overhead. Lightning flashed, revealing a man in front of her. The tall, white-headed man with a charming smile looked like Charles McAdams. Though he was dressed in a pinstriped suit, the stamp of success, he appeared humble and looked at her with tenderness.

It was Charles. He reached down to help Jenna. She put her hand into his, stood, and tightened her grip. "Please help me," she begged.

He nodded but let go of her hand.

Jenna stooped to get her cap. When she arose, Charles was gone. She looked all around and saw nothing, not even the bushes. She twisted first one way and then another. Everything she thought wonderful had disappeared. The scenery she loved to paint no longer existed.

Feeling desolate and hurt, she opened her mouth to cry for help, but nothing came out. Her body grew heavy. Her sight dimmed. Up ahead sat a man. Was it Charles? Whoever it was, he appeared to be praying. Jenna needed someone to pray for her.

Thunder crashed. Her heart beat harder. She thought it would burst through her chest. She looked around for shelter and saw her mini van. Before she got to it, a woman jumped in and drove off. The screech of tires and a constant blare of the horn made an eerie sound.

Jenna rubbed up and down her arm. As she stood there alone, she looked out across the wide expanse of space. She could see no one. Not a car was in sight. How was she going to get home? "Stuart, where are you? I wish you would take care of me." As fast as that thought came to her, one of different kind followed. "No, I don't! I want someone who loves me."

The buzzer on the clock blasted into Jenna's fuzzy mind. She jerked to a sitting position and looked about her. After a minute or two she fell back onto the bed. "That was an awful dream," she mumbled before sleep reclaimed her brain.

The buzzer went off again.

Jenna grabbed hold of her aching head. To stop the noise, she slapped at the clock until she knocked it off the table. With having to fumble around to find the offending piece, she came fully awake and saw the time. *Ten thirty! It can't be.*

She jumped from the bed and dashed into the bathroom. While the shower water warmed up, she dialed the number for the Hendersonville Country Club. She talked to the Christian Women's Club president. "I'm running late," Jenna said. "But I promise I'll be there in time for my part of the program."

Bathed and dressed in her good-luck outfit, she quickly drank a cup of good morning tea to refresh her senses. As she straightened the teal blue hat with a narrow up-turned brim, she took a look at her full-length reflection and smiled, recalling the day the bought the calf-length, teal blue dress, embroidered with bright gold and white flowers.

She was in bad need of something new to wear to a fundraiser. While thumbing through a sales rack in a local department store, this dress practically jumped off the rack and into her hands. It fit perfectly. She had to have it. When she wore it to the Women's Lions Club dinner, she received many comments on her great look. Her quick sketch of local scenery helped the ladies to raise a thousand dollars for the blind. With those results, she claimed the dress to be her lucky charm. She hoped it brought her success today.

In the passenger's side of the van, she stuck in an easel, some canvases, and art pencils. The crafts left over from the festival that was still packed in the rear barely registered with her. Her mind was centered on driving to the country club without getting a speeding ticket or having a wreck.

During the past year she found herself more and more to be pressed for time to various functions in which she was a featured speaker. Something had to change. She needed better order to her life. She can not continue to go on like this. It was a wonder she ever presented a decent program. She did, though. Her programs had been accepted well. She often received thank you notes from people who took up art as a hobby or chose to make it a career because of something she said.

The knowledge that she could share her God-given talent to others enriched her love for art even more. As with all the other programs, she looked forward to today's meeting. But for the moment, Jenna could not concentrate on her part of the program: she was concerned about last night's dream. It terrified and confused her. First, Charles offered help then he left her stranded. Next, a woman stole her van and left her stranded. What did it mean? Was she going to be left standing all alone somewhere?

Jenna's dreams seldom stayed with her so vividly. Could the loss of Stuart and a possibility of a closer relationship with Charles be the reason for the dream? Is that why it seemed so real?

She arrived at the club with a sense of relief. She bowed her head and prayed. "God, here I am again, needing your help with my presentation. Let it bless someone."

After taking a deep breath and exhaling slowly, her nerves relaxed. Jenna entered the large dining room with a spring in her step. The fifty-some women were still having brunch. The aroma from the sausage and egg casserole made her stomach growl. She could not set up her display fast enough.

With a plate full of food, she spoke to a few women on the way to the head table. There she was able to finish the casserole and mixed fruit before starting to talk about her favorite subjects, God and art.

She began her talk about biblical gifts. "The bible tells us that as the

Spirit of God works within us, we become more like him and reflect his glory. We bring him glory by serving others with our gifts. Each of us was designed by God and given talents, skills, and abilities to benefit others by the way they are used."

Jenna cocked her head sideways and added, "I believe that God gave me the "gift of gab" and the ability to paint so I could help others by teaching them art."

The reminder that she had not returned to work at the college gave her a jolt. It was of her own choosing that willingly let Stuart's behavior override her love to help students appreciate art. The word, hypocrite, came to mind. She admitted her error. "Because of a personal situation, I did not return to the job I love, but I plan to do so very soon. I want to encourage you to think about your abilities and how you can use them to serve God.

"We are told in the scriptures that as God blesses us from his great variety of spiritual gifts, we are to manage them in such a way that His generosity can flow through us. I wonder if you have any idea what yours is."

She smiled gently to her audience and asked, "Have you been led to help someone in some way and you neglected to do it because you were unsure of your ability? If you ask God for help, he will grant your request so that he will be glorified. Whether you believe it or not, you do have a gift. Perhaps it's to design or decorate a room, to write poetry or stories, maybe to draw, paint, teach, or to comfort others with words. Whatever you feel your spiritual gift is, don't let it die of neglect. God expects you, and I, to share it because it's a great privilege for us and a blessing passed on to someone else."

Jenna sketched a single rose bud. "A gift begins like this tiny bud. It is small, barely noticeable. When it's nourished and given special attention, it grows and becomes more recognizable."

She added more petals to make the bud look like a small flower opening. "The more the gift is used, and the more it grows toward maturity as the rose does when it's showered with sunshine, water, and plant food."

An outer rim of petals to her flower gave it a full-grown look, the way a beautiful mature rose should be. "A well defined flower or gift should be shared with others. To become fully-grown spiritually, the way a mature Christian should be, takes hard work, but it's worth it. Don't reject any opportunity to use God's gift, because he enjoys watching you use your talents and abilities. Anytime we reject any part of ourselves, we are rejecting his wisdom in creating us."

She went on to tell how she got into painting and how she had shared her work with others. Today she gave an oil painting of a round vase brimming with all sizes of pink roses to the women's club for their auction.

When the meeting ended, a young lady in her mid twenties approached Jenna, wanting the new sketch. "Would you sell it to me? After listening to you, I've decided to go back to college and get my art degree. The rose would be my inspiration to keep going."

A look of pure joy filled Jenna's face, making her green eyes glow like jewels. She picked up the drawing and placed it into the woman's hands. "It would be my pleasure to give it to you."

When the young lady moved on, other members rushed forward. Conversations flowed from one topic to another: Jenna's art classes, some of her students, her daughter, and her life as a single woman. The last part caught Jenna off guard. Here she thought no one would know about her husband's death. Did they also know about his affairs? She could not read pity in anyone's face. She had to get over her feelings of inadequacy and get on with her life. She had not done anything wrong, so why should she stand in the shadows and hide. Admitting this was another boost in wanting to go back to teaching.

While signing autographs she accepted invitations to other civic and church meetings without checking her calendar to see if she had already scheduled something on a particular day. She vowed to herself that she would not overlap anymore engagements. She knew it was not fair to the groups she had to cancel. The desire to share her talent with others for Christ's sake apparently was not enough drive to spur her to get to places on time. She wished she knew how to be a more efficient person.

Jenna was reminded of how badly her morning had started off and how great it had ended. Smiling now with relief and pure pleasure, she was so thankful that God had given her another victory. She thought, "I know how to be a more efficient person. God will give me a lot more victories when I exercise more faith and let him teach me how to take control of my own life."

While driving to another meeting, she looked at her watch and shook her head. Unfortunately her control had not gone into affect yet. She was late again, but thankfully the women in her mission group overlooked her tardiness. However, it was inexcusable to constantly keep people waiting. *God, with your help, I promise to do better.*

Jenna whizzed by a white Lincoln Town Car. She took a quick look at the driver and thought the man looked familiar. Was it Charles McAdams? She did not have time to make sure. When she turned into the church parking lot, the car pulled in behind her. The driver had made a quick turn around when he saw her turn in at the church.

Jenna was gathering up her pocketbook and notebook when Charles pulled open her door. "Hello, Jenna. Where are you headed, to a wedding?"

She stepped out and stood looking up at him. He left her breathless for a minute. She finally answered, "I've got a mission group meeting in the fellowship hall."

He stood quietly, looking her over from head to foot.

Jenna had the perfect taste for an artist. Her daintiness and prettiness brought femininity out in spades. He rubbed his chest as if trying to still the rapid beat of his heart. He swallowed as if trying to push down a lump that had lodged in his throat.

Jenna saw him looking her over and looked down at her clothes, too, expecting to see something wrong. Seeing nothing out of the ordinary to her she said, "No, I'm not going to a wedding. I was the guest speaker at a Christian women's club this morning. Now I'm on my way to meet with women of my own church, who will be dressed casually. They are used to seeing me dressed completely different from them. I sometimes appear in a painter's smock, or a stovepipe-type hat and knee-high striped socks, or even a clown's outfit. I dress to fit whatever the occasion calls for at a morning program and then come straight here for my mission meeting."

Charles' eyes twinkled. "I like this outfit and know of another place you should wear it."

Jenna shut and locked her van. "Where?"

"Dinner. Would you join me tonight? There's a nice restaurant across town called The Stafford House. It's decorated with paintings by some of the best artist. Perhaps you know of it." At the shake of her head he added, "I'm surprised that your paintings are not hanging there, because you have some very good pieces."

Jenna laughed. "Charles, can't you have one conversation without turning on the charm?"

He looked affronted. "I'm sincere, Jenna. Your paintings are outstanding."

"Thank you. I do appreciate the compliment, Charles. About dinner, it would be lovely. What time?"

"Is seven o'clock okay?"

"Perfect," she said and looked at her watch. "Right now, though, I've got to run. I'm late for my meeting.

She ran up the extended walkway, and with every step she berated herself for agreeing to see Charles. *I shouldn't have said yes, but he turned on the charm.* Apparently she was susceptible to the spells he wove after all.

All during the meeting, her mind reverted to Charles McAdams time and again. She heard little about the plans to raise money for the youth mission trip in August, but as hands went up in a vote of confidence for something, Jenna's hand raised, too. When the women laughed, she found out for what they were voting. They wanted her to be the guest speaker at a dinner where tickets would cost twenty-five dollars a plate.

Jenna lowered her hand. "I guess this means I'm in favor of myself being the speaker."

Everyone agreed and the meeting was adjourned.

Jenna was in the process of changing into jeans and a T-shirt when Debbie bounded into the bedroom and flopped onto the bed.

"What gives, Mom?"

The bed looked so inviting. Jenna pushed Debbie over and lay down, too. "It's been one of those days, partly good, partly bad. It started off with me waking from an awful dream, but then I received an uplifting experience from my meeting. I gave my drawing to a young lady who wanted it as inspiration to continue with her art career." She hurried over the next part. "Charles asked me out to dinner; then I voted for myself to speak at a fund raiser."

Debbie bolted up in bed. "Whoa. Hold it. Back up a step. Did you say Charles invited you to dinner?"

"Yes."

Debbie leaned forward and repeated, "Charles McAdams invited you to dine out?"

"Yes."

Debbie sat back against the headboard. "Are you going?"

"Yes."

Debbie bopped Jenna on the head in frustration. "For a very talkative woman you're not saying much. Where are you going? What time is he picking you up? Which outfit do you plan to wear?"

Jenna rubbed a hand up and down her arm and said, "Charles is taking me to some place called The Stafford House."

Debbie's eyes popped wide open. "The Stafford House is not simply some place. The world-class restaurant with a four-diamond rating is quite ritzy."

Jenna stared at Debbie. "How would you know? I've never heard you mention the place before."

"Chuck mentioned it. It's only been open about a year. I guess with all that's been going on with us, we lost out on the finer things of life around here. Anyway, the McAdams men go there for the Buncombe County Detective Association meetings." Debbie hugged her mother. "I'm so glad you are finally getting out, hitting the social scene. Charles will be a great date."

The smile slipped from Jenna's lips. "How did things go between you and Chuck? Did you manage to have a civil conversation without drawing the attention of everyone in the room?"

"Actually we did. We cleared the air. Everything we'd heard about each other's love life was a misunderstanding. He's not dating anyone and neither am I, so we may pick up where we left off when he went to college."

"I'm so glad. You two were meant for each other. But I'm not quite ready to hit the social scene. Tonight's dinner is just a one time thing. Charles may never ask me out again."

Debbie held a straight face. "Right, Mom. What are you wearing tonight?"

Jenna frowned. Se felt doubtful about going now. She wished she had never made the commitment. People will talk. But she had said yes to Charles so she would go, this one time. "The dress and hat I wore today," she said, pointing to the colorful print hanging on the closet door. "Charles liked it and said I should wear it tonight."

"Mom, you look great in anything you put on, but you need to wear something else." She slid off the bed and started rifling through Jenna's clothes. "What time is Charles coming?"

"Seven o'clock. Maybe I should stay home. I think I'll call tell him something came up."

Debbie flipped around. "Don't you dare. If for no other reason you must go see the art gallery. Chuck said it was something you would enjoy." She pulled out an emerald green faux two-piece gown. Its sleeveless top embellished with shimmering beads topped a flowing mid calf georgette skirt. "In this, you'll knock the socks right off Charles."

Jenna's lips twisted into a half smile. "I don't want to knock anything off Charles McAdams, except maybe his easy come, easy go charm. I never know when he's serious."

"Mother, don't worry about his ability to put you on the defensive. Go and take a long, bubbly bath, and I'll bring you a cup of relaxing tea. Think positive thoughts and prepare yourself for a good time."

Debbie had those same words said to her by Jenna when she impulsively accepted dates with guys because no one else would go out with them. Chuck had nothing on her by inviting Penny Hornbuckle to his college dance.

Debbie took the tea to Jenna. "Mom, remember when you used to tell me to think about my escort first. Okay, Lady, it's your turn. Make Charles think he's got the best date ever with him."

"Oh, get out of here."

Debbie giggled and ducked her head when Jenna's wet sponge came flying her way. She jumped through the doorway and shut the door just in time.

From the kitchen phone she immediately called Lynn. "Girlfriend, it was touch and go for awhile." In a voice full of enthusiasm she added, "But it's all set now. Mom is going with Charles to The Stafford House tonight."

"So you know? Our plan is working. I've heard that they have musicians who go to tables and play strictly for certain customers. Didn't Chuck go to school with one of the violinists? Do you think he would arrange for a song to be played for the two of them?"

"Okay, I'll ask him," Debbie responded and grinned. "I know that you know everything between us has been settled. I just thought I'd be polite and let you have a go at him." She giggled and added, "I've always been the polite one. Don't you dare say when pigs fly."

"Thanks so much for helping me with this scheme, but we better remember that God has control over it. Let's say an extra prayer, though, as an additional reminder of how anxious we are for our parents to fall in love."

Chapter 8

Charles and Jenna were seated in a dimly lit room of the renovated two-story Mount Vernon-style house. Candlelight flickered from every table set with fine linen, bone china, and crystal stemware. Soothing music played in the background.

Jenna felt a little sad. The last time she ate by candlelight she and Stuart had been celebrating their fifteenth wedding anniversary. They were at home listening to old favorite songs on their favorite radio station. The words "love me tender, love me true" stirred her heart, just as they did on their first date.

The song meant more to her the second time around because Stuart was singing it, too. If she had known then what she knew now she would have told him to forget the pretense when he reached across the table and took her hands and sang, "Oh my darling, I love you and I always will." Jenna thought it had been a life time commitment, but she could not have been more wrong.

She looked at Charles, blinked back tears, and grabbed up a glass of water to cover the moment. The last thing she wanted now was to burst into tears in front of her date and all the elite people dining around them.

"Is something wrong?" Charles asked. "Are you disappointed with this place? We can go somewhere else."

Jenna apologized. "Oh, no. No. It's nothing like that. Forgive me, Charles, for letting my mind wander. It's not that I don't like your company or where we're dining, it's that…" Jenna glanced around and then changed her mind as to what she was about to say. "This is a remarkable restaurant. I'm in awe. I recognized some of the names on the paintings, but I had no idea there were so many talented artists in this area." She smiled brightly, maybe a little too bright. Although Charles did not comment on her actions, he said, "So you think I've made a good choice in coming here."

Her laugh was soft when she agreed. "You couldn't have chosen a better place. I was almost speechless when John Paul asked to see some of my paintings. Thank you for this opportunity. If we were to leave right now, I would still be happy." She looked him in the eye and said, "You've truly made this date special."

He held his glass of tea up and saluted her. "As you've made mine," he said in a husky voice. "Earlier today you questioned my sincere comments, but I was dead serious when I said that your paintings are as good as those upstairs. Each picture leaves special feelings in your heart. Some of them make you smile or even chuckle while others give you a sense of peace and warmth." He leaned back in his chair and gave her a heart stopping smile. "I was sure that John Paul would be interested in seeing your work. Peaceful Existence is a great one to bring here."

Jenna's face lit up with an endearing smile. "I was thinking the same thing."

Charles drank his tea and watched Jenna as she took note of the other diners, most of whom were politicians. He had considered running for commissioner, but there were several things he needed to consider before making a decision. Should he tackle all the work that goes with being a politician? Could he make a difference to society? Would Jenna like it? Would she think it was only for show? Whoa.

His thoughts came to an abrupt halt for a full minute and then went into a tailspin. It did not matter what Jenna thought of him or his plans. Or did it? He could not help but wonder if she came out with him because he was a celebrity in his own field. He hoped not.

News reporters were everywhere, taking pictures. Jenna did not shun the attention. Although she did not pose and try to get in every shot, having her picture taken seemed to please her. It surprised him in a way, because of all the publicity that had been in news, covering Stuart's death.

Even if Jenna had not been in the limelight at that time, for good reasons she deserved to be now. She was most attractive, but she had more than looks. When she slid to a stop at her spot at the festival, she appeared to be a scatterbrain. To those who did not know her, she may have looked too incompetent to run a booth. She appeared to not have it all together, running back and forth to her van for first one thing and then another. Charles had never seen this side of Jenna, but he knew she had style, design, and talent. He was confident, given time, that her work would be displayed to perfection. With time running out she had needed help, but Debbie had deserted her when she needed her most.

Couldn't she have waited fifteen minutes before rushing off to talk to Chuck? Charles wondered. *Kids, they can be so inconsiderate sometimes.* He decided to help Jenna.

It was not long before the feisty woman showed lots of spunk. He smiled to himself when he recounted her attack on him. There had been a difference of opinion as to why he was helping her, but they recovered and got on with the program. Jenna's genuine love for others showed in the way she handled her customers. Most people would have been surprised as to how this foxy lady treated the lower class. Her show of affection toward the scraggly-looking boy who had been admiring her paintings was not a surprise to Charles. He knew that she loved kids. She loved the McAdams kids, and they loved her.

Yes, his dinner guest was an intriguing woman that needed to be brought into the light more often so everyone could know all about her. He needed to know more. It would be fun for him to learn what made Jenna tick. To uncover each fact would be like working a puzzle or solving a case and being full of anticipation for what he would discover.

Before Charles went to pick up Jenna tonight, he wondered how she would react to spending time with just him. She would not have Stuart watching her every move while at the same time keeping an eye on another woman across the room. Would Jenna have second thoughts about being seen in public with him? Would she tell him she had changed her mind? He thought about these things until he reached her porch.

Charles received a surprise when she opened the door. It almost sent him into a state of shock, just as it had the first time she appeared at his door. She, along with Stuart, had come to his home for a Christmas part. In a simple but elegant black pant suit she stood out above every woman in the room, and she was doing the same tonight. Seated across from him now was not the artsy-looking woman that he saw most of the time but the classy lady he knew she could be.

The green party dress accentuated the color in her eyes, giving them a mysterious look. This inquisitive detective wanted to be absorbed into their depths where perhaps he could discover more about her. It was not altogether her dress making him speechless, but her hair got his attention, too. She did not have on a hat this time, and the soft, loose curls topping her head like a burnished crown flowed down to her shoulders. One side of the shiny, coppery-colored hoar was pulled up above an ear and held in place by a pearl studded comb.

What a beautiful package, Charles thought. Jenna takes takes his breath away. He inhaled deeply before turning his attention to the meal the waiter was placing before them.

Charles smiled and whiffed appreciatively when the steamy hot aroma of mixed foods passed in front of his nose. Jenna had let him order for her. At first she was hesitant to eat the soft shell crayfish and pasta, but it looked so good and once she started she kept eating. Smiling she murmured, "Mmmm." The sautéed ostrich on a potato crisp with grilled onion and apple compote also had her sighing with contentment. She seldom tried new foods, especially meats, but she was willing to do this for Charles. She would not embarrass him. She would rather force the food down before pushing it away.

She was glad that she had tasted of everything. "It's all so good, Charles. I don't know what I expected ostrich to taste like, but I never thought it would resemble beef."

With good food and a nice companion, Jenna was glad that she had accepted Charles' invitation. It felt right somehow to be dining with him in public, yet, at the same time, it made her uncomfortable. This man's masculinity caused her to want more of his attention to the extent that it made her nervous. She picked up her coffee cup with caution. She wondered how it was possible to be comfortable and nervous at the same time.

"Jenna?" Charles said, reclaiming her attention. "This young man wants to play us a song."

She looked up into the pleasant face of a violinist. "Thank you. That would be nice."

"Do you have a favorite song?" Charles asked.

Jenna shook her head. "Not really."

The violinist said, "If neither of you object, I'd like to play one of my favorites."

Charles and Jenna looked at each other and nodded for him to go ahead.

As soon as the familiar tune, You're The One, began to float from the instrument Jenna realized that the violinist hoped to help make the evening romantic for them. It bothered her so much that she would not look at Charles. She kept her eyes focused on the hands orchestrating the music so wonderfully.

When he finished, Jenna smiled and asked, "Aren't you Bryan Weinberger, Professor Richard Weinberger's son?"

The young man bowed and answered, "I am the one. I am honored that you recognized me."

Jenna glanced at Charles and then back at Bryan. "When you played for the community college teachers' appreciation day, I thought you had done an exceptional job. This was equally as good."

Bryan smiled proudly. "Thank you, Mrs. Wilson. I hope you and Mr. McAdams enjoy the rest of the evening."

"We will," Jenna said, barely looking at Charles. "You have a wonderful talent, the ability to make people happy and relaxed with the stroke of a bow."

While everything she said was true, Jenna knew she was babbling, but she had to prolong the moment when she would be left alone with Charles. Should she laugh and make a flippant remark about them looking more like an old married couple than a couple on their first date? Or should she apologize for the misunderstanding on Bryan's part?

She did neither. Charles took the problem out of her hands. "I'm sorry if he thought we were more than friends. Did it bother you, Jenna?"

Since he did not look mad or embarrassed, she sat back in her chair and relaxed. "I'll admit it bothered me some, but only because of you. We know what we are to each other. It doesn't faze me if others think there's more between us, unless there's a woman somewhere in the wings."

The sudden realization that Charles might have a special lady friend bothered Jenna. Until now she had not thought about Charles' personal life. Could there be a woman waiting at home for him to call her? In a way Jenna hoped not. She enjoyed being with Charles, but she could not think of them having anything more than a casual relationship. Even as friends she would be uncomfortable dining out with him if he were seeing another woman.

Charles watched Jenna closely, finally he said, "Since Francine, I hadn't found anyone unattached that I wanted to get involved with. You know the saying, 'The best are taken.' I do date occasionally, but I'm not seeing anyone on a regular basis...so far." He glanced around the room and then back at Jenna. "I'm glad you don't worry what others think about us. It tells me that you're happy with who you are."

Jenna shrugged and spoke without much enthusiasm. "I used to be very happy with myself, but when I found out that I was not enough woman for Stuart, I lost a lot of self esteem. I wish I were different. Perhaps if I'd been prettier or knew how to use my brains more effectively, he wouldn't have turned to other women. I honestly don't know what happened to us. I get so frustrated when things go wrong and I can't figure them out. Sometimes I feel so stupid." With a look that was brighter than she felt she added, "It must take a brainy person to be a good detective."

Charles' brows drew together. He knew she was not stupid. His children and various friends have sung her praises in different ways. Her talents in the art field proved that she has plenty of smarts, he thought. Maybe she has a problem here or there but who doesn't. No one is perfect.

He gave her a twisted grin and said, "I don't know if brainy is the description I would use. A day late, I've learned that caution is major vice." He rubbed the side of his neck and said, "See this scar? I got it by not being cautious."

Jenna held a shiver in check. "What caused it?"

His whole body appeared to tense up. "I was tailing a guy who had swindled elderly people out of their life savings by promising to do some major repairs around the house. After he got them to pay up front, he fled. When I caught up with him, I wrestled him to the ground, getting ready to cuff his hands when some kids fighting in the next yard diverted my attention. I loosened my grip enough for the man to break free. He then got me in a clinch and put a knife to my throat. It took only one slit to drop me."

Jenna gasped and spoke barely above a whisper. "How awful."

"You can say that again," Charles said and assumed a relaxed position. "I guess you could say it's my badge of valor for carelessness."

With a smile and look of awe, she said, "It's good to see that you can joke about it."

He shrugged. "I can because I enjoy my work and don't want to feel intimidated by the public. I think that having a love for solving a mystery, to find out who did it and why, is what makes being a detective special to me." His face filled with excitement. "When I'm on a case, I don't think of much else. I normally go about solving the mystery as though a life depends on it being done. Most of the time someone's life *is* at stake."

The next hour flew by as Jenna and Charles talked, never running out of topics to discuss. One subject flowed into the next. She told him about being reared on Lucianna Island. She explained how she hung out at the docks as much as her parents would allow.

She talked about her fascination with the fishermen: watching them unload their boats when they came in from a day's trip and then hearing about their experiences on the water. She had hung onto their every word when they told of experiences catching snapper, lobster and shrimp.

"They made fights with giant waves and frightening winds sound like a thrilling challenge," she said, "but the idea of being way out from shore when a storm came up never interested me. I know I would be having a fit to get back on land."

She then went on to tell how she had studied about the mysterious ocean, the United States, and the country abroad, even the Florida mainland she could see in the distance. While they were interesting subjects, even romantic places to read about, she had never wanted to see any place bad enough to leave Lucianna. Her father offered to take her on business trips to the mainland, but she always refused to go. She loved the island.

Without warning, though, the fateful day for her to venture away from home arrived. Reluctantly, a devastated Jenna went to Florida. After getting settled in her new home and school, the awful separation from places and everyone she knew soon receded into the back of her mind, and life changed for her.

"Did you meet Stuart in school or college?" Charles asked, never taking his eyes from her face.

"In school. He helped me overcome being homesick. I grew to love Florida and lost interest in returning home to the slow pace of island life. Even though I missed my parents, Stuart became my life. We got married after college, and I vowed that where he went, I would go. His life would be my life. Together we promised to spend our lives serving God, but somewhere along the way, Satan slipped in and destroyed our marriage."

Jenna turned her head away and blinked to hold back the tears, still hoping and praying that God and time would bring her peace.

Charles reached for her hand. "I'm sorry, Jenna. I wish I could do something to make your pain go away."

Jenna looked him in the eye. She had no idea how much time passed before they broke contact. She only knew that the gentle caring look in Charles' face, and the rapid beat of her own heart kept her pinned in place. She felt that the nice Charles McAdams could also be dangerous. His exciting job, his talent as an interesting conversationalist, and his handsome looks drew her interest, as well as the interest of many women around them. Like her they probably wondered what it would be like to be kissed by him. Her imagination caused her mind to travel a road that she should not take. She removed her hand from his clasp and reached for a spoon to stir milk into her coffee.

"Lynn used to talk about all the detectives in your family," she said between swallows. "I believe your father and mother worked in the same agency."

"Yes. Dad got all of us interested in case scenarios," Charles said with a rueful grin. "Chuck and Kenneth, Lynn's husband, are working for me. Tina is the secretary for her husband Edward who is a railroad detective in Arizona. Last but not least, Lynn had to get in the act, too."

Jenna smiled and said, "Even with all her desire to find answers to seemingly impossible problems, it's been hard to see that lovable child as a hard nose detective."

"Lucky for me that she is," Charles said. "I often have to send her to department stores. While it may not seem like catching shop lifters as a dangerous job, some situations have been dangerous for my young daughter. I have been reluctant to send her out several times, but she wouldn't have forgiven me if I had. When a manger calls about a rash of stolen articles, Lynn goes in to help." Charles chuckled. "Fortunately, some incidents have been light hearted, even funny. At one store, Lynn caught a woman wearing several layers of underwear, men's underwear."

"You're kidding," Jenna said.

Charles grinned, shaking his head. "It's true. We've all dealt with some unusual cases."

His rich baritone voice caused Jenna's heart to flutter. She sat down her coffee cup with care and listened as best she could to every word he said about his investigation in the Case of the Grove Body. "A woman wanted to surprise her neighbor who had knee surgery. She knew it would be a while before the man could get out and work in his yard, so she decided to plant some flowers around the yard to make it look livelier. While digging in a grove of trees she unearthed the remains of a man's body."

Jenna cocked her head and looked Charles over from head to…as far as she could see before running into the table. His broad lean shoulders and strong looking chest looked so good to her. Like Chuck, she figured he probable exercised on a regular basis, too.

While Charles had Jenna's supposedly undivided attention, he told her about a case that Tina's husband had worked on. "For three nights, Edward camped in a train car before catching the notorious ostrich gang."

Jenna giggled. "I believe you're making up these cases."

"I promise you I'm not," Charles said with a grin. "The eight boys, ages twelve through sixteen, were not notorious but troublesome. They didn't like the idea of the birds being killed for restaurant meat. So each night, in about the same location where the train slowed down before coming to a complete stop, the boys would turn about a dozen loose."

With a devastating smile he added, "I don't think any one of us would change careers. You could say we're a family with questioning minds. Not questionable…then again perhaps that is the appropriate word." He raised his eyebrows at her, expecting some remark. When she just smiled he added, "I guess anyone who takes chances and goes after criminals single handed probably does have an unsettled mind."

Jenna leaned back in her chair and looked around the room to take her eyes from his heart-stopping smile. When she turned back toward him, she shook her head and said, "I believe you are quite sane. What's most remarkable to me is that you all are in the same profession and you're a close-knit family."

Charles nodded. "When Francine died, we all pitched in to take care of the home and of each other. Of course Rose Ingram came to help us, but with Tina being nine and Chuck six, they helped look after Lynn who was just three. But you know all that."

"Yes, and I also know that you got a gem when Rosie came to work for you. From our first meeting at one of your parties, I saw how good she was for all of you. Not only her cooking was delicious, but it was evident how much she respected you and loved those children. I suppose she's still with you."

"Oh yes," Charles said with conviction. "I won't let her go; she's like a dear aunt. Rosie tells me all the time that I should marry so I'll have a younger woman to run the house. I told her, even if I did marry, I'd want her to stay. Besides, she has no family. I couldn't tell her she was no longer needed."

Jenna tilted her head and gave him a thoughtful look. "Rosie is fortunate to have you taking care of her. Stuart used to take care of me. He did all the financial statements, reminded me of appointments, and practically pushed me out of the house so I would get to my meetings on time. That was a great help. I only wish that he had done it because he loved me."

Her heart swelled with an angry feeling and a great ache. He took care of her all right. He made sure that she was out of the house and out of his way. It would not have been to his satisfaction for her to have been home when Sheila or some other woman arrived, nor would it have been in Stuart's best interest for Jenna to know how to keep financial records.

While fumbling in her pocketbook for a tissue Charles asked, "Jenna, would you like something else to eat or drink?"

She nodded. "Yes, thank you. I would like more coffee."

After Charles ordered more coffee for both of them, Jenna asked, "Have you heard anything about Howard Bookman lately?"

Charles sighed. "Yes. He's getting out soon. Once again, he'll be free to come and go as he pleases. I help put prisoners behind bars and other officials help get them out. Sometimes the system doesn't seem fair."

"Are you still angry with him?" Jenna asked. "I know I'd be. Even though Stuart and Sheila were having sex when he had his heart attack and she was not the one who actually took his life, I can't forgive her for being with him."

Charles gave her a look of sympathy. "I understand how you feel, but no, I'm not angry with Howard anymore." He exhaled, blowing out a puff of air, smelling like vanilla coffee. "I'll pray for you and Sheila, that one day you'll be able to forgive her and move on with your life. I'll also ask God to let her see the joy of serving him in your life and may it encourage her to make a spiritual change."

Tears filled Jenna's eyes. "I'd appreciate that, but for now, how about if we get off a sad subject and liven up our conversation again. I don't want people around us seeing me cry all night and think that you are being mean to me."

He laughed and waggled his eyebrows. "I agree. I don't want to ruin my reputation with the women."

Jenna shook her head and returned to discussing children. "You must be grateful for the three wonderful kids that God has given you."

With a twist of his lips Charles' humor had definitely returned. "I just never counted on them being mischievous, especially Lynn. To this day I never know what she's up to. I hope that one of her children will be a carbon copy of her."

Jenna laughed a tinkling sound. "I'm sure you don't think it would be a terribly bad thing to have another Lynn."

Charles agreed. "You're right. It would be another beautiful child to help keep life interesting."

"Have you ever considered marriage again?"

For a moment Charles did not respond. "Yes," he finally answered. "There was one woman but she was already married. I've had to ask God time and again to remove the desire."

When Jenna said, "That must have been difficult," he looked deep into her eyes and presented her with one of his most charming smiles, "It was, but I'm not above thinking about it again, now. To be honest, until recently I hadn't cared to go on dates much less think about getting married. Where do you think I should look for a soul mate?"

"I imagine," Jenna began, adopting a casual tone of voice, "that your children would be willing to advise you."

He threw up his hands and said, "Heaven forbid. I'd rather they didn't get involved in my life that way. If I'm ever lucky enough to have the love of a special woman, I'd prefer to acknowledge it on my own. I'm afraid with their help I'd get saddled with a dumb broad who wouldn't know when to come in out of the rain." On a more serious note he said, "Actually, I've turned my life over to God. If he should give me another wife, I will know she is the best one for me."

The last remark did not reach Jenna's mind. She had latched on to the part, dumb broad who wouldn't know when to come in out of the rain, and it bothered her immensely. Those words played over and over in her mind. Stuart had said the same thing when he talked about her to Debbie and his friends. But he had not been as smart as Charles who would never get saddled with a blind, trusting fool like Jenna. He would not want a wife who could not think rationally and sift through material for solutions to problems. It was a fact that Jenna could not solve her own problems much less someone else's.

Charles did not appear to see the pain in Jenna's face. "I get a lot of satisfaction out of trying to solve cases," he said. "It's an ongoing challenge that consumes much of my time. I doubt that many women understand how full and active a detective's life is unless they are in the business, too."

Jenna bit the inside of her jaw to keep from speaking out and saying the wrong thing. Instead, she said to herself, *Right. We women are too dumb to understand anything outside the realm of our own small existence.* She resolved that if and when she should marry again, that it would be to someone who respected her and did not think she was dumb. Should there be the slightest chance that a special man did come into her life, she hoped she wouldn't look for problems in their relationship. For instance, was there another woman that he didn't want her to know about?

Jenna looked at Charles as if she expected him to read her mind, but all she saw was a thoughtful expression. She figured he was either wishing that someone more entertaining and interesting was sitting across the table from him or wished that he was alone to do whatever he pleased. She knew that if she were to leave, he would most likely hook up with the first available woman that came by. That would not take long either. Women, single and married, threw themselves at Charles all the time. That could be good for him though; it would be the perfect opportunity to delve into each woman's character as he looked for that special lady. Searching their character could be like solving a mystery.

But to let another woman into his life that had no interest in detective work would never happen. Like Jenna, at times Charles was a loner. He often crammed work into every hour of the day. Jenna knew, in a sense, how he felt because a heavy schedule suited her, too. It appeared that both of them were destined for solitary lives. Perhaps that was the way God intended for them to live.

"Jenna?" Charles said to get her attention "If you're ready, we'll go."

She nodded and stood. He put a hand to her back and headed toward the exit, but friends stopped them along the way. Jenna noted how the women touched his arm, trying to claim his attention. He greeted each one with his captivating smile and charm.

Charles introduced Jenna. Some of the people knew her by reputation and the men who didn't instantly wanted to know more about her.

"She's a wonderful artist," Charles told them. "Keep looking upstairs, you may see her work hanging there in the near future."

His words and the men's flattery brought an instant rush to Jenna's heart, but she did not let any of it go to her head. She knew they were in the same league with Charles, as great charmers. Politicians flattered people to get votes, and Charles flattered people to get information.

What Jenna could not understand was why Charles went out of his way to charm her? She could offer him nothing, no brainy thoughts, no valuable information, not even her dignity. Stuart had seen to that. No matter how Charles felt about Jenna, she liked him. It was not his smile that got to her. Nor was it his polished good looks and interesting conversation that made him so overpowering and it was not because of his money either. She loved his gentleness and attentiveness. She soaked it up like a sponge. The attention he paid solely to her at the moment made her feel special and important.

At her house, Charles waited for Jenna to unlock the door and turn on an inside light. His gaze never left her face but moved to her lips when she turned to say goodnight. The look of adoration shining from his eyes took her breath away. When she felt her pulse kick into a rapid beat of excitement, she turned away from him to take in a great gulp of air and then exhaled to calm her nerves. It was a trick she learned in the early years of her speaking engagements. Every time she was to stand before a large crowd she got butterflies. A seasoned speaker told her how to calm her feelings. "Inhaling and exhaling always worked for me," the woman said. It also helped Jenna then and it worked for her tonight. Almost. With hands that were no longer shaking, she stuck one out for a handshake. "Thanks for dinner."

Charles took her small hand and gently pulled her closer to him. He seldom kissed a woman on their first date, but Jenna was different. He knew her and had been secretly in love with her for a long time. All evening he had wanted to be close to her, hold her in his arms. He had to kiss her before he left, even if it were only a little peck.

The moment their lips met, something like electricity shot through him. Charles wanted to pull her closer into his arms and to deepen the kiss. Jenna Wilson had knocked his socks off. In other words, she had made a more powerful impact on him than he ever thought possible. *Did she feel the same?* He wondered. In the dark, it was hard to tell. When she pulled away, she seemed to withdraw from him. He decided to move slowly and treat her with care or she may never go out with him again. Now that she was available, he wanted to make her his one priority. He was going to make her a constant figure in his life. For now, though, he let her go. "I enjoyed the evening very much."

She stood there in a stupor but murmured, "I did too." She went into the house feeling dazed. What just happened? Was Charles trying to close the case on The Disillusioned Widow?

CHAPTER 9

Remembering Charles' quick but unforgettable kiss caused a shiver to skitter along Jenna's spine. She finally moved from the door where she had leaned for endless minutes. She headed toward her bedroom only to stop after going a few steps. She placed fingertips to her lips.

Hold it, girl. That kiss meant nothing to Charles. It was only another way to express his undeniable charm. With sagging shoulders she prepared for bed.

In all fairness she admitted that the kiss meant something very important to her. She did not want it to, but for some reason it did. Although it had been a brief show of affection to Jenna, it was sensational. It was not the pressing, devouring touch of the lips that she would have expected from Charles, and she was unprepared for the polite, gentle and oh so ecstatic kiss. Since it seemed so secondary to him, an act that probably occurred with every other woman in the world, she gave the good night show of affection a dismissal and went to bed.

In a matter of minutes the bedroom door flew open and Debbie rushed in and jumped onto the bed. "Good. You're not asleep yet."

Jenna propped on one elbow and glared at her daughter. "Would it matter if I had been?"

Debbie grinned. "Nope." Now sitting in the middle of the bed with her elbows propped on her knees, she said, "Tell me everything."

Jenna slid into a sitting position up against the headboard. "You were right. The Stafford House is a classy place. Artists, well-known businessmen, gorgeous women, and politicians were everywhere. I didn't see any of the candidates running for an upcoming office table hoping to make their presence known. However, on our way out, I did meet some of them. One was a senator and one was a house of representative. I was glad you talked me into wearing something more suitable for the occasion."

"What about the paintings? Did you see any?"

Jenna nodded her eyes bright with excitement. "They were there all right. The whole upstairs floor served as a show room. Charles and I wandered from one end of the gallery to the other, viewing at close range every magnificent piece of art. There were many decorative pieces of either molded or sculpted busts or vases, but the majority art work was paintings. The only time I thought of eating was when Charles' stomach growled." Jenna laughed and grabbed Debbie's hand. "The most fascinating thing happened. Charles told John Paul Montague, the proprietor of The Stafford House, about my work. He told me to bring some pieces for him to see, that he might consider hanging one in the gallery."

"Mom, that's terrific. What will you take?"

"I'm leaning toward Peaceful Existence. Charles thinks it a good choice. What do you think?"

"You have some really good paintings, but I agree with Charles. The woman reclining on a lounge in the flower garden should be at the top of your list. How did you and Charles get along?"

Jenna hesitated before admitting, "We had a pleasant time. The meal was fabulous. A violinist came to our table and played the romantic song: You're the One." Jenna drifted off into a world of her own, wishing that she could find someone with whom she would be considered *The One*.

Debbie's snapping fingers got Jenna's attention. "Mom, tell me more."

"We talked a lot, mostly about our children," Jenna said. "He talked about Francine's death. It made me sad and thoughtful. I think the conversation got to Charles, too. We sat for a while, neither saying anything."

Debbie's mouth gaped open and her eyebrows rose to her hairline. "Mom, you didn't? You were out with one of the best looking men in town and you sat there thinking about Dad and how mean he was to you."

Jenna shrugged. "Yes. I'm afraid I did. A lot of the things he said and did reminded me of Stuart and the way he treated me. I couldn't help it. Painful memories just popped into my head."

With a look of pity Debbie said, "I'm beginning to think that you are hopeless. Dad always thought you were, but I knew better...until now."

Jenna looked puzzled. "What do you mean Stuart thought I was hopeless?" She knew what Stuart thought of her, but she had no idea that Debbie had knowledge of his real feelings...

Debbie hugged Jenna and apologized for being insensitive. "I'm sorry, Mom, for hurting you. Dad did more than enough to drag you down. Some of it you probably don't even know about. The way he pretended to be a loving husband around the church and then made fun of you to his friends was disgusting."

Jenna's face turned red. "How did you know that?"

"The first time I overheard him on the phone telling someone you didn't know which end was up. If he wasn't here to run everything, it's hard telling what would happen to you." Debbie winched at her mother's hurt look. "Do you want me to go on?"

Jenna nodded. "I need to know all that you know."

"Dad didn't manage the household accounts so you wouldn't have to trouble your pretty little head about such trivial matters. I know he used to tell the choir members that. But he really did it because he thought you were incapable of keeping records. I know that because I overheard him telling some people in the office one night during a party at our house. And of course you found out that he did it to keep you from knowing where the money actually went."

Jenna began to shake. She was furious. In a tight voice she asked,

"Did he ever find out that you knew these things?"

Debbie nodded. "Oh yes. I confronted him a couple of times. The first time was a night when you were late coming home. Remember you had been to a speaking engagement and drove up on a multi-car pile up on a back road? You got out and helped some people until an ambulance arrived."

Jenna nodded. "I remember it well. Two children were terrified when their mother wouldn't wake up. I sat with them until their aunt arrived."

"Dad said you were probably off somewhere running your mouth. If you had to be late you should be coming from a classroom where you were learning something useful like math. I told him that you were smart and didn't need to know math, and that people enjoy your talks. He laughed and spoke with a sneer, saying that they enjoy listening to you as much as they like hearing me yap. According to him, neither of us could hold an intelligent conversation. At that moment, I knew for sure that he didn't care much for either of us. I ran from the room and went into the dining room. I stood at the window in the dark, wishing you'd come home."

"You never said anything about the conversation when I did get home."

Debbie shrugged. "I know. I didn't want to hurt you. If I'd told you about every conversation, there wouldn't have been any peace in the house."

"Were there really so many bad experiences?"

"Oh yeah." Debbie answered. "For instance, I had been looking for something in the hall closet outside his office and heard him say, 'If I don't keep a close eye on the dumb broad Jenna won't know when to come in out of the rain.' I eased up to the door to see who was in the room with him. He was standing with his back to the door, talking on the phone."

Jenna gasped. "Did he know you were there?"

"Not that time." Seeing her mother's strained features, Debbie added, "I'm sorry, Mom. I was afraid to confront him."

"Why?"

"Once before, he had waited until you left for a meeting, before going over to Mavis' house. When he came home, I got up enough courage to say something to him about it. But there was no talking to him. He was the head of the house and he could do what he liked. When I said he was being unfaithful to you, he raised a hand to slap me. When I said I was going to tell you, he headed toward me, looking fierce. I didn't know what he would do, so I ran to my room and locked the door. After that, he used hitting as a weapon. He never hit me, only threatened to. He said if I didn't keep my mouth shut that I'd wish I had."

Jenna grabbed Debbie and hugged her close. "Oh, my darling. I had no idea that any of that was going on."

Debbie chewed on a fingernail. "I was afraid, but one time I tried to bluff my way along. I told him if he hit me I'd go to the police. He said that they wouldn't believe me, because of his standing in the community and college. He also said if you or I dared to move out we would regret it. I was already regretting that I had to call him Dad. I'm sorry; Mom you had married a monster. "

"I knew it, but I had no idea that you did. I wish you had told me about your conversations. Regardless of what happened to me I would have gotten you away from him." Jenna said. "We would have gotten another place to live, even if it had been in Lucianna."

Debbie smiled ruefully. "I'd have missed school."

"True."

"Anyway, I didn't have to suffer his abuse the way you did, because I left for college. But I often wondered what was really going on here. Since nothing came out in the open, I figured that you never found out what he was doing. I prayed every night that God would take control and get you away from him."

Pain pierced Jenna's heart. She paced the room. How could Stuart treat his own child so badly? Did he not love her? The lump in Jenna's throat felt permanently lodged there. She swallowed with difficulty. Some of the pain caused by Stuart had started to fade. Now due to learning about Debbie's grief, it was all coming back.

"I thought I was the only one he put down," Jenna said. "It goes to show how dumb I am. I had no idea that he no longer loved you either."

Tears ran down Debbie's cheeks. She didn't attempt to wipe them. "It's all right, Mom. I know that you love me and always have." She slid off the bed and went to the kitchen. "I'm going to get us a cup of tea."

Absentmindedly Jenna murmured, "Thanks, honey. That would be nice." She was feeling too much hurt, disappointment and frustration to think half way straight. *Because I was not Mrs. Perfect did not give Stuart the right to make fun of me. He knew my limitations before he married me.* Neither did he have to embarrass their only child by letting her hear him tell others that she was dense. Anger had caused freckles to stand out on her nose and cheeks. With a fierce look she shouted, "I am not dumb!"

She took the cup of tea that Debbie handed her and drank half of it before setting it down. "I guess it was wrong of me to let Stuart do a lot for me that I should have done for myself. Actually there were several things I would have preferred to handle my way, like choosing my clothes and the way I wore my hair, but I went along with him to keep peace. He was so unrelenting in letting me choose even one outfit for myself. 'You've done a lousy job so far, what makes me think you can do a good one now?' he asked. I told him he could look at it before I bought it and he agreed. But that was a no-go from the start. He complained about everything. The color made me looked washed out. The cut made me look too fat. The style was too old for me. He went on and on until I walked out of the store with nothing, not even my dignity."

Tears once again filled Debbie's eyes when her mother said, "I'm the world's biggest fool." She linked arms with Jenna and said, "Mom, let's talk about something else. You are the greatest, and life must go on. What you do with it from now on is what will make you or break you." She smiled sweetly. "Sound familiar? You told me those same words when Chuck and I broke up. I think what I have done with my life so far hasn't been so bad, has it?"

"Definitely not," Jenna answered and laid her head on Debbie's shoulder. She had concerns when Debbie linked up with Steven Bailey, but when they parted ways after a month or two, Jenna relaxed. She was so thankful that Debbie did not have a long relationship with the drug dealer and got away from him before he got her involved with his activities. "I believe you'll be a great influence on the students you will be teaching."

Debbie sighed. "I know you're still upset over what Dad did, but I hope it won't keep you from sharing a life with another man. You need someone to grow old with."

Jenna's eyebrows rose to her hairline. "May I guess whom you have in mind? Could it be Charles McAdams?"

Debbie grinned. "Do you know of a better prospect?" Counting on her fingers, she numbered his attributes. "He's nice, extremely charming, owns a new suburban, and a Lincoln Town Car. He has a sprawling home big enough for me to stay in when I come home from college and still not get in your way. He's got a prosperous business and his own hair and teeth. What more could you want?"

"His own teeth you say? That's the deciding factor," Jenna said. "I'll take him."

"Hurray!" Debbie said, and slid off the bed. "I'll call Charles now and see if we can move in with him right away."

"Deborah! You'll do no such thing. Have you lost your mind?"

"Mother, I was teasing. I want you to get on with your life and meet someone who will treat you right. I don't want you hooked up with another monster. Charles is the greatest. I hope you two do hit it off. If not, well…God will send you a good man." She hugged Jenna, looking her in the eye. "I love you, Mom, just the way you are: a procrastinator, ignorant of record keeping, and always late to meetings. I only want to see you happier, worry and stress free. You really are involved with too many activities. It would be great if you could cut back. At the rate you're going, you could have a heart attack yourself."

Jenna argued, "I like being involved."

"I know, but do you have to take on the world. Get out socially a little more. Have fun."

"Deborah…"

Debbie tried the stern look but ended up looking funny. When Jenna laughed she said, "I'm serious, Mom. If Charles asks you out again, don't turn him down. Keep in mind that no two people are alike, even look-a-likes. Chuck and Charles favor yet they are different. Look at us. We're alike but very different." She smiled brightly and added, "You did have fun with Charles tonight, didn't you?"

Jenna left Debbie waiting with anticipation. Her feelings were mixed. She liked Charles because he was a great father and had always been good to Debbie. As for her herself, he was a little too charming, but she did want to see him again. The hold back was her fear of being hurt again. She recalled his attentiveness and the sincerity she heard in his voice each time he talked in a serious vein. And she appreciated not being looked down on as if she was beneath him socially and financially. The kiss clenched her decision and she answered, "Yes it was fun. Charles showed me that being with a caring man can be pleasant and interesting."

"Good," Debbie said with a glowing look. "Promise me one thing."

"What?" Jenna answered in a deadpan voice, wondering what was coming next.

"Promise that you'll think about going out with Charles at least one more time."

"Okay. I promise," Jenna said, getting back into bed, "but not tonight, okay?" She pulled up the cover, dragging it up close to her chin.

Debbie kissed her forehead. "Okay and I'm sorry to have brought up the subject of Dad. I feel sure he must have loved you a little bit. I hope you get a good night's sleep. Dream of seeing your paintings in the gallery at The Stafford House." She blew her mother a kiss before closing the bedroom door. In her own bedroom she called her best friend.

"Lynn? I think we're making headway. Mom said she had fun with Charles tonight. She got dreamy eyed as she talked about the violinist playing a romantic song for the two of them."

Debbie positioned the receiver in the crook of her neck and continued talking while removing make-up from her eyes. "I guess we have to wait and see what happens. Keep praying and keep me posted about Charles' feelings. Playing cupid requires a lot of work."

With Debbie behind closed doors, Jenna felt free to let her true feelings out. Between sobs she spoke aloud. "Stuart, why couldn't you continue to love me as you did when we first got married? Was I so unlovable? Were you pretending about your feelings when you asked me to marry you?" *No, you loved me, truly loved me. I know you did. If you didn't, you were the best actor in the world.*

Painting together had been fun for both of them, but the occasions did not last long once the bloom faded from their marriage. Stuart's desire to stand at an easel soon waned. He produced fewer and fewer pictures until he was no longer painting, so Jenna thought. One day she went by the college to join him for lunch. There was no one in the room. While waiting for Stuart she walked around the room. The closet door was partially open. She started to shut it and something caught her eye. She pulled the door open and saw several paintings of a beautiful young lady. As Jenna looked at the pictures she saw that each one got more seductive. The girl lost a piece of clothing with each pose. Before she got through the stack she threw them down and ran out of the room. She knew Stuart had painted them. The style was distinctively his.

For days, Jenna avoided Stuart as much as possible. She was afraid to confront him. She knew he would turn the tables on her and blame her for being noisy, saying she had no reason to go through his closet at school. Because of his anger he may hit her again like the time his fist made contact with her eye. She had gone to school the next day with a black eye and cheek. She told everyone that she had tripped over a throw rug and hit her face on the brick hearth. Some teachers gave her looks of pity while others looked doubtful; she had the feeling they did not believe her story.

While Debbie was away at college, Jenna decided to leave Stuart. She would not involve her friends and ask to stay with anyone, and she was afraid to tell the police or her pastor about Stuart's abuse. She got a motel room but was afraid to go to sleep. She stayed awake until her eyes closed. She had just fallen into oblivion when someone knocked on the door. When she asked, "Who is it?" Stuart said, "Come on, Jenna, open the door." To the manager he added, "She's not well. If she misses her medicine she wanders off and sometimes gets lost. I'm so glad you had a room. If you hadn't she could be anywhere by now." He kept talking patiently to Jenna and coaxed her into opening the door.

On the way home, he did not say a word, but once they got inside the house, he threatened to do her physical damage if she left again. "Your pretty face will be scarred for life."

The only thing she could do to get Stuart out of her mind for even a little bit was to pray. Once God got her over the rough period she felt compelled to paint. It was an addiction. In order to avoid talking to Stuart she painted more than usual. Her students were a blessing in more ways than one. She loved talking to them and encouraging them to see the joy one received by using a brush. She helped many students explore their skills and realize that they were gifted with a natural talent to paint.

In the early years of her marriage, Stuart let Jenna go off alone to paint, knowing she enjoyed capturing the beauty of every scene around them. She would get caught up in sketching, photographing or painting and lose all track of time. At first, when she was late returning home, he went looking for her, and then he gradually let Jenna return home at her leisure.

Because of her deep concentration, she lost track of time and was often late to important meetings and parties. Usually they pertained to something going on at UNC Asheville. To Stuart, they were most important. For Jenna, the college functions were not her cup of tea. When she did attend a party, after chatting to a few teachers she soon sneaked off to an empty lounge to read or nap. As soon as the party was over, Stuart went looking for her and usually found her asleep on the sofa.

Recalling her actions, Jenna gasped and sat up quickly in bed. *Was that when Stuart's devotion turned from love to obligation? Was that when he started looking elsewhere for companionship? Was that when Sheila entered his life? Dear Lord, what kind of wife was I?*

Stuart had seemed content with their lifestyle. Each time he found her asleep in the teacher's lounge, he teased her awake and carried her lovingly out to the car. *Was it all a show for those hanging around the doors? He acted as though he liked to take care of her. Could it have been an act so he would have something to laugh about with his friends? How could she have been so naïve, so blind?*

Jenna slammed over to the other side of the bed and beat the pillow. She wished it were Stuart's head. She gave the pillow one more jab.

Once she learned of Stuart's behavior with Sheila, she could hardly look anyone in the eye. Though she was not the guilty party, Jenna felt like it. She should have noticed the change in her husband long before she did. Jenna berated herself for not being more observant. *Where did her common sense go? When did her marriage actually fail?*

While twisting and turning into a more comfortable position, Jenna figured her common sense went into the shadows with everything else she failed to acknowledge. When she did not want to face a situation, she pushed the matter aside. She honestly planned to take care of her newspaper articles on time and to return the growing number of phone calls, but she put it off until she absolutely had to do something.

Most of the time, she waited for Stuart to urge her into taking care of all projects except her painting and working with plants. When she was not dabbling with paints she was working in dirt. Behind their house was a greenhouse that the former owner had used for plants and vegetables. Jenna used it for storing her repotted flowers and shrubs that she took when visiting patients. One shrub in particular she kept for herself. She watched and petted it like she would a baby. She had taken cuttings from two different shrubs, a red and a yellow, and joined them, trying to come up with something unique. The way the reddish-gold rhododendron grew made her as proud of it as any medal she had won for a painting. But she did not share it with Stuart.

He had no interest in getting his hands dirty and stayed away from the greenhouse. Jenna was glad; she had an ideal place to escape and be alone.

Stuart was not as perfect as he thought he was, but she admired his ability for being organized. As much as she had loved him and wanted him to love her as he once did, she could not be the systematic planner that he wanted her to be. She had too many other things on her mind, preferably painting. Since he was an artist, too, she thought he would have understood her drive to paint but apparently not. *I guess he didn't understand a lot of things about me.*

Before sleep claimed her, Jenna realized that the major problem in her marriage lay with her desire to be alone. She also realized that she did not have any common sense or she would have known how Stuart felt about her desire to become the best artist she could be. As he claimed, she was a hopeless case.

CHAPTER 10

At about 10:30 on Wednesday morning, Jenna finally got a chance to unload the arts and crafts from her van. Halfway through the placing of her stock into a closet, her hand froze in midair. After a minute or two she moved and covered her mouth with a shaky hand. Despite her efforts to keep from getting upset Jenna became panicky. Peaceful Existence was gone.

She dug into every storage box, shuffling and tossing out items. If any of the carefully painted items got scratched, it was the least of Jenna's worries. She had to find her favorite painting. Jenna ran back out to the van. It was empty. Not a single leaf or a magnolia bloom lay on the floor. Back inside the workroom, no amount of searching through everything a second time revealed the painting. Dear Lord, where could it be? She wondered.

The answer she came up with was, "Someone took it." There was no other explanation for it. She knew the painting had not been sold at the festival, or was it? Jenna ran to the telephone and called Debbie.

When Debbie took time off from her studies to stay with Jenna, she had to do more than stay around the house and hold her mother's hand. With their finances in bad shape, she had to get a job. Debbie loved to exercise and always did great in gymnastics. Although she did not try out for the Olympics as her instructor had wanted her to do, she continued practicing on a regular basis long after she got out of high school. She enjoyed her accomplishments of winning on levels throughout the state, but she knew to go higher in competition, it would take more dedication and time to be the best. There were too many other things she enjoyed doing, like dating, shopping with girlfriends, and taking trips with the youth at church. To keep involved with gymnastics to some degree, she chose to work with children when she was home from college.

At work this morning, she was helping a new girl through a series of flips when Jenna's call came in. "You try these exercises on your own," she told the preteen. "I've got to take a call."

"Hi, Mom. What's up?"

When Jenna heard Debbie's perky voice, she immediately took charge of the conversation. "I'm sorry to bother you, honey, but I'm looking for my painting. Do you know where Peaceful Existence is? Did you take it from the van? Is it hidden somewhere in the house?"

"No, Mom. I haven't seen it since Saturday. The only time I've even thought about it was when we discussed that it would be the best one to show John Paul."

Jenna raked fingers through her curly hair. "I'm stumped. I don't know where to look for it. I guess it's been stolen." An old familiar touch of helplessness began to fill her. "I don't know what to do now," she wailed.

"Don't get in a tizzy, Mom. I'll do something." Debbie called Charles McAdams and explained Jenna's problem. He promised to see if he could help.

Dressed in an oversized sweatshirt, faded jeans, and an equally worn straw Panama hat, Jenna went out to clip dead limbs from some rose bushes. She thought if her mind and energy was directed on other things maybe the tension in her body would leave and her back would no longer hurt. Perhaps then she could think more clearly and realize what really happened to Peaceful Existence. With clippers and a bucket in hand, she was walking toward a rose filled flowerbed when she heard a car door slam. It sounded as if it came from her driveway.

Jenna smiled. Company was always welcome. Visitors gave her excuses to prolong certain jobs, like trimming roses. She loved the beautiful blooms that each plant provided, but she did not enjoy getting stuck with thorns. Each time it happened she was immediately reminded of the thorns pushed onto the head of her blessed savior. If it had been her treated so brutally by men that laughed and mocked him, she would have hollered, "Stop! I can't take this anymore. Let the sinners get to heaven the best way they can." But not Jesus. He was certainly a much better person than Jenna Frazier Wilson ever attempted to be.

"I am so thankful, said aloud, that Jesus was not a coward like me," she thought. "He suffered and died on the cross so that I could go to heaven. I can't wait to kneel at his feet and tell him over and over how sorry I am that he had to suffer, but I am most grateful that he made a way for me to escape the burning hell."

By this time Jenna had turned the corner of her house and saw Charles McAdams standing beside his car. She froze in spot. No, it can't be him, she almost said aloud. She looked awful. She did not want him to see her looking so ratty, but there was nothing she could do about it now. He had seen her and was walking toward her. Her steps faltered even as she closed the gap between them.

When Charles stopped in front of her, she put on a friendly face and extended a hand. "Good morning, Charles. To what do I owe this pleasure?"

His brown eyes scanned every inch of her perfectly made up face and then did a swift appraisal of her appearance. His expression did not appear to change yet his eyes turned so dark they were almost black.

It was impossible for Jenna to judge his reaction by that look. She had the feeling, though, that he did not like her appearance. Before today, he had only seen her in clean sports outfits or dressy clothes. Now that Jenna was at her worst in a faded, stained and ragged outfit she was an embarrassment. He would never ask her out again.

A defense mechanism kicked in. Well, that was just too bad. She was in her own yard and had not invited him there. She started to tell him so when she noticed how great he looked. The neat black slacks and red knit shirt hugging his taut body made Jenna feel really frumpy. She wished she had dressed better. She had neater looking work clothes. Today, though, she was not in a caring mood. She was wallowing in self-pity. Her painting was gone.

They stood there staring at each other, oblivious to the people strolling along the walkway in front of her house. A couple people said good morning. Jenna unconsciously waved back at them. She was concentrating on the handsome man in front of her.

Charles came to his senses first. "Excuse me, Jenna, for staring, but you are the only woman I know who can dress down and still look good. Even your floppy hat is cute."

His smile caused her heart to flutter, but she shook her head in denial. There went the noted charm that Charles bestowed on every female he met. She never thought it would work on her, but she guessed she was as vulnerable as any other woman.

Jenna laughed and said, "You don't know how to be natural, do you? I know what I look like." Before he could comment, she started walking back toward her garden. "I was about to check out my prize rhododendron. If you've got a minute, come with me and look at something that will be gorgeous, hopefully, in a couple of days."

They went to the area of her yard where a mixed variety of plants grew. Near a homemade pond, numerous bushes were opening into colors of purples, pinks, reds, and yellows. In the center of the lot stood a hybrid rhododendron bush filled with half open blooms in an unusual shade of red-gold.

"I call it Evening Sun," she said. "I've worked and petted this plant for three years."

"How did you get this color?" Charles asked.

"Propagation. I joined a dark red Loki and a dark yellow Logan Damaris. It has been my first experience at crossbreeding. You can buy bushes with similar colors, but I wanted to try my hand at making my own variety. I'm so excited. I can hardly wait to see the full bloom. A committee from Fletcher's Garden Club is coming Thursday to judge it for their spring contest. "

"Best of luck," Charles said with a look of awe. "It's a beautiful plant as it is with the dark green foliage and just a hint of color peeping through the leaves."

"Do you like working with plants?" Jenna asked with great interest, hoping they had something other than their children and crafts in common.

"No. I've never had time for it. I enjoy looking at flowers and have a great appreciation for their beauty, but an experienced gardener works his magic with my yard. However, I've been thinking about cutting my workload next year. Perhaps I'll get you to give me some tips that I might try on the planting and caring of certain plants. Besides golf, I'd like to find something relaxing to do. What about you? What else do you do to relax?"

She grinned. "Besides painting and working with plants?"

Charles nodded. "I'm sure there is something else you'd like to try?"

"Actually there hasn't been. Playing in dirt and painting have been my areas for relaxing. Also they have been my downfall. I'm beginning to believe that painting came between me and Stuart. I get so involved with every phase of producing a work of art that I lose track of time and what's going on around me."

"You paint a lot now out here around your plants, don't you?" Charles asked.

Jenna's expressive eyes opened wide. "How did you know? Oh, I guess Debbie told you."

"No. I recognized parts of your garden on items you had at the festival. Peaceful Existence looked like it may have been painted in this garden."

Jenna nodded with a frown. "I got the idea when I saw Debbie napping out here. Now the painting is gone."

Charles' face filled with concern. "I heard. Do you have any idea what could have happened to it?"

She shook her head and sat down on a cement bench. "Someone must have stolen it and most likely at the festival. It could have been taken from the van, but I don't know when or how. Nothing looked disturbed when I moved the stock into the storage room. By the way, how did you know about the painting?"

"Debbie called me and asked if I would help find it."

"Would you?" Jenna asked her look hopeful. "I don't know where to begin, except to think it was taken at the festival. Now that I think about it, I don't remember packing it into the van that evening. Wait a minute. I didn't pack the van, you did." Her eyes flew open wide.

"Stop it, Jenna. Don't even go there," Charles said. "I didn't take your painting. They were all wrapped up when I began loading them. I didn't know one picture from another. Look, Jenna, I know you are probably grabbing at straws, but if we're going to find who did take it, we have to work together."

Jenna relented. "I know. But I'm still not fully convinced you didn't do something with it, but for the time being I'll give you the benefit of the doubt."

Charles grunted. "Thanks for small mercies."

Together they mulled over Saturday's event and the crowd coming and going around their tables.

"Did anyone look suspicious?" Charles asked.

Jenna removed her hat and fluffed up her curls. "No. I can't imagine anyone stealing it in broad daylight with people all around."

Charles scratched his head. "Sometimes it doesn't pay to trust anyone with something valuable." When he saw Jenna's frown, he apologized. "I don't actually mean everyone. There are some people who have God in their heart, and they won't disappoint you. Anyway, did you notice how people looked at the picture? Did anyone take it down and move to a different light or perhaps turn it this way and that to observe it from each angle?"

Jenna thought for a moment. "A little gray haired lady did, but I saw her hang it back up. Later she bought a tissue-cover box with a tiny flower garden painted around the four sides. It was a good thing I took a large supply of items decorated with rhododendrons to the festival because they sold fast."

Charles nodded. "I could tell by the way you set up your display that you'd draw a crowd. Besides the paintings, all the plants hanging from the folding racks and huge bowls of flowers sitting around made your area look like a garden. Once customers left you, they wandered my way. Perhaps I should set up beside you next time."

Jenna quickly responded, "I hope you do. If I need help unloading, I won't call you a thief if you pick up one my boxes."

They laughed, and Jenna added, "When I thought you were stealing my crafts, I was on the verge of calling for help when you turned and dropped the box at my feet. I simply lost my voice. I felt so bad. Will you forgive me?"

Charles took hold of her hand. "You were forgiven before you even asked. The only thing I hope to steal from you is your heart."

She slipped her hand from his light grasp. "There you go again, dishing out hogwash. Back to my painting, please. I don't know if my picture thief is beautiful, handsome or ugly. How will you go about looking for him or her?"

"When I go to the police station, I'll look through their files to see if anyone was ever apprehended on a similar case. If I find any suspects, I'll have you look at the pictures to see if you recognize anyone as being an attendee at the festival." He stood up and looked down at her. "Try not to worry. I'll make this case my priority."

Jenna rose, putting on her hat, and said, "Thank you so much." As they strolled toward the front yard she added, "I set the price high on the picture because I didn't want to part with it. It's gone now, and I didn't even get a penny for it. Perhaps it's God's way of telling me I shouldn't put great importance on things that I should be more concerned about what is of great value for the hereafter."

Charles put a hand on her shoulder, and she shivered. He bent to look under the brim of her hat, appearing to have not noticed her reaction to him. "I don't believe you were overly concerned about parting with the painting or you wouldn't have taken the chance of selling it at any price."

Jenna gave Charles a look of gratitude. "You're right. I enjoyed painting it and I'm thankful that other people have liked it. If I don't get it back, I hope it finds its way to the home that deserves it."

"But, if it's in the area, I'll find it, Jenna. I'll be in touch with you soon." With a wink he added, "Don't fill up your calendar. We've got to have another night on the town."

He left, and Jenna went to sit on a front porch step. The man's a menace; she thought but sighed and smiled in amazement. She could not believe how much better she felt after being with Charles. His winning smiles and complimentary words soothed yet disturbed her. They made her too aware of him.

Yes, Charles McAdams was gifted with charm. While she felt gratitude for his help, she could not take his personal attention seriously and let him become an important part of her life. His actions had a practiced technique, apparently one that he had used over and over again. Charming the ladies came natural to him, and she could not tell where the genuine man began and where it ended. Jenna stood abruptly and marched back to her flower garden.

While at work, off and on her thoughts returned to Charles. She decided that he was harmless. She had nothing to worry about where he was concerned. To see him again on a social level would never happen because they traveled in different circles of people. Besides, her life was full. Maybe more than it should be, she admitted.

To attend every appointment and fill all obligations began to bother Jenna. She was feeling burned out. She wished the newspaper would terminate her column because each piece was getting harder to write. He mind knew what she should write but putting it onto paper and turning it in to the editor on time worked on her nerves. The problem had gotten worse since Stuart's death. To be honest, she had been thinking of resigning from the position but knew Stuart would have objected if she had mentioned it. He would have called her a quitter. It did matter that she was overextending herself and was afraid of it affecting her health, according to him; if you took on a responsibility you were to see it through.

Debbie jabbed the clippers into the ground and muttered, "Then why wasn't he responsible enough to see through to the end his commitment of being a faithful husband and a loving father? I know. He just got tired of constantly pushing an unorganized person through life." She grabbed up the clippers and starting clipping more branches while continuing to talk to herself. She was glad that her neighbors were not close enough to hear her murmurings. She knew that Debbie was right about her being a genuine grade A procrastinator, but to some extent Jenna found it to be a good thing.

When she delayed writing or finishing a sketch, a new idea often presented itself, and her articles and paintings turned out better than she would have imagined. Also, by being this way, she felt it made her more sympathetic toward her students.

At workshops, Jenna never pushed them to finish a project before the two-week period ended. She preferred that they learn the basics in class and then put it all together at home whenever they could. In college, Jenna and her classmates liked art better when they were allowed to work on it at their leisure rather than being rushed to finish it by a dead line. When she became a teacher, she used the same technique on her students, and they were more productive.

For Jenna, spending time with people ranked a close second to painting. Stuart had complained when she went to the hospital or nursing homes to visit the sick and lonely or talked on the phone to someone she had not seen in a long time. He said she gave too much of herself to others. Jenna shrugged. She could not help it if she liked to talk, nor did she mind being interrupted from work. Often times she got ideas for articles from the people she met, but then again interruptions did occasionally cause her to neglect important facts.

One time her spaghetti sauce burned while she was on the phone. Another time she had left the lawnmower running because it was difficult to crank, and while talking to a neighbor the mower ran out of gas. Instead of going to the store for more gas, she went to the kitchen and opened a jar of prepared sauce that was almost as good as her recipe and ate some spaghetti.

Jenna recalled her father talking about her free spirit, the way she flitted from one place to another in search of new things to learn or do. On the seventy-mile-long island called home lived some talented people who willingly taught her what they knew.

Her enthusiasm to learn the dying art of tatting, the making of necklaces from black coral, and weaving of hammocks from rope made on the island impressed the old folks and they looked forward to her visits. They all began to expect her to come around more often than she could.

She also failed to show up to help her father pack some herbs for shipping, because she was biking off to one place or another. Some days she met friends to play tennis or go swimming for the famous wilks, black and white shells that were hidden under rocks in the sea. Diving and hunting was a time consuming activity, but she loved it.

Personal discipline was hard for Jenna to conquer; it had been all her life. Since Stuart's death she has begun to see that all along she should have tried harder to gain willpower and determination to make more decisions for herself.

When it became a drudge to whip out a 250-word article she should have quit. The editor never made her sign an agreement to write for any certain length of time. She could have quit any time. But because she had promised to fill in while the previous columnist was out for surgery, she felt obligated to stay until the woman returned. But the columnist had complications and could not continue to work. Jenna agreed to continue writing for a while. But, the more she wanted to paint, the harder it got to write.

Stuart wrote articles for the university newsletter. He explained to her how he developed a suitable system for writing. Every Tuesday he got up at 5:30 a.m. and wrote. But it was not all that he did. He said he also went out to exercise.

Anger filled Jenna's eyes. Exercise! Ha. Keeping her from finding out about Sheila was some exercise. "Girl, you didn't know your own husband did you?" she asked herself. "What a dumb wife you were."

Frustrated, Jenna jumped to her feet, which was a mistake. She could not move. While standing still to let the pain in her back ease off, she looked toward a neighbor's house behind her. She decided to not let thoughts of Stuart drag her down today. Once the pain receded, she gathered up a bouquet of flowers to take to the elderly gentleman who had just arrived home from the hospital.

Jenna watched as his daughter helped him into the house. When she figured that he was safely settled in bed she went over and welcomed him home. After a brief visit, Jenna went to her workroom.

The unpainted items drew her attention. Where should she start? A case of lampshades would look great with outdoor scenes on them, she thought, and the tote bags could use some flowers or women's heads with red hats on them. She passed over them for a couple of plain vases.

One day while searching her favorite craft and novelty store for something unusual to paint a delivery of supplies arrived. She stopped plundering to watch the store owner unwrap everything. She liked what she saw and bought some of everything he took from the boxes. She knew that the ladies of her mission group could use some decorative vases for the flowers they took to shut-ins. "They might sell pretty well at the festival, too," she told the clerk, and took home three dozen 12-inch tall glass vases.

In no time at all, Jenna was involved with her painting. Most of the designs were feminine-looking, but a few had boat scenes suitable for men. She put them aside to dry and picked up some plastic bookmarks to fix for Mother's Day and Father's Day. On the ones for mothers she put a long stem rose and wrote With Love to Mother. The ones to fathers, she put a water wheel and a creek. While she was in the process of writing Number One Dad a crack of thunder caused her to jump. The brush took a streak of black paint across her perfectly written letters.

"No," she groaned, "I don't have time for this."

Debbie entered the room with a tray, containing hot coffee and chocolate cake. "I believe it's time for a break," she said, frowning at her mother's frustrated look. She gave Jenna time to eat a bite before saying, "Tell me, did Charles come by?"

Jenna nodded and took a swallow of coffee. "I'm glad you called him." She began eating the cake and then mentioned Saturday's festival and her painting.

Debbie could not recall anything out of the ordinary. "Of course, I saw some weird looking characters hanging around, but they didn't appear interested in the paintings. Actually the girls, or was it guys, don't know what they were, but after a brief look at your items they moved on."

A clanging noise outside interrupted their conversation. The women looked at each other and froze.

"What was that?" Jenna whispered.

Another clash of thunder boomed. A cat squealed. Rain pelted against the windows.

Debbie blew out a puff of hot air. "Storms and cats. Boy, they make me jumpy."

Jenna picked up the book mark and started to paint it all over again. "Me, too. At least I know what to expect now. Maybe I won't jump every time I hear a strange noise. I can't keep repainting everything. I don't have time."

Debbie yawned and stretched. "You can have the noise and the painting. I'm going to bed. You coming?"

"Not right now. I've got a lot to do. Since I've finally started this, I think I had better keep going. Sometimes I think if I didn't need the extra income to pay off the bills that your father left behind, I wouldn't do anymore consignment stores or festivals and just stick to painting canvases."

"Mom, you can't quit. I believe and start paintingyou may have hooked some regular buyers."

Jenna's eyebrows arched in wonder. "You think so?" When Debbie said, "If you quit now, you will never know for sure," Jenna grinned and asked, "What would I do without you?"

Debbie's brows drew together as in deep concentration. Finally she said, "Make the wrong decisions?"

Jenna chuckled. "You're probably right, but let's pray that I'll soon learn how to make good moves for myself."

Debbie stretched as high as her petite body would allow and headed toward the door. 'I'm really bushed. Good night, Mom."

Jenna was already concentrating on the book mark. "Night," she mumbled, her voice barley audible above the noise outside.

Thunder boomed and lightning flashed near the window where Jenna sat. She jumped and smeared paint on another book mark. She threw up her hands. "I give up," she grumbled and went to bed, too.

CHAPTER 11

"Mom, come here!"

Jenna bolted upright in bed. Was she dreaming or did Debbie actually call her? She tried to shake the haze of confusion from her mind and go back to sleep, but Debbie continued to call her. With it came the sound of pounding feet running into the house and across the floor.

"Mom, something's happened to your garden. The rhododendrons are gone. A whole section is empty."

From a nearby chair, Jenna grabbed her robe and shoved her arms into its sleeves as she ran to the back door.

She rushed outside, barely touching the steps. Sure enough the yard looked awful. Bushes no longer sat ready to burst open in full bloom in the area farthest away from the house. Mulch lay outside the flowerbed. A trail of dug up grass ran across the yard to the road.

"Dear me, "Jenna whispered. Oblivious to the wet grass soaking her bare feet, she stared at the garden where she alone had done a tremendous amount of work.

Anger kicked in and brought her out of the trance that had her rooted in front of several holes.

She kicked at mounds of dirt, sort of aiming it toward the holes. She knew it would not repair the disorder, but she had to take her anger out on something. With her hands jammed onto her hips, she threw back her head and shouted, "Where are my plants? Where is Evening Sun?"

The younger version of herself stopped starring at the garden and wrapped an arm around her mother's waist. Debbie chuckled and said, "It looks as if you've been rhododendron burglarized."

Jenna jerked away and glared at her. "That's not funny."

The smile faded from Debbie's face. She held up her hands in a way of apology. "I know, but you were about to lose it. I want you to lighten up."

"I don't need to lighten up. I've every right to be angry. In the span of one night someone's made hard work look like a waste of time and energy. The plants friends gave me as house warming presents are gone. All I have to show for the hours spent out here is one big mess." Jenna kicked another mound of dirt toward a hole. "That's where my prize bush is supposed to be. Do you see why I don't think this is so funny?"

"You're right, Mom. It's not funny," Debbie said, failing to keep a grin from pulling at her lips when she added, "but I've never heard of anyone digging into someone's garden and stealing bushes. I'm going to call the police." She turned toward the house before Jenna saw her expression and grew livid. A safe distance away she called over her shoulder, "Don't you need some shoes on? How about changing clothes? They might send a man."

Jenna had started mopping along behind Debbie but stopped at those words and jammed her hands on her hips. "My goodness, Debbie, I might be in shock, but I'm not stupid."

Debbie turned and gave her mother a hard look. "I didn't say you were. Do you want my help or not?"

"Of course I do, but give me a little credit for knowing that I should change clothes before expected company arrives." Jenna watched Debbie march on toward the house. She was surprised at her daughter. Did Debbie think like Stuart after all? Had she been like her father all along, thinking that her mother was dense?

Jenna took a couple steps and then stopped to look back at the empty spots. Her shoulders dropped another two inches. Who wanted to hurt her so much that they would take her favorite painting and then attack her garden? With her eyes still open she prayed every step she made back into the house. *God, you took care of me when Stuart failed me. You didn't let me crack up then, please don't let me do it now.* Her prayer continued as she dressed. *Please send Charles to help me. He's the only one I trust at this point. I don't know where to go next.*

Although she did not feel like dressing up, her mother's words of encouragement came to mind. "When you're troubled and feeling low, dress up physically, mentally, and spiritually, as if you're preparing for battle. You'll then be armed to face what comes before you."

By the time she had a sailor hat settled on top of her braided hair much of her anger was gone. She was giving her self one last look in the mirror when the doorbell rang.

For someone who looked ready for sailing, a boat ride was the last thing on Jenna's mind. She could not get over the previous happenings. Although she was no longer wanting to strangled her robber she could not help but be afraid that the robberies were a prelude for something worse to come. *Dear Lord, she began to pray again, whatever the reason is for this mystery, please give me wisdom to face the future objectively and with a Christ-like spirit.*

In the kitchen, where Debbie had taken their guests, were the police chief and Charles. "Mom, you remember Richard Shelton."

Jenna smiled, but it did not reach her eyes when she said, "Thank you both for coming." Looking at Charles she added, "I don't understand why such crazy things are happening to me."

"Would anyone like coffee?" Debbie asked. "We also have hot tea. I don't think Mom could live without it."

Jenna reached for her tea and wound both hands around the mug. While starring into the green liquid she wondered if tea had any bearing on her actions. Did it affect the mind? Maybe it was what made her stupid and act unintelligent. She blinked and took a swallow. No. Nothing was wrong with tea. It was good for you or her father would not have sold it. And there was absolutely nothing wrong with her that would not affect anyone else in her position.

Charles' deep, wonderful-sounding voice broke into her train of thought. She smiled tentatively when he said, "I'd like to have some tea, please."

"I'll take coffee," Chief Shelton said, "with a little milk."

Jenna sat down her cup and then asked, "Have you gotten any leads on my painting?"

The chief shook his head. "I'm sorry, Mrs. Wilson, but nothing positive yet. Ever since we first heard about the missing painting, we've been looking for it everywhere we could think to look. Charles wants to check out an idea when we leave here."

"Pertaining to what?" Debbie asked and set a coffee cake on the table. "Does that mean the picture is still in the area?"

"I'd rather not talk about it at this point," Charles answered, looking at Jenna. "If it's a good lead I'll tell you all about it as soon as I can."

Chief Shelton pulled out a note pad and pen. "Tell us about your plants."

Debbie sat down beside her mother and did the talking. "I found them missing this morning. After the awful storm last night, I thought I'd take a look outside to see if the wind and rain had made a mess with tree limbs and leaves. When I opened the back door, I couldn't believe my eyes. Mom's garden looked like it had opened up in spots and swallowed her plants." She shook her head in amazement and added, "Some nut wanted her plants awfully bad to dig in the rain, and at night."

Charles looked at Jenna's downcast expression. He stood and held out his hand to her. "Let's go and take a look at the garden together."

The chief and Debbie stayed behind so he could question her some more. For the next fifteen minutes, Charles talked with Jenna, discussing every aspect about last night.

"Did you hear any unusual noises?" he asked.

Jenna stared at Charles, looking to see if he had two heads. What a crazy question. Storms always make unusual noises. But she decided it must be an appropriate question or the smart detective wouldn't have asked it. She knew he would not do or say anything to make himself look inept at his job, so she said, "With all the thundering and lightning, I could barely keep from jumping out of my skin. That was more than enough noise for me."

"I'm sure that's true," Charles said but urged her to think about all sounds, those above and beyond the storm. "Can you recall anything at all that was different from the usual pop and crackle?"

She shook her head. "I'm sorry, Charles. I didn't sleep well, and I'm having trouble reliving last night's happenings. There was a clang…Debbie and I were in the workroom at that time. It sounded like metal hitting metal. A cat screeched and sounded as if it had knocked something over. We decided that the noise came from a stray animal looking for shelter, but it must have been the robber."

Charles moved about the grounds, examining every spot until Chief Shelton and Debbie came out of the house. The men walked to one side of the yard, comparing notes. Charles pointed to the ground and began following a trial. A patch of grass, roughly dug up, ran from the garden to the road where the trail ended.

A moment later, he rose from a squatting position. "Looks like a wheelbarrow or some other piece of equipment with one wheel dug up the grass," he observed and traced the path onward to the edge of the road. "It looks like something with a jagged edge, perhaps an old wheel, may have done the digging."

The others followed him to the curb. He wrinkled his forehead and turned to Chief Shelton. "Maybe my assumption is wrong, Anthony. The pavement on the road should be dug up or at least scratched, but there's not a consistent marking. Then again maybe I'm right and the wheel barrel was stopped at the curb in order to transfer the bushes to a truck."

Just when Jenna was beginning to have faith in Charles' ability to solve the most puzzling mystery he came up with a most discouraging comment. "My goodness," Jenna groaned, shaking her head, "so this is going to remain an unsolved mystery, too."

Spurred into action by Jenna's depressive attitude, Charles wrapped an arm around her and started walking back toward the house. "Jenna, do you have any faith in my abilities as a detective?" When she looked

130

at him without commenting, he said, "I'm going to do my very best to find out what's going on here. I won't quit. I intend to find the person or persons responsible for your grief?"

The chief promised that he too would keep working on her case. "I'll let you know of results as soon as something is legitimate," he said and then left.

The phone rang. Debbie went to answer it, leaving Jenna and Charles to say their good-byes.

Charles placed his hands on her shoulders and smiled into her upturned face. "Are you busy this afternoon?"

She shrugged. "I had thought about working on some crafts. I'm certainly not interested in doing yard work. Why?"

"I'd like to take you to the lake." He removed his hands and stuffed them into his back pockets. Looking her over, he added, "Your outfit reminded me that I haven't been sailing in a while. If you'll go with me, I'll get Rosie to pack us a lunch. How about it?"

Jenna knew better than to agree, but she wanted to go. Before she could talk herself out of it, she said, "Yes, all right. What time?"

"Give me time to get to the office and get some men working on my ideas for finding your plants and to check on a lead about the painting. I'll be back in an hour."

The hopeful light in his eyes along with an encouraging smile caused butterflies in her stomach. She was afraid to speak, fear that her nervousness would make her voice squeak, but she sounded calm when she said, "I'll be ready."

She watched Charles back out of the driveway, and waved. Her feelings contained a mixture of excitement and concern. She was worried about going out in a boat but looked forward to being alone with Charles. His unforgettable kiss still lingered in her mind. She smiled and then frowned. Why did she act like a teenager around Charles? Her reactions to him really bothered her.

With a snort of self-disgust, Jenna went into the house. Several minutes passed before she realized that she could not get Charles off her mind. She washed up the cups and saucers, and then flung down the dish towel. "What a bother," she fumed. "What's the matter with me?

I should be trying to figure out a way to cancel the date. I shouldn't encourage Charles. A relationship with him will never be more than friendship." But she could not stop herself from wanting to be with him. She enjoyed his company. He was nice to her. Even with all the charming words he dished out, he seemed sincere with her most of the time.

The phone rang again. Debbie grabbed up the receiver and then held it out to Jenna. "It's the doctor's office."

Jenna moaned. "You might know I'd have to work when I have plans."

"What plans?" Debbie mumbled, searching through her pocketbook for her car keys.

Jenna stood with the refrigerator door opened, looking but not getting anything out and answered nonchalantly, "Charles invited me to go sailing."

Debbie's head flew up; a bright smile filled her face. "Great! Maybe you won't have to go into work until tomorrow morning. You know how they call in advance o see if you'll be available."

"Yeah. And you know the number of times they've called on the spur of the moment."

With an encouraging look, Debbie held out the receiver and added in a whispered voice, "Cross your fingers. Gotta run. If you do go out, smooth sailing."

"Thanks," Jenna said over her shoulder. "Hope you have a good day."

After a brief conversation, Jenna hung up the receiver with a disappointed look. She enjoyed her job but wished the call had been for another day. Just this once she wanted to do something fun and different. While dialing Charles' number she figured it was probably for the best. She most likely would have gotten sick anyway. She remembered getting seasick once. After that experience she had vowed to never go out on the water again.

She and Stuart had taken a cruise on The Holiday ship. While heading toward Cayman Islands a storm came up. The ship did not rock excessively, but it was enough action to upset Jenna's nerves and her stomach. She felt so badly that she could not go to supper. Stuart went alone. At the time, Jenna knew he would be okay. Their table companions the night before had been very friendly and talkative. It was not until their last night on the ship that Jenna overheard a conversation on deck where two ladies had been talking about Stuart. The blonde woman said he was a great dancer and the tall, dark haired beauty said he was a great kisser.

Jenna then realized why Stuart had returned to the cabin late and was humming when he unlocked the door. He admitted since he had not wanted to go to bed earlier, he had made his rounds of the ship and ended up in a lounge where people were dancing. But he had not revealed all that he had done that night. And she would not have known about his "fun" if she had not heard those women talking. Recalling the episode made her angry.

She also recalled that she was in the process of calling Charles. She took a deep breath to dispel the anger and dialed several numbers, never getting to talk to him. He was not at the police station, at his office, nor at his home. So she left word with Rosie. "Tell Charles that I'm sorry about the outing. Maybe we can do something another time."

She hung up, thinking that perhaps it was for the best that sailing was not going to be on their agenda today. A green face and vomiting all over the place was not an attractive picture she cared to show anyone, especially Charles. If she ever ruined a trip for him, he would probably never invite her to go anywhere ever again. Should he ask her on another date, she hoped they would do something other than sailing.

Jenna went to work and spent the afternoon taking calls, making appointments, and collecting payments. It left little time to dwell on Charles, herself, and her problems. The office closed at seven. She got home much later than normal because she had to stop at the grocery store.

After she put the milk and eggs away, she played the answering machine and listened to Charles' message. *Jenna, I'm sorry, too, that we can't go sailing. I've also got unexpected work. I have to go to South Carolina to check out some information on a missing person. I hope*

you will think about me a little while I'm gone. I'll call when I get back.
Another thing, the lead pertaining to your painting failed to produce
positive results. I'm sorry.

Debbie had come into the room shortly after the message started playing. Jenna gave her a resigned sigh. "He's never going to find it."

"He'll find it," Debbie said with distinct optimism, and then presented a mischievous grin. "Do you plan to think about Charles?"

"I guess I'll have to with you around to constantly remind me, won't I?" Jenna answered and swept out of the room.

When she shut the bathroom door, Debbie went to the kitchen to call Lynn. "Hi girlfriend. You won't believe what happened today," she said, giddy with excitement.

"Give me time, I'll tell you." She laughed and continued, "Mom agreed to go sailing with Charles. That was a major decision for her, since she vowed to never step a foot on another boat. Unfortunately for our plans the excursion never materialized. Mom had to go to work and apparently so did Charles. He left a message on the answer machine about going out of town on business. He sounded as disappointed as Mom looked. Let's pray that his trip makes them both miss each other."

The days passed quickly while Jenna worked on crafts. All the painting consumed much of her time. At one point she called it quits so she could go out and search the area for signs of her bushes. She could not find a single trace of her plants. None of the yards looked to have new bushes and not a one had been tossed to the side of the road. Like the painting, they have disappeared.

The police did not have any news and neither did Charles' office. Jenna talked with Chuck who apologized profusely. "I hate to disappoint you, Jenna, but I can't tell you anything yet. I really am sorry."

Jenna wished that Charles would hurry up and come home. She wondered, though, would he jump on her case as soon as he returned. With a wistful look she thought how wonderful it would be if he did care enough to claim her losses as his major problems to solve. She recalled his personal request: Would she think about him while he was gone?

Try to think? Ha. How could she not think about him when the solving of her robberies rested in his hands? Jenna could not think about her painting or shrubbery without the man coming to mind.

More to the point, members of the beautification committee were supposed to come for a judging of Evening Sun. She dreaded having to call and cancel the meeting, but it had to be done.

She apologized to the club president and ended her call just as the doorbell rang. Chuck McAdams grinned at her from the other side of the threshold. He greeted her with a kiss on the cheek and a quick hug before saying, "Hey, gorgeous. Thought I'd never get here to see you. We're swamped at the office, but I walked out, telling our secretary that I had to go see my favorite woman."

Jenna smiled. He looked so much like his father that she could not stop the smile from spreading into a wide grin. "Like father, like son, charming. Come in, Chuck. I'm always glad to see you. How are you?"

"Fine," he answered, wiping his brow in a mock weary gesture. "We've been terribly busy with Daddy away. I needed a break from the mound of paper work that he usually helped with. Instead of the stack of reports going down, it seemed to be getting higher. Before it buried me I jumped into my car and started driving." With his arms spread outward he added, "Look where I ended up. Like old times. When I needed to get away from something troubling me, I always ran to you."

"Ever since we had out first private conversation, I looked forward to your visits, even if it was just to listen to your ramblings."

Chuck noticed her paint smock. "Have I come at a bad time?"

"Never. I'm always here for you. But first, have you got anything to tell me about my painting and bushes?"

Chuck shook his head. "Sorry. I know Dad will jump back on the case as soon as he gets home."

"It's what I expected to hear so let's talk of better things." Jenna looked puzzled when she got Chuck a glass of iced tea. She poured herself a cup of hot tea. "Tell me something, Chuck."

"What's that?"

"Who's paying your father to work on my robberies?"

He pulled the glass away from his mouth and smiled. "Actually, no one."

Jenna looked distressed. "I hope he's not expecting me to pay him. I don't have the money."

Chuck reached across the table and squeezed her hand. "Don't sweat it. Daddy is doing it just for you." He stressed the last word. "If he wasn't, I'd pay him out of my pocket." With a serious look he said, "Jenna, you're the mother I always wished I had. I will do anything for you."

Tears filled Jenna's eyes. In a choked voice she said, "You know I love you." At his nod she added, "I thought you were going to be my son…in-law. It broke my heart when you and Debbie broke up."

He grinned and said, "We're back together again. One way or another, I expect we'll be mother and son."

She grinned but did not comment on his last statement. Instead she asked, "Are you ready to hear about my hat collection?"

Chuck looked at the ball cap on her head. "They look so cute on you, but why hide that beautiful red hair under them. Don't you like people, especially men looking at it?"

Jenna shrugged. "I haven't thought about it from that angle. Matter of fact, it feels good to get a compliment on my hair once in a while. I'm at the age where I need all the attention I can get," Jenna said with laughter in her voice. "No. The truth is, I like hats, but I didn't always."

"What caused you to start wearing them?"

With a twinkle in her eye she said, "I'll tell you if you promise not to laugh."

He crossed his heart and held up his hand. "I swear."

Jenna chuckled. "Don't swear except in court. Okay. Now. It began with a plane trip. You know what happens when I get on a plane."

Chuck made a face. "Don't I? That time you went with my senior class to New York, you upchucked all over me."

Jenna faked remorse. "I'm so sorry."

"Yeah. Right."

With a more serious look Jenna said, "I still get airsick nearly every time I'm on a plane. Shortly after Stuart's death, I was asked to speak at Fort Smith's Christian Women's Club in Oklahoma. My back hurts a lot due to some disk problem, so I submitted to flying rather than driving the long distance. Debbie volunteered to go with me."

"Good Old Deb to the rescue," Chuck said with a smile.

Jenna's eyes squinted almost shut. "Who? My daughter? Debbie helped me get the embarrassment of a lifetime."

Chuck's eyebrows waffled. "Sounds interesting. Tell all," he said and laughed at her pained expression.

Jenna slapped his arm and then continued her story. "After we checked in at the airport I went to the gift shop. While paying for my purchase, Debbie grabbed my arm, saying, 'We have to hurry and get on the plane.' So we took off toward the exit. Just as I was having my luggage scrutinized I heard my name being called. 'Mrs. Wilson. Jenna Wilson, wait a minute. You forgot your package.'

"I stopped. Debbie stopped. Everyone behind us stopped. At the booths, the guards' heads snapped around. All eyes watched the young girl push her way through the crowd. 'Mrs. Wilson,' she called again. 'I thought you might need this before you returned.'

"In the shuffle to get a package into my hands, the plastic bag turned upside down and out tumbled the bright red slip I had just bought."

Between Chuck's rise and fall of laugher Jenna added, "The salesclerk, Andrea Lang, was a former art student of mine. I used to think of the girl with fondness because she was so adept with oils, but now I remember her more for helping to embarrass me in the airport. The other person was Debbie.

"There I stood among all those strangers, gaping at the heap of red silk at my feet. Debbie picked it up and held it so everyone could tell it was lingerie and said, 'Yep, it belongs to Mom. She will need it for her hot date tonight.' That was one time that my face was redder than my hair. I wanted the floor to open up and swallow me. I could have died. Instead, I found myself being stared at by an airport full of travelers who were grinning from cheek to cheek."

"I guess Debbie laughed, too."

"Of course she did. You could hear her over everyone. I marched over and snatched a big wide brim hat from her hand. She had bought it to wear when we got to Oklahoma, but I made good use of it first."

While Chuck was wiping tears, Jenna added, "To hide from the numerous broad smiles, I plunked her cowboy hat onto my head and pulled the brim low over my face like this." She demonstrated by pulling the brim of her ball cap over her forehead and marched into the plane. "I took my seat without speaking to anyone."

"That must have been hard," Chuck said, trying not to smile, "not to talk, I mean."

Jenna bopped his shoulder. "I had no idea Debbie wasn't behind me until I looked back. There she stood at the plane door telling the stewardesses about me and my slip." Jenna shook her head. "My fear of flying left me as I juggled an overloaded carry-on bag, my pocketbook, and the plastic bag with my red slip while at the same time trying to keep my face covered and step over a big lady on the outside seat who didn't give an inch."

Chuck burst out laughing again. Jenna joined him this time. About five minutes later they were reduced to the giggling stage and wiping tears. Jenna manage to say, "Pretty silly, huh?"

Chuck answered, "Silly, no. Funny, yes. You're not still embarrassed about the slip are you?"

"No. Not really."

"What has the plane trip got to do with wearing hats now?"

Jenna drank some tea before answering. "Once I settled down, I liked the feel of the hat on my head. When I made myself talk to people around me, I received lots of compliments on it. Because the passengers engaged me in conversations, I didn't have time to worry about the flight, nor did I get the least bit airsick.

"More and more I began to wear hats to my meetings. People now identify me with hats. When I enter a room, someone usually says, 'Here's the hat lady.' I almost feel naked without one on."

Chuck reached over and tugged on the cap brim. "I admit they do suit you. I agree with Daddy. He said you look great in anything you put on. You could probably make a feed sack look like a ball gown."

Jenna's eyebrows rose nearly to her hairline. "That's stretching the compliment a bit too far." She changed the subject. "I hope my painting is found soon. I'd like to show it to John Paul Montague. You do know he may hang one of my paintings in his gallery."

Chuck nodded. "Of course I know. Deb told me." Looking anxious he added, "But you better count on another painting. Peaceful Existence may not be in the area anymore. If it is, it may not be in good shape."

"I guess my bushes left town, too," she said, flinging her arms outward.

He began to move through the house toward the front door with Jenna following slowly behind. Chuck turned toward her. With a sincere look he hugged her and said, "Don't give up hope, Jenna. If anyone can solve this case, it's Daddy. I'm not being prejudiced, but he can dig up information when the rest of us feel there is absolutely nothing to be found."

Jenna felt sure that Charles would need a miracle. If by some divine intervention he did find the painting and plants, she knew they would no longer be in good shape, especially the rhododendrons. She knew if they were found, they would be dead. Not even the great detective, Charles McAdams could save dying plants. He knows nothing about caring for them much less do restoration work. Women are his specialty. When they fall at his feet, he just charms them back to life.

She smiled innocently and said, "I've heard a lot about Charles' reputation, in more ways than one."

With a twisted grin Chuck said, "I know what you mean, but he is a terrific guy."

She mumbled, "If you say so."

"I do say so, honestly. One of these days I hope you will be able to say the same thing."

She ignored that remark verbally but silently thought, I hope so, too. Aloud she said, "Thanks for coming by, Chuck. I've enjoyed your company."

"It's been like old times, when just the two of us would sit at the table talking for hours. You let me spill my guts to you and never once criticized anything I did. I've missed those talks."

In a choked voice Jenna said, "Me, too. More than you know."

Chuck looked at his watch. "It's time I got back to work. I feel so pepped up that I might actually accomplish something this afternoon."

She walked outside with him. When he cranked the car, the ringing of the phone could barely be heard outside, but Jenna heard it. She ran inside and grabbed up the receiver. "Hello," she said in a breathless voice.

"I hope that sexy voice is for my ears only," Charles said.

His voice made her pulse race, and it caused her to talk with more enthusiasm than she had intended to do. "Are you still in South Carolina? Do you think you'll be home in time for supper?"

"I'm on my way now and coming straight to your house. I'm taking you out to eat, so be ready."

"Sounds good to me," Jenna replied with a wide smile. "Maybe neither of us will have to cancel this time. Drive carefully." She wanted to add, "I'm looking forward to seeing you again," but for some reason she held back the sentiment.

Charles, however, did not withhold his feelings. "I can't wait to see you, Jenna. It's making me ride the gas pedal a little too heavily. So far I haven't gotten a ticket."

Jenna liked the way he said her name. It made her feel incredibly special. She wished that Charles did think she was special, someone worth knowing. Sometimes, like now, with all that has happened in her life, she felt she was nothing but a bother. Yet she could not help feeling a little giddy with excitement. While she looked forward to seeing him, Jenna was determined to fight against falling under his spell, his charming words and actions. But, she still worried about him.

"Please be careful, Charles," she begged. "I don't want to have to visit you in the hospital...or funeral home." The last part was said almost in a whisper. The thought of him being killed sent a chill up her spine. *Please, dear Lord, take care of Charles. Bring him home safely.*

As much as Jenna was beginning to care for Charles, she was afraid that his feelings for her were not serious. While he may be drawn to her now, she knew that the attraction would not last long. She was convinced that if her own husband could not love her, no other man certainly would. Her faults were too many for an educated woman to have. *If I'm so book smart, why couldn't I have realized that Stuart's feelings for me were not what I thought they were?*

Jenna was standing in front of a body-length mirror. She had stopped to take a good look at herself. She saw the light in her eyes and felt good about her looks. She was liked by lots of people, even loved by Charles' children. So what was wrong with this reflection?

She talked to herself, "Jenna, don't get weighed down tonight of all nights by looking for trouble. Think positively about having a wonderful evening with Charles." She smiled and gave a little nod to the mirror. "Thanks self, I will."

With a lighter step she went to take a shower. Back in the kitchen she looked at the clock. From squinted eyes she gave the clock a second look. Didn't those hands move at all while she was bathing?

Time seemed to stand still. Wearing green satin lounging pajamas, Jenna beat a path from the front door to the kitchen to the bedroom. Around and around the house she paced. With each trip the beat of her heart got faster, not from the exertion of walking but from the expectation of seeing Charles. She wanted to see him, to talk to him, to laugh with him.

Charles was an interesting man. He had a great sense of humor, and he was a great conversationalist. Words in his deep voice rolled right off his tongue. It was when he spoke softly, saying her name, that goose bumps covered her arms.

Jenna rubbed her arms and tried to concentrate on other things beside the time. What would she wear tonight? Should she wear a hat? No, she would go without one. The last time they dined out, Charles commented about her hair. He liked it hanging in loose curls.

We probably won't be going anywhere fancy since he won't have time to put on a tux, so I better dress casually.

While slipping on the navy pantsuit jacket over a white tank top her thoughts continued to dwell on Charles and the ground he was covering. The distance between North Carolina and South Carolina lasted long enough to have her in a state of anxiety. She twisted around and shut the closet door with a snap. *Forget Charles. Forget his driving. Forget the steak house that he'll probably suggest. Get your mind on something constructive and calm down.*

She began pulling out paint supplies. For some time Jenna had wanted to paint Asheville's Grove Park Inn. When she first moved to this tourist spot, she often made a special effort to drive by the beautiful inn. Last week she finally took some pictures of the place. She took them from a file and spread them out on her sketching table.

She pulled the extending lamp over so she could see each one in the best light. The inn's roof looked like a red cloak folded over the vast unit of rooms forged from mountain boulders. She hoped to capture its likeness as she saw it. With legendary proportions, the Grove Park Inn sat like a grand lady at the base of the majestic mountains behind it.

She smiled with assurance. *It would be an ideal painting to replace Peaceful Existence.* She was getting excited about starting work on it. She was kind of glad she was in the sketching stage. Nice clothes or not she would have probably gotten out the paints and been so deeply involved with the picture that she would have refused to give it up for a meal with Charles had there been time.

Charles. He was on her mind again. She smiled and looked at the clock. "It won't be long now," she whispered, and the phone rang. Thinking it was him, she snatched up the receiver. "Hello, Charles. Where are you? Oh, I'm sorry; I thought you were someone else. What's the matter? Did I mess up again?"

The same bank officer was once again calling Jenna about her checking account. Unless she made a deposit today, two checks would show on overdraft and an extra charge would be added. A friend at church who had overdrawn her account several times was offered a personal checkline reserve application for overdraft protection.

"You never have to worry about overdrafts again," the woman said. "There's no charge to establish this account. Finance charges only accrue when you actually use it."

Jenna had been offered the service, too, but quickly refused it when the finance charges were mentioned. With her low income, she was afraid that she would be tempted to advance herself funds a little too much, which would be a God send until the statement arrived and she owed the bank more money than she could afford to pay. She would stick to running to the bank every month to beat an overdrawn charge rather than chance getting into more trouble.

"I want to learn to handle my checking account without falling victim to temptation," she told her banker.

As of now she was susceptible to an overdraft charge if she did not get to the bank. She grabbed up her pocketbook and while counting out the appropriate amount of money, she looked at the clock and saw the late hour. "I'm on my way," she told the book keeper. "Thanks for calling me."

Should she take her checkbook and get the lady to show her the error. Not this time, she decided. No one could make sense of her record keeping, and it was happening too often.

"I should expect the smiles each time I go into the bank," Jenna had once told Debbie, "but I don't know if the tellers are just being friendly or if they actually know why I'm there. It's so embarrassing."

As Jenna headed up the road toward the bank she prayed aloud, "Dear Jesus, please send me some cost-free help. Debbie messes up her own check register, so she wouldn't be of much use to me. Not only do I need help with my records but also with my stolen goods. My life keeps getting more muddled. Show me a way out of this mess. And one more thing, help me know when, or if, Charles is sincere in his feelings for me."

After her trip to the bank, Jenna stopped to place an ad in the newspaper. She offered a reward for information pertaining to her painting. While she was hurt and disappointed with the loss of her rhododendrons, she could not afford to give away any more money just to learn that a mischievous boy thought it would be fun to mess up her yard. Who else would be crazy enough to dig in a garden during a thunderstorm? She figured the prankster would remain anonymous.

With both items taken care of, she returned home feeling better until she saw her garden. Her heart sank, leaving holes in it, much like the plant-free spots among the bushes and patches of flowers. Her yard was such an eyesore. She needed to get out there and do some replanting. She was afraid, though, that if she set out new plants that she could not afford to buy, they would disappear, too, and she would be back to square one. She also knew that once she began working in the soil, she would not stop until she had completed the job; then she would be bedridden with back pain. Another thing, a very important reason for not working in the dirt, she wanted to be dressed and ready to go when Charles arrived. She did not want anything to cause her to cancel this date.

CHAPTER 12

Jenna pulled up in front of her house and stopped. Her mouth flew open. Her heart began to race. Something was wrong. A truck and several cars filled her driveway. Other vehicles lined the curb in front of the house. What did it mean?

She could not park and unbuckle her seat belt fast enough. On unsteady legs she somehow managed to get to the front porch. She pushed open the door expecting to see a roomful of people, but she saw no one. She ran and looked into each room, finding nothing unusual except in the kitchen. Delicious-looking desserts and casseroles covered the table.

Jenna stood still, looking puzzled. Cars outside, food inside. Who was responsible for this? Had she forgotten about a meeting that was supposed to be here?

Her heart began to race. The only time that cars flooded her yard and people brought in food happened when Stuart died. No one was dead now, so what was going on?

Footsteps echoed on the back porch. Jenna rushed to open the door. There stood Frances Walker, president of her church mission group. The woman's sandy colored hair was secured into a no-nonsense bun, but her blue eyes twinkled from a smiling face that was smudged with dirt on one cheek.

"Jenna, you're home," Frances said, stepping into the kitchen. Her expression sobered when she saw Jenna's puzzled look. "My dear, what's wrong?"

"What's wrong? Not that you're not welcome, but why are you here? I'm confused. Where are all the people who belong to those cars out there? Why is all this food here? Are we having a meeting that I don't know about?"

Jenna, my dear, don't get so worked up. Your friends decided to do a little mission work, starting right here in your yard."

"What do you mean?" Jenna asked, standing on tip-toe, trying to peer around Frances to look outside.

"Come with me," Frances said, leading Jenna to where she could get a full view of the women restoring order to her yard. "We know it's a lot of work for one woman, and with you having back problems, we planned this little surprise for you." Francis spread her arm outward toward the ladies and added, "Walla!"

Walla? Little surprise? A smile spread from ear to ear. While watching the women who were usually dressed to perfection scramble around in the dirt, Jenna said, "Ladies, you've made my day. I need my camera." She ran into her bedroom, not for only a camera but to change clothes. Back outside she jumped around snapping shots. "This is wonderful."

"Jenna Wilson, don't think you're going to use those pictures to blackmail us into doing other dirty jobs," someone said.

Jenna batted her eyelashes innocently and said, "Now would I do that?" She laughed and then added, "I really appreciate what you're doing."

"You know us," Francis responded with a smug look, "We're always looking for reasons to share a meal."

Jenna helped remove a bag of mulch from a truck bed and then helped Frances set out a large red rhododendron. The ladies were fortunate to have this woman's supervision; she used to operate a green house. Her knowledge and experience had the yard looking wonderful and they were not even through.

After thirty more minutes of labor, the garden was restored to its beautiful scenic view. As they were admiring their handiwork, a man quietly approached the group who were still squatting or kneeling.

"May I be of help, ladies?" he said, bending over Jenna's shoulder. His hot breath on her neck caused her to shiver. She turned her head to look over her shoulder and gave Charles a look of surprise.

"You're here," she whispered, and the smile she gave him was genuine.

He inhaled sharply and said softly, "I'll leave and come again if it'll guarantee I'll get that look from you again."

"Don't you go anywhere," she hissed back.

The comment seemed to please him even more.

"Hello, Mr. McAdams," Frances said, breaking into their private communication. "Sorry, you're too late to help." She fell to a sitting position and rubbed her neck. "I'll admit we could have used your help earlier. Dragging all those heavy bags of mulch off the truck was quite a job."

Jenna was not listening to Francis but was watching Charles in amazement. Her thoughts came out as single words. Charles. Here. Now. Wonderful! Earlier, at the sound of his voice over her shoulder her heart felt as if it had stopped. Now it was beating in double time. She stood slowly, with the aid of Charles' hands, and then looked down at her clothes. She brushed furiously at the dirt. Some of it shook off easily while the rest seemed destined to stay until her shirt and jeans could be laundered. She shook her hair, making sure there was no dirt on it, and then touched her face. Most of her makeup had been wiped away on the sleeve of her shirt.

Jenna resolved that however much she liked to look her best when in the presence of company, sometimes it was impossible. She was one of those people who could not work the soil without getting dirty, and she was certainly nasty. She decided that if Charles was going to keep coming around here, he was going to have to get use to the way she dressed, simple and fancy. She hoped that he could handle her unkempt appearance enough to hang around a while longer.

Ever since Charles' arrival, his eyes had seldom left Jenna. He watched her every move with that heart topping smile on his handsome face. He gently brushed a hand over her hair and came away with a piece of mulch. "Can't have this gorgeous hair messed up with trash," he whispered.

Jenna exhaled heavily and murmured in a breathless voice, "Thank you." While gazing up at him she smiled sweetly. Her happiness bubbled forth. Charles was here. She cocked her head sideways and finally spoke where the others could hear. "I'm so glad to see you. Care for a dirty hug?"

Humor crinkled the corners of his eyes when he said, "I'll take any kind of hug that I can get. After avoiding two near collisions in a rush to get here for supper, I'm grateful to be alive to receive a hug from anyone."

The ladies formed a line, putting Jenna at the end. One of them said, "We're also glad you're safe and we're willing to give a hug to someone who wants it."

"I'll gladly take them," he said, giving each one a special comment that had them all practically swooning.

With a twisted grin, Jenna thought, there's that McAdams Charm being dished out again. When it came her turn to hug him, in a casual embrace with her hands on his shoulders, she stood on tip-toe and laid her cheek next to his. "Welcome home, Charles."

Near her ear he whispered, "I want a better hug later."

Jenna backed away from him. Rarely at a loss for words, she did not respond for a minute. She finally mumbled, "Hug. Later. Hmm." At his wide grin she turned and thanked the ladies for their generous contribution. "The way I procrastinate, it's hard to tell when or if I would have gotten around to this monstrous job. Words can't explain the appreciation I feel for your thoughtfulness."

Francis linked an arm with Jenna's and said, "Now that the labor is over, let's eat."

Jenna's eyes grew wide. She and Charles were supposed to dine out for supper. She looked at him and saw his resigned expression. Disappointment assailed her. She wanted to be with him, too. All day long she had looked forward to their date, now it was not to happen. This cancellation was not either of their faults. She hoped he would understand. "I'm sorry," she said, hoping he believed her. Pointing toward the garden she said, "I had no idea the ladies were going to do it. When I came home from town, they were already working, I had to join them."

Frances' voice broke into her ramblings. "Sorry for what?"

An awkward pause followed her question. Jenna looked from Frances to Charles to the other women. She finally said, "We were going to dine out tonight."

Frances went over to link an arm with Charles and said, "You two can go out together another time. Tonight, we ladies are feeding you both."

Charles stopped walking. "I'm sorry, ladies; I didn't intend to intrude. I'll leave and let you women get on with your activities. As you said, Frances, Jenna and I can eat together another time." Under his breath he muttered for Jenna's ears only, "That is if people will quit interfering with our plans."

Something felt like it had turned a somersault in Jenna's stomach. It sounded as if Charles really was disappointed because they were not going to be alone. Would there be another time for them? Would he risk another invitation? With all her heart Jenna hoped so.

To Charles she smiled sweetly and said, "I can assure you, Charles, you're not intruding, and you won't go away hungry. These women are super cooks. They don't know how to prepare dishes in small quantities, so there is plenty of food on my table. Please stay and join us."

Charles' smile was broad when he said, "Okay, ladies, lead the way. I'm anxious to see what you've got prepared. I'm starving."

Jenna looked at him with astonishment. Charles sounded like a child getting all excited about a picnic. It was not his useful charm gushing out either. In the den, where he was eating from the coffee table, he acted like a young man who had been chosen king-for-a-day. He eagerly accepted each sample of casserole or dessert set before him. The meal was a boisterous affair with all the women, except Jenna, trying to please Charles. She watched with an amused expression as grown women acted like schoolgirls chasing a football star.

Charles had them eating out of his hands, she thought but then corrected herself. No, it's the other way around. First one lady after another shoved their favorite prepared recipe in front of him. Charles tasted of each thing, declaring it to be the best he had ever eaten.

"You ladies need to work up a tasting gala, using your favorite recipes," he said between bites of pineapple cake. The cool whip icing seemed to make the moist cake slid down his throat before he had a chance to chew. He then added, "You could also incorporate some tried and tested dishes with foreign flavor. It could be a great money-making project for missions. People, especially office employees, would enjoy something different for lunch.

The ladies' faces lit up even more. The secretary pulled out a note pad and began taking notes on how to make the event successful. While cleaning up the kitchen, the women continued to toss back and forth ideas for a theme.

"Maybe we could get the children to dress in costumes from different countries," one lady said.

Another quickly added, "Why don't all of us wear costumes, too?"

Frances agreed. "That's good. I like your suggestions."

"Perhaps choirs, soloist, or a local southern gospel quartet would perform for the event," Jenna said.

"What a wonderful idea," Frances said. "I'm getting very excited about this project."

While the women continued to discuss the gala, Jenna took the opportunity to talk to Charles. She smiled brightly. "You've done a wonderful thing. We've been trying for months to come up with a unique money-making project and all the time it's been right here in our hands."

Charles produced his charming smile and said, "I guess all it took was an appreciative male to get the ball rolling."

Jenna grunted. "Hah! It's due to all that flattery you gushed on the ladies."

Charles' expression grew thoughtful before he said, "It doesn't work on you, though, does it, Jenna?"

If only he knew. She felt delicate hairs stand up on the back of her neck. She shook her head and said, "Let's just say, I'm wise to you. I've watched you in action long before we ever got well acquainted. Your reputation at getting women to reveal secrets preceded you. These ladies seemed to melt under your disarming smile and sweet flattery. You see? I know what to look for."

Charles gave her a curious look. Deep down he cared about people and wanted them to take him seriously. He wished that Jenna saw this side of him. He made a determination to make her see him in a better light. With God's help he would do it, too.

Frances approached the couple and shook hands with Charles. "Thanks for encouraging us to have a tasting gala. I think it will be lots of fun."

Charles gave her a mischievous wink that made him look more devastatingly handsome. "Be sure to add that delicious pumpkin cream cheese pie. Regular pumpkin pie used to be one of my favorite desserts. Now that I've tasted one with cream cheese, it may become my favorite of all pies."

A petite lady with frosted brown hair had been standing to the side watching Charles reaction to the dessert. She then stepped forward, and with a giggle she said, "Thank you, Mr. McAdams. I made it. Would you like a piece to take home?"

Jenna's eyes popped open wide. She stared at the normally quite woman and thought, Dora giggled. She's not a giggler. Charles did it again.

He kissed Dora's hand and said, "I would love to have another piece of your fabulous pie."

The women soon departed, leaving the house virtually quiet. Jenna did not know what to do. This was the first time since Stuart's death that she had been alone in her home with a man.

Charles placed his big hands on Jenna's small shoulders and turned her around to face him. "Did you think about me while I was gone?"

While the low, husky sound of his voice turned her legs to jelly, Jenna laughed to cover her nervousness, and tried to make a joke out of his question. "Of course I did. Every time I thought about my lost painting and stolen bushes, I was reminded of you and wondered if you would ever find them."

"Jenna," he said, shaking her a little. "That's not how I wanted you to thing of me. Didn't you at least look forward to having supper with me tonight?"

"Sure I did, until I came home from town and found friends working in my yard. After I started helping them, supper became the last think on my mind. Fixing up my yard took priority over everything else."

Charles narrowed his eyes at her, sharpening his gaze. "You deliberately forgot our date, didn't you? I broke the speed limit to get here, and you were not the least bit interested whether I'd get here or not. Thanks for nothing."

When he backed away, Jenna reached out to him and apologized. "I'm sorry for sounding insensitive, but I really was concerned for your safety. I prayed for Jesus to take care of you. But you saw my involvement with the garden. I couldn't stand around in a ball gown and let the women do all the work."

"Had you planned on going dancing?"

"No," she said and laughed. "That was figuratively speaking. I was dressed in a pant suit, ready to go out with you when I came home and saw my friends working for **me.** I had to change and help them. Then I lost all track of time."

"But why today? Couldn't they have done it another day?" He looked so hurt that she wanted to take him into her arms and soothe away the pain as she used to do with Debbie when she got hurt. She laid a hand on Charles' arm and squeezed gently. "I didn't know they were coming. I wasn't here when they arrived. They just showed up and went to work. I thought it was wonderful! But I'm glad to see you. I really did look forward to our date."

Charles smiled. "That's all I wanted to hear. Can you give me a hug that shows you mean it?"

He stood there looking so sweet and innocent that Jenna could not refuse him. "I guess I can handle that." She wrapped her arms around his neck and kissed his cheek.

When she would have backed away, Charles cupped her face with his hands. His smile warmed her and put butterflies in her stomach. His lips came down onto hers in a brief but electric contact. It was not a demanding kiss, but it was evident that Charles sought some sort of response.

Jenna could not respond with a more passionate kiss because she was afraid of her own physical reaction. She backed away, taking his hand and leading the way to the couch.

The flush on her cheeks brought a pleased look to Charles' face. He did not comment on it but asked, "Have you been busy this week?"

Jenna did not answer right away. Charles McAdams had thrown her off kilter, and she did not know how to handle it. Her determination to be on guard against his blatant charm and good looks failed her. She could not seem to handle it as she had wanted to. Since his masculine appeal could so easily unsettle her, she decided to not fight it anymore.

"How was your trip?" she mumbled.

"I found my man, but I couldn't get here fast enough. Did you think about me?"

Jenna nodded. Was it in answer to Charles' question or to the decision she had just made?

All she could figure out at the moment was that she wanted a relationship with this man, but she would move slowly to achieve something sweet and special.

She finally answered Charles. "Yes, I've been very busy with my crafts, trying to make the week pass swiftly. Thought of you helped. Also your son helped." She told him about Chuck's visit. "I enjoyed his company; it was like old times when he'd come to visit. I was feeling good, and then the bank called." She threw up her hands. "Lord do I need help there."

"With what in particular?" Charles asked.

Jenna flung her arms out. "Everything, such as keeping records, balancing a checkbook, and making sure that I don't lose my father's business. Stuart thought I shouldn't learn about those things. Now I wonder why?"

"I would be glad to help you," Charles offered.

"Would you? I'm afraid to show you what I try to do. I don't think I can explain it, and I doubt if you could figure it out in a million years.

I was told at the bank today that they would not be calling me anymore about not having enough money to cover bad checks. From now on, an automated system is going to be handling the checking accounts. If there's not enough money to cover the returned checks, an overdraft fee will be added. If that happens, I will definitely be in trouble. I'd be most grateful if you would take a look at my books."

"Show them to me."

After spreading receipts, statements, and other records out before him Charles asked, "Have you filed your taxes? The deadline is in two weeks."

Jenna shook her head. "No. I keep putting it off because I don't know where to start."

"Perhaps I should do the taxes first," he said, opening a ledger used for her father's business.

She bit on her bottom lip and then asked, "Are you going to charge me for your services? I need your help, but I can't pay much."

Charles gave her another curious look and said, "Indeed I am gong to request payment and a big one."

Was he kidding? She could not tell if he was or not. Jenna slammed the ledger shut, catching his hand. "Forget it. I'll let the government send me to jail."

Charles jerked back his hand. "Good gracious, Jenna. Give me a break. Quit coming down on me like I'm the bad guy. I offered to help you."

She stepped back and fell onto the couch. "I'm sorry, Charles. Please forgive me. I do want you to fill out my taxes. I'll have to pay somebody; it may as well be you."

Charles frowned. "Such thoughtfulness. As I started to say before you rudely interrupted, I am going to charge you. I need something to keep me awake. A pot of strong coffee should be payment enough. Now, get on with it, woman. I've got work to do."

She smiled tentatively and said, "Don't go anywhere. I'll be right back with it." Jenna kept his cup filled. And she also kept quiet which was a chore for her, because she was anxious to know her outcome with the IRS.

154

While sitting to the side and pretending to read, she chewed on a fingernail. When she heard the kitchen door open, Charles got a reprieve from her watchful eye, and she was able to stretch her legs. She met Debbie and made her bypass the den; they went straight into Debbie's bedroom. Behind the shut door, Jenna explained her odd behavior.

"I didn't want you to interrupt Charles' train of thought," Jenna said.

With an inquisitive look, Debbie asked, "Where's his train going?"

"He's filling out my taxes," Jenna said with a bit of annoyance in her voice. "I was afraid if you started talking, he'd never finish."

"Me. I bet it was hard for you sit there and stay mum."

Jenna presented a reluctant grin. "You're right. So why don't we put our mouths to good use and pray. I hope with all my heart that I don't have to sell this house to cover expenses. If I do, we'll have to move to the island and live in my parents' house. I'd hate to make the tenants move out. That would also mean you can't go back to college."

After they prayed, Jenna crept back into the den, picking up the Bible on the way to her comfortable recliner in the corner. The pages fail open to Jeremiah Chapter 29 and her eyes immediately picked up the words in verse 11: For I know the plans I have for you," declares the Lord, "plans to prosper you and not to harm you, plans to give you hope and a future." She reread that verse several times, letting the meaning sink into her mind and heart. She was feeling elated and hopeful that life was going to be much better. Was that because Charles was there to help her?

As always, Satan was sitting nearby to drag her down. "Have you forgotten what Charles is doing? You're going to have to sell this precious home of yours."

Jenna looked at Charles and the old worries returned to plague her. She was concerned with Charles' findings. He kept his attention focused on the job at hand, only paying tribute to her when he needed an answer to a question.

Jenna could not tell what he was doing or if he were accomplishing anything. She did not want him to quit before he finished, but she wanted so badly to know where she stood with her taxes. Dare I ask him if I should make plans to sell my home? She wondered and was about to open her mouth when her eyes dropped and she saw the words, I know the plans I have for you. She knew that God cared more for her than the devil did, so she closed her lips and continued to fight the urge to interrupt Charles. He would let her know something in due time.

Jenna never thought that Charles would be the answer to any of her prayers except perhaps as possibly as the detective who would find out who stole her property. She certainly could not afford to turn down his assistance when she needed it so badly.

Without looking up, Charles asked, "What kind of business does Sheila Davis operate?"

"Prostitution."

He looked up then and right into Jenna's stormy eyes. "Excuse me?"

"She was Stuart's call girl."

Charles sat there looking confused. The man appeared genuinely puzzled. "Are you saying that your husband paid all this money for sex?"

"How much is all this money?" Jenna asked.

"He named an enormous figure."

"Oh no," she groaned and bowed her head. In prayer she asked God if this was the plan he had for her, to always suffer humiliation at the hands of Stuart."

Jenna wanted to jump and run. She dreaded to look Charles in the face and see his pity. More than enough people had talked about her situation to last a lifetime. Everywhere she went, people asked questions or offered sympathy, but few people gave her encouragement, only those dear friends at church. One day she and Debbie packed up and went to the island for a month. If it had not been for her Christian friends writing and calling to check on her she may have stayed there indefinitely. Feeling refreshed and confident that she could survive in the states, they came back to Asheville and took care of the house situations.

At the time of Stuart's death, Charles had been out of the country, too. He went to Canada to find some woman's runaway husband and had missed all the wonderful gossip about Jenna and Stuart. But Charles was here now, opening old wounds.

He wanted her to discuss the part of her life she rarely shared with anyone. All the old hurt and anguish swelled up within her. Pain from it pushed hard against her chest. She rolled her eyes upward and conceded. "Sheila may not have actually been a prostitute, selling herself on the streets, but she took everything she could get from Charles. I know they had sex." She gave a convulsive swallow and clutched a throw pillow to her chest.

"Haven't you ever talked about this to anyone, like your preacher for instance?"

"Not in its entirety. Of course Debbie and I have talked. In the beginning we couldn't carry on a civil conversation without us both getting angry. In a choked whisper she added, "I didn't know he mistreated her until recently. During one of our rare talks about Stuart, she told me the way he'd talked down to her and bad mouthed me. She hates him now."

"I'm so sorry for all that you and Debbie have suffered at that man's hands and mouth. Sometimes when you feel its right, will you talk to me about Stuart?" he asked.

"I can tell you now that I was the idiot Stuart took me for," Jenna said, "because I didn't know he was physically involved with Sheila Davis until right before he died. Boy, could he act, keeping his romances a secret from me," she added with a bitter twist of the lips. "He went into the wrong profession. Stuart should have been on a stage instead of in a classroom. If he had, though, he may have missed the heartthrob of his life."

Charles reached for her hand but stopped when she turned and moved toward the window. She stood there and looked out into the darkness before continuing. "Sheila was one of his art students. She and I are totally different. I guess that's what caught his eye. Come to think of it, I've often wondered why Stuart married me because I'm short with short legs of course and he always raved about long legged beauties."

She sat down away from Charles and wrapped her arms around her knees and started her story. "At college games he would whistle and cheer when tall cheerleaders executed perfect dismounts from their quadruple stacks. On television shows, when beauty contestants walked out in bathing suits, he commented on their legs. 'Have you ever seen more gorgeous limbs on a body?' he asked. When we went to the beach, his eyes were constantly drawn to women's legs."

Jenna could not sit still another minute and paced the room as she talked. "I guess his number one favorite pair of legs belonged to Sheila Davis, a girl young enough to be his daughter." Besides having long, shapely legs, her height of six-feet-two easily topped my five-feet-two. I admit that she is beautiful with a statuesque figure and lovely flowing black hair." Jenna continued to talk nonstop and pace, back and forth across the den.

Charles did not comment the whole time but sat and watched her, as if he were trying to read between the lines of what she was saying.

She stopped suddenly in front of him and asked, "Can you believe that I caught them together in my bed? After my last class at college I went to the doctor for my regular checkup. From there I stopped at Frances' house to pick up some typed reports for the mission meeting that night. A friend of hers had died and she was going to the funeral and couldn't make our meeting. Several other members couldn't make it for one reason or another. Frances had been trying to call me, but I didn't get her messages because I left my cell phone in another pocketbook."

Jenna looked at Charles and shrugged. "Anyway, I went on home. That was a very stormy night, not weather wise, but emotionally," Jenna added. "I don't know if it was the worst night of my life or Stuart's or for his mistress. I just know I felt like I'd been knocked for a loop."

Charles attempted to talk, "Jenna, if you want to stop..."

She appeared to have not heard him and continued talking. "There was a strange car parked in our driveway. I figured that a student had stopped by to talk about an assignment. With the study door shut, I assumed they wanted privacy so I went on to our bedroom. Stuart had company all right, just not in his study."

"Jenna..." Charles began.

She stopped him with a wave of the hand and turned away, going back to the window. "If only I hadn't gone home, maybe I wouldn't have known about Stuart and Sheila's affair and wouldn't be experiencing this awful heart-wrenching pain." She pressed a balled fist to her chest and rubbed around and around.

"How did you handle the confrontation?" Charles finally got to ask.

"I yelled, calling the woman in my bed every name in the book, very ugly names, I might add. I yanked her hair, slapped her, and tried to pull her away from Stuart. It should have been Stuart I was beating on, but, at that moment, I totally blamed Sheila. I couldn't have been more wrong." Bitter tears rolled down her cheeks in full force. Great wracking sobs shook her body as she fell to her knees.

Charles knelt beside Jenna and wrapped her in his arms. He did not speak but let her cry. His features tightened with exasperation. He looked ready to do something destructive himself. The whole time she talked, each sentence had made him angrier with Stuart. He had seen Stuart in action. The times that the Wilson family had come to his house for parties, he saw Stuart flirt with tall, shapely women. While he had never actually made a move toward any of them, he did plenty of smiling and winking. Charles wondered at that time if Stuart had ever cheated on Jenna. Now he knew the answer.

He closed he eyes and inhaled deeply. He needed to keep his feelings in check for Jenna's sake if not for any other reason. Something caused him to open his eyes and look toward the door. There stood Debbie looking wide-eyed. She looked ready to jump in and clobber him. Charles held up a hand and mouthed, "She'll be okay." When Debbie slowly turned away, he gave a weary sigh, sat on the floor, and cradled Jenna on his lap.

"Poor baby," he thought. "She's not only weary with the load of her own burdens, but she's carrying the weight of her husband's indiscretions and they are weighing her down."

Charles could not understand Stuart and why he would do such a terrible thing to his family. When the man died, by his very thoughtlessness, he left behind the wreckage of two precious lives, Jenna's and Debbie's.

Jenna moved from Charles' arms and stood up. She reached for the tissue box on the end table beside the couch. "I'm sorry for crying all over you," she said. "When I recall the way he looked at me with contempt, I still feel like dirt."

"You're not the guilty party," Charles said.

"I know, but I felt like it then and still do at times."

He saw her look of self-loathing and raised a hand as if to pull her back into his arms, instead he wiped tears from her face.

His words were so wonderfully sweet to Jenna when he said, "I wish I could take a handful of those tissues and wipe away all your hurt."

Touched by his tenderness she started crying again. After a minute or two she slowly raised her head and looked him in the eye. "You may not be able to wipe it all away at once, but you've helped more than you'll ever know. I needed a shoulder to cry on, and yours now has the weight of my world on it."

In a husky voice he said, "Jenna, I want to do more; tell me how."

She was calmed by his concern. She presented a weak smile and asked, "How about my taxes? How are you coming along with those? Is my father's business going to be okay? Do I have to sell this house and my car to pay IRS? Can I get a job in their office? Will they take IOUs?"

Charles chuckled and made his way back to the desk. "Anymore questions before I start talking?"

"No, I guess not. I'm nervous about the outcome of things." She pointed to the pile of papers in front of him. "How much do I owe?"

He showed her the paper that she had to sign.

She gasped. "It's not fair. Why do I have to pay for Stuart's sins? Now I'll have to sell this house, too."

"Jenna, you don't have to do anything drastic. I can lend you the money."

Jenna shook her head, over and over. "No. No way am I going to take from you." She sat down on a straight back chair and grasped the edge of the seat. She could not get involved financially with this man. "I appreciate your offer, but I can't take it."

Outside, the rain fell in sheets, sluicing down like a waterfall. Crackling flashes of lightning lit up the whole sky. Thunder rolled. Its prolonged crashing and tumbling sounded as though every tree around them would soon be plummeting to the ground. Jenna barely heard it. Her mind stayed preoccupied with money matters. What was she going to do?

She moved across the room, far away from Charles. The last thing she wanted was to be obligated to him. What if she took his money and couldn't pay it back? The interest alone would grow to an astronomical figure? She had to get the money elsewhere, but where? The banks and loan companies were out. A wave of despair swept over her. Dear Jesus, she silently prayed, please help me to come up with a solution for this problem. In the Bible, you said that you had plans for me to prosper, how can it happen when everything around me is being taken away?

Charles passed a distracted hand through his hair and then rubbed the scar on his neck standing out like a bad growth. "My goodness, Jenna, it's only a loan. What's wrong with a friend lending you money?"

"That's the problem, Charles. Friends should not lend each other money. It can break up friendships?"

Charles threw up his hands. "I'm the one offering it. You didn't ask for it. I don't care when it's repaid. You can take all the time you need."

Jenna's face filled with anguish. "Charles, you don't understand. I may never be able to pay you back, unless you need a fulltime secretary. You could keep part of my salary."

Charles smiled. "I would love to hire you, but I don't have an opening. Take my loan, and when I do have a job, I'll call you."

Jenna knew it would never happen and said wearily, "Thanks, but no thanks."

With a heavy sigh, Charles said, "I didn't mean to get you stressed out. I thought my loan would be the best way to go."

While standing there staring at each other, somewhere close by a tree crashed with a tearing sound. This time the noise penetrated Jenna's hearing, and she jumped. "Did that hit my car? Maybe it fell on yours." She ran to look outside. Their cars were safe and so far was her house.

But the strange undercurrents filling the room made Debbie stop in the doorway. She gave her mother and Charles an anxious look. "Man, what noise. I don't know where the most tension is coming from, here with you two or outside. Is World War III about to erupt?"

Charles grinned and said, "I offered to loan your mother money to pay her taxes, and she acts as though I'm trying to buy her affection."

Jenna frowned at him and said, "Charles, I'm not doing any such thing, and no matter what you think I still can't take your money."

The noise outside and inside was silenced as if everyone and everything was waiting for a solution to a portion of God's plan for Jenna's future.

Finally Debbie said, "Mom that sounded like pride talking. We prayed earlier for God to make it possible for us to keep our home. You need the money. Charles is offering his help. Take it."

Jenna gave Debbie and then Charles a puzzled look. "Is pride such a bad thing? Maybe for once I want to take care of myself."

Charles responded. "No. Pride is good to a certain degree. But sometimes you have to let others help you." He caught the stricken expression on Jenna's face and added, "I promise you there will be no strings attached. There won't be a dead line for you to repay it. You can handle it your way in your own time." He looked as anxious as she felt.

Jenna sighed and apologized to God out loud. She talked as if no one else was in the room. "Here I've been praying for help and now I'm turning it down. It's as if I don't trust you, Lord. You want to answer my prayers and I throw it back in your face. You sent Charles to help me, and I am most grateful. Let me feel that it's right to borrow money from him."

When she heard Amen coming from Charles and Debbie, she looked at them and smiled. "Okay, Charles. I appreciate your offer and I welcome your loan."

He hugged her, looking relieved. The light glowing from his eyes made him look years younger, and the scar less noticeable. "Good. I'm glad that's settled. Both of us will feel better because of it."

His comment made her feel important and valued, and he sounded as if he truly meant it. Jenna blinked back the water that stung her eyes.

Debbie smiled brightly and kissed her mother's cheek and then

Charles'. "Since the storm has subsided and money matters are being handled effectively in here, maybe I can get some sleep now." She left the room with a wicked look on her face.

Charles put on his sports jacket and said, "I'm going to leave so you both can get some rest. Jenna, if you want me to I'll come back one day and show you how to keep your checking account on the computer."

She flashed him a smile that seemed so convincing. "You will? Thank you so much, Charles. I don't know what I'd do without you."

"That's what I wanted to here," he said, appearing thoroughly pleased. "It's my pleasure to bring a sparkle of joy to those beautiful eyes." He cupped her face and lowered his mouth to hers for a brief kiss.

When he raised his head, Jenna felt like pulling it back down to hers but fought the urge. Instead, she led him to the door. "Goodnight, Charles. You have been a God send."

He gave her another quick kiss. "When I take a look at my office calendar, I'll call and see if we can eat alone without being interrupted."

While Charles and Jenna said their good-byes, Debbie called Lynn.

"You won't believe the miracles worked here tonight," Debbie said. "Your father was an instrument of salvation for Mom."

The one sided conversation continued with Debbie apologizing. "I'm sorry: you didn't know Charles was back? I guess he couldn't wait to see Mom. He filled out Mom's taxes, listened to her talk about Dad and Sheila, and then let her cry on his shoulder. I know it's not only sympathy and gratitude we want them to have for each other, but caring has to start somewhere."

She was still talking to Lynn when she left the bathroom, heading toward her bedroom. "And, Lynn...oops. Wait a minute." She ducked into her room and easily shut the door. "They were kissing. Romance is in the air!"

CHAPTER 13

Jenna sat glued to the book in front of her. Because the scriptures had pulled her into their story line, she was oblivious to all sounds around her. After the doorbell rang several times, the musical tones finally penetrated her mind. Coming back to her surroundings, she shut the Bible and answered the summons.

The visitor was not a close acquaintance, but she knew him. She had met him at work when he came with his wife for her follow-up appointments after having surgery.

"Mrs. Wilson, I know you are looking for a certain painting. I have some information you might be interested in."

She was uncertain as to his intent. Until she knows more, Jenna could not brush him off. She had to know if he really could help get back her painting. Jenna smiled tentatively as she looked him over. He seemed harmless, so she invited the slightly bald-headed man of early middle age into her house. It was a mistake: not because of any danger but because of his body odor. He was in desperate need of a bath. Jenna almost grabbed hold her nose. The awful smell nearly sent her falling backwards. She twisted around and led him into the middle of the den in order to keep the offending odor behind her.

Reluctantly she offered Josh Harrington a chair. "Won't you be seated, Mr. Harrington?" hoping he would sit on the wooden chair that she pulled forward. He bypassed the hard chair for the plush easy chair near the window. Jenna took the wooden chair herself because it was the one furthest away from him.

Since she let him in the house, the only thing he said was, "You've got some nice paintings." He kept looking at them with a little too much interest to suit Jenna. She was beginning to wish that she had not invited him in. It was common knowledge that he could not keep a job. She did not know if it was due to health, education or lack of interest in earning money the traditional way. She had heard that he would to do simple jobs to get paid on the spot.

He finally broke into her thoughts. "I believe you'll be very interested to learn what I know, you will want to pay for it."

"What is it that you know that would be worth a dollar or two?"

"Ha!" he said with a raspy laugh. "It's worth more than a measly few bucks." Mr. Harrington settled back on the comfy cotton covered seat and crossed a stained, denim clad leg over the other. The tips of his fingers on one hand joined the other hand, making a five-point steeple. Every fingernail looked chipped and dirty. His air of self-assurance did not match his unkempt appearance.

Jenna wondered if she would ever get the smell and dirt out of the fabric on her chair. While she studied him, he said, "I was relieved to see your ad in the newspaper yesterday. If it hadn't been there, I wouldn't have known where to turn with my information."

"What **is** your information?" Jenna asked, ready to shake it out of him. She felt anything but the calmness she tried to exert. She did not know whether to get excited over the possibility that this man did know something or be angry that he was there to con her. "Why didn't you go to the police with your information?"

His eyes again circled the room. Jenna felt that he was obtaining a mental picture of everything in there. She knew that he had observed the antique vases and small pieces of furniture that once belonged to her grandmother. After Stuart's death, she and Debbie had gone to the island. She chose the items in her parents' house that she wanted and had them shipped here. No one, not this sleazy man anyway, was going to get his hands on a single one of them. And she certainly was not going to sell them in order to pay him for information.

"Listen. If you're not going to tell me anything of value, I must ask you to leave," Jenna said, standing.

The lines around Mr. Harrington's mouth tightened, and his look hardened. "I believe in taking valuable information to the person who is personally involved. The police may not think that what I have to say is worth hearing."

"In other words the police wouldn't pay for your information. Is that right?"

"You are exactly right. But I know you want to find the painting bad enough to pay for it." He glanced around the room again, and made a significant gesture by rubbing this thumb and forefinger together as he spoke. "I'll tell it to you for five hundred dollars."

"Five hundred!" Jenna gasped and then quenched her immediate desire to kick him right out of the house. The man's self-satisfied look made her want to slap it sideways, but she kept her temper under control. With determination she spoke with calmness. "I must know what your information is before I give away an enormous sum of money like that."

"A valuable painting of yours disappeared from the Asheville Arts & Craft Festival. I saw it there," he said with every shred of confidence in what he said was true. "This nice picture stood out among all the other beautiful paintings hanging around. The woman in the garden looked familiar, but I couldn't place her."

Jenna's hand began to shake. Perhaps he did have some information, then again maybe he knew only what she had put in the ad.

"What else did you see in the picture?" she asked. "Did you see the cat peeping out from a rosebush?"

Mr. Harrington quickly agreed. "Of course I did."

Jenna's heart sank. There was neither a cat nor a rosebush in the picture. "Where is the painting now?" she asked.

"Do you know where the old...wait a minute," Mr. Harrington said, jumping to his feet. "You haven't said you'll pay. You're not getting my information without paying for it."

Jenna stood, too, marching toward the door as an indication that he should follow her. "Good day," she said in a stilted tone. "I've decided not to buy your information. You don't know what is in the picture except what you read in the newspaper ad. You thought it would be a good way to capitalize on an unsuspecting woman, but you thought wrong."

The man looked as if he could not believe his ears and murmured, "If that's the way you feel, then you don't deserve to get it back."

"I am, but I'm not as desperate as you think," she said, looking him straight in the eyes. "I suggest you leave before I call the police."

Without another word the man left, looking dismayed.

Jenna felt tempted for a moment to give him some money. If he used it to get cleaned up or eat a decent meal, she would not mind helping him. She doubted that he would put it to good use and let the matter drop.

Disappointed and somewhat aggravated, Jenna returned to her desk and began reading again 1 John 3:7, "Little children, let no man deceive you." She thanked God for paving the way with His words so she would not be taken in by Josh Harrington and deceived into giving away money that she could not afford to throw away.

It took her a few minutes to put the man and the meeting out of her mind. After last night, having to make an important decision about Charles' loan, she could not be blamed for being less than on the top of things this morning.

She had awakened during the early hours, dwelling on the time spent watching Charles work on her taxes and then relive her feelings for Stuart and Sheila Davis. She appreciated Charles letting her cry on his shoulder without him taking advantage of her vulnerability. Sometimes she felt nothing but anger and hatred for her dead husband, other times she felt as if their married life and Stuart's death had happened to someone else and she was just an observer.

Jenna knew she needed to keep hold of reality, but it was difficult. At times she did not know which end was up. What did she know about anything? For a year she had ventured from one aspect of life to another, looking for peace and happiness. Nothing really helped her except the Bible, but she felt there was something or someone who could help her even more. Her talks with God proved beneficial. She believed that He sent Charles into her life. His talent, brains, skills, and desire to help her have worked a miracle. She wondered, though, if she should pull in the reins on their growing relationship. It would be so easy to reach out to this man who was financially secure and good to her, but would she find herself mixed up with the wrong person again?

At one time, being with someone with lots money would not have bothered Jenna. Shortly after she and Stuart married, he had been left a large inheritance by an uncle. Stuart took advantage of his new wealth and spent it freely. Jenna could not stop him.

"It's my money," he told her in no uncertain terms, "and I'll spend it as I please."

Jenna did not fight him over it and shared somewhat in his lavish spending. Just to say she had shopped in New York, she and some friends flew there two weeks before Christmas and spent a couple days taking in shows and buying extra presents. Such unnecessary extravagance, she thought, and wished she could go back and change some things.

If an abundance of money fell at her feet today, she would not spend it foolishly. She would never again feel comfortable spending it on furs and expensive jewelry, things she did not care for or even need. The lack of such desires did not come about because of her low income but because of her experience with the church mission group. After working with the indigent, she learned the value of money and that others needed it to survive not to have a good time. Her priorities have changed greatly.

With Charles being a Christian, she felt sure he would feel the same way. Through his work he has seen the way the lower class lives. For years he has served on the board for Help, Inc., an organization for the abused, and worked with the Salvation Army, helping the less fortunate.

"That's the reason I make and sell crafts," he told her, "to raise money for needy organizations."

Frowning, Jenna admired Charles for his contribution to society but felt selfish when she recalled her own situation. She had to make and sell crafts so that she would not become part of a needy group. She wished she could do like Charles and give the money she collected at the craft fair to the home for abused wives. "Maybe someday I'll be in a position to help them."

A thoughtful expression filled Jenna's face. Had she been so terribly wrong about Charles? She wondered if behind all his charm there was a caring person that you could trust with your life.

Was she ready to look for the real man in him? She wanted to because she believed that something of incredible intensity and depth was developing between them. First, she wanted to be absolutely sure that he would be the same two years from now as he was last night. She could not stand another shock of knowing she was involved with a loving man one minute and a two-timing abusive monster the next.

Jenna shook her head, trying to keep the pain at bay. Every time she recalled Stuart's thoughtless and selfless behavior, her heart broke all over again. After Debbie was born, Stuart began focusing on ways to look younger. He went on a diet, exercised, and colored his graying sideburns. Also, surgery tightened his double chin. As time went on he changed more and more in ways that she would have never dreamed possible. Her expectations of a wonderful loving husband and father were ruined when he got involved with Mavis Witherspoon. There had been other women, mere flirtations that hurt Jenna, but she accepted them because they were just passing fantasies. The attraction with Sheila Davis was more involved. He was on the verge of leaving Jenna, so he said when she caught them in her bed.

"It was just a matter of time," Stuart said. "I was waiting for the right moment."

When Jenna recalled him telling her about his parental teaching to keep a pristine reputation, she was dismayed to learn that he let Sheila help him lose his reputation and career at a phenomenal price. Not only did he give the woman outrageous sums of money but threw away the most important thing in his life, his relationship with God. His spiritual life seemed to have been severed. He knew God frowned on adultery, yet he willingly committed the sin.

Jenna turned to the second chapter of Philippians. Various questions popped into her mind as she read. *Does your own life in Christ give you strength? Does his love comfort you? Do you have mercy and kindness toward others? Do you and Christ share in the spirit?*

While pondering those questions, God's direction came to her. *If so, Jenna, make me happy by sharing the same love and having one mind and purpose. When you do things, my child, do not let selfishness or pride be your guide. Instead, be humble and give honor to others than to yourself. Do not be interested only in your own life, but be interested in the lives of those who need Christ in their lives. I didn't promise days without pain, laughter without sorrow, sun without rain, but I did promise strength for the day, comfort for the tears, and light for the way.*

In open prayer, Jenna said, "God, forgive me where I failed you. Help me to be a better and stronger Christian. Please, help me to put the painful experience with Stuart behind me. Help me overcome my hurt and anger against him and especially with Sheila. I want to make the effort to rid myself of such feelings, but I can't do it alone."

The telephone rang. Time and again it rang. Each conversation left Jenna more distraught. It caused her to lose the close communion she was having with God. Frustrated, she grabbed up her pocketbook and car keys and left the house. While behind the wheel of her van, she thought about the numerous prank calls she had just received. Everyone wanted money for nothing. She wished that she had never put the reward notice for her painting in the newspaper.

To make sure she was not at home to get more of those phony reports, Jenna kept driving. An hour later she found herself pulling into the front entrance of Montreat College where Sheila now worked in the office. Jenna got out and stood beside the van a moment before marching straight toward the building, never breaking stride until she reached the secretary's office.

"Hi, Mary, is Sheila Davis working today?"

"Hi yourself," the middle aged woman answered and then hugged Jenna. "Sheila had to take a phone message to one of the students.

She'll be back shortly. It's so good to see you again. Are you coming back here to teach? So many new students who have been referred to your class by their friends hope you'll be here by the next semester."

Jenna nodded and said, "I do want to. Can you work me in to see the chancellor?"

With a broad smile Mary said, "I can. Ms. Blakely can see you in thirty minutes."

Jenna looked at her watch. "That will give me just enough time to talk to Sheila. I'll get out of your way and wait for her in the lounge across the hall."

On the way to the teachers' lounge, Jenna hoped that Sheila would join her before she lost her nerve. With each step, the lump in her throat grew larger. She swallowed with difficulty.

When Sheila did arrive she stopped at the door. Jenna motioned her in. "This will only take a moment," Jenna said in a casual voice. "I'm not going to make a scene. Would you like to sit down?"

Sheila shrugged. With a safe distance between her and Jenna she went to the plastic covered sofa. She sat down on the edge of it and drew her long legs up close to the cushion. She folded her arms across her chest and gave Jenna a guarded look. "What do you want with me? I thought I'd be the last person you'd want to see."

Jenna saw the worried expression in Sheila's eyes and came to a major conclusion, causing her own nerves to ease up and her tense features to soften. "I'll admit I'm quite surprised at myself for being here, but it's something I feel I should do. Sheila, what you did in the past must remain in the past for both of us to move forward and go on with a normal life. Of course I wish the clock could be turned back and my life be changed, not only in what you and Stuart did, but in the things I did or did not do to make Stuart happy with me."

Jenna noticed Sheila's skeptical expression but continued talking without commenting on it. "I feel that I'm as much at fault for the failure of my marriage as Stuart. I'm not apologizing for the way I behaved when I caught you two in my bed, but I am sorry for putting all the blame on you." She stood and walked around the room, ending at the doorway. She turned back toward Sheila and smiled tentatively. "I don't expect you to say anything. I felt I should say this to you in order to remove the bitterness from my heart. It would be a good idea for you to try making a better life for yourself. If at all possible, please consider this one thing very carefully, God loves you."

When Sheila sat there, not commenting, Jenna left. Out in the hall, she looked back and saw Sheila still sitting on the sofa and starring at her. There was something thoughtful in the gaze.

After leaving the building an hour later, having arranged to return to teaching in the fall, Jenna stopped by the cemetery. She went directly to Stuart's gravesite. The lawn was being mowed and men were removing all the dead and faded flowers from the graves. The grounds keeper took good care of this cemetery, unlike the way Stuart took care of his life.

For the first time since the funeral, Jenna allowed herself to step inside the wrought iron fence surrounding the cemetery. Sunshine brightened the place. The day of Stuart's funeral was entirely different: cold and rainy.

She recalled the large crowd at the funeral, huddling under umbrellas, listening to the final words the minister said about Stuart. While she recalled the scene, his kind thoughts had washed right over Jenna's head. While they may have been true to him, they were not completely true to her. She could not help thinking that Stuart got what he deserved.

But she had cried. While standing by his grave, staring at his coffin, tears ran unchecked down her face. She could not tell tears from raindrops. It did not matter, though, because neither washed away the hurt and pain she felt. Depression descended upon her like a black cloud. She was not crying so much because Stuart was dead but for his ruined life.

In the early years of their marriage he had purchased two grave plots and ordered a double tombstone so they could be buried side by side. After the way he had treated her, she never wanted her body to lay beside his again, in life or death. She did not want Debbie standing at the graves, loving one, hating the other. It was a waste, but the double tombstone was changed to a single. Fortunately the selling of the extra plot helped cover the funeral expenses. She walked away from his grave that day, leaving him alone. She would no longer have to look him in the face and wonder what he was planning to do next. God had his own plans for Stuart, nothing that involved her now.

Today the bright sun helped to fill her with peace. Jenna no longer felt like knocking over Stuart's tombstone or stomping all over his grave. She knew they were useless feelings and was so glad that God had removed them and was restoring her joy.

As she walked along the paved driveway, her steps were slow as she wondered what her life would have been like if she and Stuart had not entered the art world. Would they have met? Would she have Debbie? Not watching where she was going she stumbled over a footstone. A thought came to her: *Consider the moment, Jenna, instead of dwelling on unanswerable questions.*

She stopped at the foot of Stuart's grave, holding a bouquet of artificial flowers. They were some she had on the front seat, planning to give a sick friend. She would take the woman some fresh ones instead of these artificial. She knelt to put the flowers in the empty urn and then sat back on her heels and talked to Stuart. "I know you can't hear me, but I feel that I must say some things." She looked around to see if anyone was watching her before continuing. "At your funeral, Stuart, I was stunned by the amount of hatred I felt for you, because I have never hated anyone in my life, except for Sheila. I once loved you more than life itself, but it changed when you changed, trying to control me and then mocking me by blatantly showing your feelings for other women. I'll never forget your abuse, but I'm hoping to forget how much it hurt me. More importantly, you will never again hurt our daughter. What I'm trying to figure out is did you ever love me at all?"

While attempting to stand, Jenna got the impression that Stuart spoke to her. "Jenna, I loved you a lot during the early part of our marriage, but somewhere over the years my love drifted away. Money became more important and with it I could have things I'd never experienced before. During that time is when I put God in the backseat. I let the Devil back into my life. Try not to hate me forever and learn to love again. Find a man who will cherish you."

Jenna knew Stuart did not speak to her, but those words from an inner voice gave her encouragement. She knew now that she could move forward with her life and whispered, "Good-bye, Stuart."

The van ate up the distance back across town. Jenna smiled and began to sing with a recording by her favorite Southern gospel singers, Called Out Ministry. A warm glow of joy exploded through her. It erased the last dark vestiges of doubt about herself as a woman and a Christian and blended it with an incandescence of a million lights. Her future looked brighter and much happier. Her relief knew no bounds...until she remembered the phone calls that had bothered her earlier. They came in so fast that she could not get any painting done. When she could no longer stand the thought of being bogged down with more money hungry callers she left home. Knowing there would be more calls she went to the recreation center and to watch Debbie put students through a routine of exercises. She gently but firmly helped a beginner with a difficult move. Jenna admired her daughter.

She could safely say that Debbie was the best thing that came from her failed marriage. *Thank you God for not letting her father's behavior destroy her attitude and good nature.*

Jenna smiled and settled her western hat more comfortably on top of her head. She stood and waved bye to Debbie. On the way out of the gymnasium, she saw a young boy and two younger girls enter the front door.

"Hello," Jenna said in passing.

With shy looks the girls grabbed hold of the boy's hands. He mumbled hello and then pulled the girls along in his haste to get across the room.

Jenna's brows puckered into a thoughtful frown. Who was that? Where had she seen that boy before? With a shrug she walked off dismissing the children from her mind. As she ran errands and browsed through some stores at the shopping mall, the day passed swiftly. It was about six o'clock when Jenna finally headed toward home.

Parked in her driveway was Charles' blue Suburban. She jumped from the van and ran up to his window. "Have you got any leads? Did you find my painting or my bushes?"

He climbed out and stood close, looking down into her upturned face and said, "Hello to you, too." Shaking his head he added, "No, Jenna, I haven't found them. Can't I come to see you unless I have news you want to hear?"

Jenna apologized, "I'm sorry. Of course you can," but she still wished he would quit dragging his feet and get on with the search. In a small voice she asked again, "Haven't you any idea where my things could be?"

"At the moment I really don't." He wrapped her in his arms and added, "I promised to let you know when I found something concrete and I will. Please try to be patient. I'm not giving up, honestly I'm not."

Jenna backed away from him and let a smile slowly spread across her face. "I believe you. It's just that I'm not a very patient person. I'm trying to become one, but it's so hard." The adoring look on his face made her heart swell and fill with more happiness. "Come inside, Charles, and I'll fix us something to drink."

First she excused herself and rushed to the bathroom. She flipped off her hat and tossed it onto the clothes hamper; then she fluffed up her curls. Her eyes needed some repair, as did the freckles across her nose.

Jenna could not freshen up fast enough. With anticipation of a pleasurable evening, her fingers became all thumbs. She straightened her clothes on her way out to join Charles and found him in the kitchen preparing tea. He set a cup of hot tea before her. "You looked as if you could use this."

The enticing aroma of cinnamon had her sniffing and smiling appreciatively. "I did." She took a sip and sighed. "Delicious. It's been a full day," she said and explained the events.

"I wish I'd been with you. Apparently you didn't need anyone, but I could have given you support." His look was clearer than words and far more exciting. He really cared about her.

Jenna's face glowed. She looked like a woman facing the prospect of real love for the first time.

"You can't imagine how it feels to know that you are concerned about my wellbeing," she said, smiling with confidence. "Thanks for wanting to give me support, not because you feel I'm a nitwit and couldn't handle the situation but because you care."

"I do care very much. And no, my dear, you are not a nitwit." With a playful smile he added, "You may be a little feisty but definitely not a scatterbrain."

They laughed and talked, sharing many of their hopes and dreams for the future. Charles talked about his early life when he pursued a career in politics. He thought he could help change things back then. It was during the time when people first started dealing drugs openly. Some of his friends had become dealers, tearing their homes apart. He hated their lifestyle.

His words contained a touch of irony. "I was young and idealistic with dreams of changing the world. My desire was to get my friends back to legitimate work and their families together again."

"What was wrong with that? I think it's admirable."

Charles shrugged and answered, "Nothing was really wrong, but I now have a more realistic, spiritual philosophy about life. I feel that whatever I'm doing I should brighten that corner of my life."

Jenna looked him in the eye and smiled gently. "You certainly do it by finding missing people and bringing loved ones together again."

"I wish I could take credit for bringing us together."

A sense of delightful expectancy filled Jenna which left her with no room for regrets. Even the loss of Stuart began to fade a little more into the past where it belonged. She decided that now was the time to take another step forward. She no longer felt like a dumb bunny and looked forward to learning how to take care of her checking account on the computer.

She gave Charles a look of excited expectation and asked for his help. "Have you got time to show me something on the computer?"

"I do. Pull up a chair and let's get down to business."

Her enthusiasm pleased Charles. "Did you know you need a tax number to use when you reach a certain amount in the sell of art and crafts?"

Jenna nodded. "Yes. That's one item of interest I handled myself."

When Charles shut down the computer, Jenna hugged him. "I appreciate your help. I feel that I can do this work by myself now and it helps to restore my confidence. I've prayed a long time for God to send someone to help me, and here you are."

"Anytime you need me, all you have to do is to let me know." He stood up. "Let's go get the steaks we missed due to your mission friends' poor timing."

Jenna did not think of refusing but eagerly accepted this date with Charles. Their relationship seemed to have a life of its own. It was growing by leaps and bounds. Jenna gave a sigh of complete contentment. No way would she continue fighting what so obviously was meant to be.

While climbing into the suburban, she noticed a stack of wood in the back. At closer inspection she saw the unpainted birdhouses. An idea pooped into her mind.

"Charles, how do you plan to finish those birdhouses?"

"The way I usually do. Stain them."

"Do you mind if I paint some for you?"

He smiled. "If you want to."

"I'd love to. It would be a way to repay you for your help." Before he objected to that remark she added, "I haven't bought birdhouses to paint for myself, but I've wanted to do some."

"I admit I'd like for a few of them to have a different look. My customers buy plain birdhouses to hang in trees for wild birds. While riding through housing developments, I've notices some decorative ones hanging in flower gardens or at the edge of porches. They looked pretty and inviting for the birds who didn't object to the paint."

Their discussion on birdhouses ended at the steak house. The leisure dinner could not have been any better for Jenna. She sat there, thriving on the wonderful attention Charles paid her. It made her feel special. With his help she no longer felt incompetent like someone who would not know when to come in out of the rain.

CHAPTER 14

The next few days and nights blew by in a hive of activity. Jenna felt alive and invigorated. She produced a lot of work.

She turned Charles' hum-drum-looking birdhouses into cottages, store buildings, schoolhouses, and barns with horses peering out windows. She also replenished her own stock for the upcoming festival at Black Mountain. Each night she went to bed tired but happy and never woke up until daylight.

When the bright sun peeped through the Venetian blinds, she stirred. It took some blinking and rubbing of her eyes to get them open. Once she did, the first thing she saw was the flowers Charles had sent her. They looked so adorable on her nightstand; she could not resist fingering the pink rose petals. This made the second bouquet to arrive this week. Jenna's heart skipped a beat when the thought came to her that perhaps Charles did care for her after all.

The telephone rang. She nearly crushed the roses between her fingers when she heard the words, "Good morning, Jenna. Hope you had a restful sleep and ready to get up and going."

At the sound of Charles' deep voice, quick flutters erupted in her stomach. She put a hand on it to calm the excitement so she could talk without sounding short winded. "Good morning to you, too, Charles. I was just laying here admiring my flowers. It was so thoughtful of you to send my favorite color rose."

"You're more than welcome," he said. "I also have something else for you to feast those beautiful eyes on."

"What's that?"

"Your painting and shrubbery that were stolen."

Jenna's heart stopped for a minute and then kicked into a rapid speed of beats. The news kicked into her stomach an entirely different feeling from the sound that Charles' voice caused. She felt her pulse go into an erratic dance of dread and excitement.

Charles had found her stolen items. Jenna could hardly take it in. For too long now she had wanted desperately for Charles to find them. Now that he has she did not know what to think other than the plants must look awful. They must be in terrible condition. Because a gardener would not have dug them up without patience and care and an inexperienced person without horticulture knowledge would not have haphazardly uprooted them up during a rain storm.

What kind of person digs in gardens at night? She was most interested in seeing her experimental rhododendron, Evening Sun, but then again she was hesitating to see it. She was afraid it would be all dried up with leaves falling off it. But she had to see it to satisfy her curiosity, along with the thief.

Another emotion overrode the urgency to see the person who stole from her, and was excited at seeing Charles again. She could hardly wait to be near him and to watch as his eyes filled with warmth when she walked toward him. Ever since he let her cry on his shoulder, their feelings for each other have been more open; it was evident that they liked being together.

But should she have this exquisite feeling bursting forth at the thought of seeing Charles? It definitely was a precious gift for her to cherish. It had been a long, long time since Stuart looked at her with appreciation, so she could not help eating up the attention. The longing to be thought as special by a man who cared for her once again had been fulfilled and she did not want anything to spoil it.

God, please let this relationship grow with your blessing and guidance, she prayed. She wanted desperately for a solid relationship with Charles to last, but only if he stays the same and never changes as Stuart did. *Can you guarantee that Charles won't let me down?*

Jenna frowned. She recalled him saying that he was not looking for a wife. "Since Francine, there has never been but one woman who could hold my interest, and she was married. I have been praying that God would give me another soul mate. Maybe some day soon my dream girl will realize that I'm just around the corner waiting on her." He laughed. "Does that sound corny?"

She was afraid that he may never consider her good enough to be his partner in marriage, even if God granted her the chance. His interest in her now will probably vanish once she gets back the painting and plants that he worked so hard to find. Since he also got her established with record keeping on the computer, he may decide that there is no reason to come around anymore. The thought of not being with Charles anymore made a pain shoot through her heart. For his sake, she could not let him know about it, so she put on a brave face. "I think it's a wonderful idea to put all your trust in God. When he has complete control, he will make sure you and the right woman meet. She may already be around the corner waiting on you."

"I know that God will work everything out right. For now, I'm on my way to pick you up and take you to see your painting and plants. Are you ready for it?"

"Of course I am. Are they close by? Are they in good condition? Who took them? Do you have him or her or them in jail?"

Charles interrupted Jenna's swiftly shooting questions. "Hold it, Jenna. I'll be there shortly to take you to where they are?"

"They who? My belongings or the scoundrels who took them?"

"Both, the person and the items. In about ten minutes, be at the door and we'll go relieve your anxieties."

"O--kay." Jenna ran to her bedroom to put on a tan safari hat that went well with her tan shirtwaist dress. She smiled at her reflection in the mirror. After one final look she ran to the front door and was practically dancing when she saw Charles turn into her driveway.

He had barely stepped onto the porch before Jenna was pulling him into the house and plying him with more questions. Before satisfying her curiosity he took a step to close the gap between them. He framed her face with his hands and said, "I'd rather be doing something other than talking."

A shiver coursed through Jenna as she looked into the warm brown depths of his eyes. She felt his breath, feather light against her skin. When his kiss came, it tasted like breath mint. He smelled like soap, and his arms that wrapped around her were comforting. She prayed that he would continue to enjoy her company after this day was over.

Charles held her at arms length away from him and said, "If you'll quit distracting me woman, I'll take you to see for yourself who the robber is."

She quickly stepped toward the door, saying, "Well, come on man, and let's go. I've been waiting for this moment for ever."

They drove to a rundown neighborhood.

For several blocks the house numbers could be read on the door, and then there were no more. Charles mentioned why many houses bore no signs of an address. "The numbers are either faded or torn from the doorframe along with other parts of the houses, apparently done by vandals. It's a sad looking neighborhood. I came here earlier today to find the house. There were a number of kids playing ball in the street. I talked with them awhile; all seemed interested that I wasn't trying to sell them drugs. If I had been, they would have had to sell their souls to pay for it."

Charles pulled over to the edge of the road in front of a little frame house. While the boards appeared to be in good shape, the paint was fading and peeling in spots. Banisters on the porch were loose and the grass needed mowing.

"A little work would certainly brighten up this place. I thought I had problems. I'm rich compared to the people living here," Jenna said, talking in a hushed voice, but Charles heard her.

"I agree that this whole neighborhood could stand a face lift. I've been thinking of getting an organization to do some mission work here. I know many church groups go out of state to do the same kind of work that's needed here. I'm a firm believer that we should also take care of our own."

Jenna smiled at him. "You're so right. I just had a great idea. With all the kids around here, Debbie and I could arrange to have a backyard Bible club. It would be so much fun for these children and they could learn more about Jesus in the process." It bothered her to see families from low income families forgotten because they were not news worthy. "They need a politician, like you, Charles, to be their champion."

"First things first. Ready to go meet some of these low income people?"

Jenna nodded. She would soon be facing the person who stole her painting, but she was no longer angry. Instead, she was filled with compassion. She rubbed her arm in an unconscious gesture of concern. She quickly prayed, *God, take control. Don't let the person be a habitual thief or a convicted criminal. I don't want anger to override the situation.*

When Charles came around to open her door, she willed her legs to move and carry her forward. He knocked on the door of the house. In a whispered voice he asked, "What will you say?"

"I honestly don't know. I have to see the person first," she answered and waited with anticipation for someone to open the door.

A boy swung it open. He halted abruptly when he saw Jenna and stared at her with widened eyes. With a quick look toward the closed door of an adjoining room, he moved to allow his visitors to step inside.

Charles made the introductions. Jenna, this is Sammy Walker, a great admirer of your work. Sammy, this is Mrs. Wilson."

He immediately apologized to Jenna. "I'm sorry for taking your painting and plants, but I had to."

For an instant Jenna could not identify the boy, but his voice brought back their meeting. He was the one at the festival that she had given a flower to for his mother. She also had seen him with two little girls at the gym. Jenna frowned.

Charles stood in a relaxed stance. His face remained passive while waiting for Jenna to interrogate her thief. He knew what to expect because he had gotten Sammy's confession earlier. Though it cost him some effort, Charles waited to let Jenna handle this situation herself. He felt sure that she would want to in order to keep her pride intact.

But his protective instincts made him want to take over because he needed to keep Jenna from suffering more stress. He could not prevent those feelings from surfacing, nor could he keep Jenna off his mind. At work, the mere thought of her interrupted everything he attempted to do. Every time he focused on her qualities, he saw sparkling green eyes, a teasing smile, her energetic personality and willingness to help others.

Charles knew all this about Jenna from way back when his children were small. Ever since their first meeting and spending just a few hours with her, they have continually sung her praises. He felt sure that today he would see more of her Christ-like spirit for himself. She would be shocked to know that ever since Stuart's death he has prayed for God to give her to him as his wife and soul mate. He felt close to the edge of confessing his feelings to her but knew it was too soon. She had to gain confidence in herself and trust in him. Her feelings came first. With a fierce intensity that he had never experienced before, not even with Francine, he made Jenna's concern his priority. "But, dear Lord, don't make me have to wait much longer," he prayed and then returned to the matters at hand.

He nodded to Jenna and said, "This young man wants to talk to you, to explain why he stole from you. Go ahead and ask him whatever you need to. It won't be as bad as you may think."

To Sammy she asked, "Why did you say you had to do it?"

He ran small fingers through his hair and muttered, "My mama's sick, real sick. The doctors can't help her." In a choked voice he added, "I-I was desperate, Mrs. Wilson. Mama's been in bed a long time. She doesn't have the energy to get up and walk far. She always looks so sad. I just wanted to see her smile."

In a sympathetic voice Jenna said, "It must be hard for you and your sisters to take care of your mother all the time."

He shrugged thin shoulders and nodded. "We'd do anything for her.

Mama loves flowers. You saw our front yard. It's ugly. But the back yard looks better…now." He dropped his head and mumbled, "I thought if she could look out the window and see something pretty she would get better. You were so nice to me and have so much. I didn't think you would miss what I took." He looked at Charles then back at Jenna. "Mr. McAdams explained that what I did was not the way you treat people, especially someone who's been nice to you. I'm sorry. I really am."

Two big tears rolled down his face. He turned away to blow his nose and then added, "I know you're here, Mr. McAdams to take me to jail. I haven't told Mama where I got the painting and flowers. I told her an angel let us borrow them."

A slight smile crossed Jenna's lips. "How did you get the shrubs here?"

"In my sisters' wagon."

Jenna turned puzzled eyes upon Charles. "What made the digging marks in my yard?"

Sammy spoke up. "My shovel did it. I got it hung under the wagon and didn't know it 'til I got to the road. I'm sorry about that, too."

Jenna sized up Sammy. "I don't see how you got some of those bushes out of the ground."

Sammy stretched to his full height of four feet. "I know I'm not big for a fourteen year old, but I'm strong. When I'm determined to do something, it seems like my strength doubles. And I wanted very much to get Mama some plants that would have lots of flowers."

Jenna could not help but feel sorry for the boy and at the same time admire him. For a moment she stood there looking dumbfounded. What should she say? With raised eyebrows she looked at Charles. He simply looked back and smiled gently.

She turned back to Sammy and asked if she could see his mother. "I want say or do anything to upset her. I promise."

With a look of anxiety he led Jenna and Charles into a sparsely filled bedroom. In one corner sat two little girls, playing with dolls, and curled on the bed beside an uncovered window lay a short, thin woman with dull brown hair.

Jenna knew it was rude to stare, but she could not stop looking at the woman. With a healthy appearance this woman would be pretty, she thought. She then looked up at Charles and caught a sympathetic look on his face as he watched Sammy work with his mother, trying to rouse her up.

"Mama," Sammy said in a low voice, and patted the pale face. "Mama, can you wake up? There's someone here to see you."

The woman opened her eyes and tried to push up in the bed. When she focused her fading blue eyes and saw Jenna, the stranger became her focal point. Her solemn face filled with curiosity, but it was with great effort that she said, "Sammy, you should have given me some warning that we have guests." The hand she tried to raise toward her hair fell back on top of the much-used cover.

Sammy took the fragile-looking hand in his and said, "Mama, you've met Mr. McAdams." With apprehension he introduced Jenna. "This is Jenna Wilson, the artist who painted the picture on the wall." To Jenna he said, "My Mama, Edith Wilson."

Jenna turned toward the wall behind her and saw her painting Evening Sun for the first time since Asheville's festival. A gasp escaped her lips before she could stop the sound. She looked at Charles and then at Mrs. Walker who was also looking at the painting. A flicker of interest lit up her full eyes. A gentle smile raised the corners of Edith's mouth. Gently she said, "You do beautiful work, Mrs. Wilson."

Her reaction did not help Sammy to relax. Even though Jenna made him a promise he did not know her well enough to believe she would keep her word. His eyes kept darting to her and then to Charles and his mother and then back to Jenna. Every time Jenna opened her mouth he wrung his hands. When Jenna finally walked over to the bed, his little eyes opened wide as saucers. Beads of sweat popped out on his forehead.

Jenna kept her promise and talked about his mother's health all the time. "I'm pleased to meet you, Mrs. Walker. I'm sorry that you are not well. I hope you will be feeling better soon."

Charles eased up beside Jenna and reached for her hand. She wrapped her fingers around his and squeezed hard. He knew she appreciated the contact because she immediately relaxed. He believed that she may be willing to trust him now and his heart swelled with happiness.

The experience was a new and daunting realization. With heartrending certainty he knew his feelings for her were right. With all his heart, mind, and soul he loved Jenna. He wanted to marry her, to take her home with him and make plans for a future together. But it was a matter to set aside for now. With squared shoulders, he slipped an arm around Jenna's waist and spoke to the invalid. "How are you today, Mrs. Walker?"

"Not much better," she whispered. "I don't have any energy."

Jenna picked up the hand lying across her flat stomach. She cradled it in both of hers. "Mrs. Walker, I thing you should know that your son is willing to move mountains to make you feel better. I wish too that I could help you in some way."

Mrs. Walker looked at Sammy before saying. "I don't know what I'd do without him." She turned back to Jenna and took a breath. "Forgive me for starring, but you remind me of my mother. Like you, she always dressed like a fashion model."

"Thank you," Jenna said and smiled. "I'd like to meet your mother."

Tears gathered in the fading eyes. "I wish you could, but I don't know where she is." Sobs came forth and shook the small body.

Jenna immediately cradled Edith in her arms. She rocked and talked in soothing tones until the little woman fell asleep. Jenna laid her back onto the pillow and tucked the thin coverlet over her shoulders.

Outside, she talked to Sammy about his mother. "I didn't mean to upset her. Do you think I look like your grandmother?"

Sammy dropped his head, making some long strands of hair fall across his eyes. When he raised his head, he did not attempt to move the hair aside. He looked so sad when he said, "I don't know. Maybe a little bit. I've only seen some old wrinkled pictures; I've never seen my grandparents. When Mama and Daddy married, Grandpa Reynolds wouldn't have anything else to do with Mama. He told her not to come back home, not even if she had a child to show them. Mama said Grandma pleaded with him to take back his words but he wouldn't."

Sammy did not see the frown Jenna gave Charles because he was watching his sisters play. Absentmindedly he kept talking. "Mama said Grandpa was mean because Daddy was a country preacher, traveling to two churches every month. He said Reverend Ted Walker wasn't good enough for the daughter of a cigar manufacturer. He would never make enough money to keep his daughter in the way she was use to living. 'I'll never give you a penny as long as you're with that man,' Grandpa told her. She said she didn't want his money, she only wanted his blessing, but she never got it.

"God ordained out marriage," mama also told her daddy. "It was meant for me to be Ted's partner in life and with his ministry. If we never have a lot of money and have to live from hand to mouth it will be okay because I love my husband. God will take care of us."

Sammy continued to explain his mother's situation. "When they left to come to Asheville, she never heard from her Mama and daddy." His eyes watered up. "I believe Mama would feel better if she could talk to grandma."

Jenna brushed the thatch of hair hanging in his eyes to the side of his forehead and asked, "Where is your daddy?"

"He died last year in a car wreck," Sammy answered on a choked sob.

Jenna gathered him in her arms. He wrapped his thin arms around her and burst into tears. She cleared her throat and said softly, "You were then forced to become the head of the house."

He nodded and wiped his nose on his shirtsleeve. "It wasn't bad 'til Mama quit trying to get well."

Jenna gave his shoulders a squeeze. "Perhaps we can help you in some way," she said, pointing to Charles and herself.

Sammy's expression filled with doubt. "You, Mrs. Wilson? After I stole from you?"

Charles, Jenna, and Sammy had been strolling around the house. By this time they were in the backyard with Jenna's transplanted rhododendron bushes. They were not planted in an orderly fashion suitable for Jenna, but they were thriving and blooming, even her hybrid bush.

Jenna fingered a few petals of Evening Sun before answering Sammy. "I'll forget about what you did if you promise to never steal again, not just from me but from anyone. Ever!"

Sammy's eyes and mouth flew open wide. "You would do that?"

"Will you make a promise and keep it?" she insisted.

"I promise," he said, crossing his heart and holding his hand upward. "I will never steal anything ever again. I know it's wrong and I asked Jesus to forgive me. I wouldn't have done it to you this time, but everything you have is so nice. I wanted mama to have something pretty so she would feel better."

Jenna looked puzzled. "There's something I don't understand; how did you know where I lived?"

Sammy looked guilty when he said, "The little card attached to the flower you sent to Mama had your address on it. I asked a guy at the grocery store about the street, and he told me."

With an amazed look Jenna said, "You are quite a gutsy boy to walk a mile across town with a wheel barrel at night."

"I prayed for safety all the way home," he explained. "My daddy said if I ever needed protection to ask God for it and he would help me. And He did."

Jenna hugged him. "You bet He did."

"I admit digging up the plants again will be more hard work, but all I need to do is take the picture off the wall. I'll tell Mama that the angel's reclaiming her loan."

"No. That won't be necessary, Sammy. You keep them all as a gift from me. Leave the painting where it is for your mother to see. I don't think anyone else would appreciate it as much as she does. I'll pray that each time she looks at it her spirits will be lifted up, even if it doesn't help her get well."

All of sudden Jenna's eyes lit up and she turned to Charles. "Did you notice that the woman in the picture resembles Edith?"

He nodded and answered, "I saw the likeness yesterday. I wondered how long it would take for you to see it. It was as if she posed for the picture."

"I agree," Jenna said and chills ran over her arms. "Had the robberies been God's way of getting us here to meet this family?"

"Could be. He works in mysterious ways," Charles answered. "What about The Stafford House? Wasn't that the painting you wanted John Paul to see?"

Jenna shrugged. "It was, but I'll come up with something else."

Her thoughts were now centered on a way to help this family. "What if Edith and her parents were brought together? Sammy, do you know where your grandparents live?" Jenna asked, becoming excited at the prospect of finding them and possibly helping Edith in the process."

"I believe they're in Pittsburgh, Pennsylvania. They may not be living now. Mama didn't have friends or relatives who would tell her things about Grandma and Grandpa." He shrugged and added, "My sisters and me never saw any of our grandparents. Grandpa and Grandma Walker died when Daddy was a young man. There's only us."

Only us. How lonely that sounded to Jenna. She could relate to this family. She had never met Stuart's family until he died and her only living relative now was Debbie. *We can cope without relatives, but these kids can't.* She had to come up with some way to help this family.

Sammy's sisters, who looked to be about eight and five, sat down and began digging in the dirt. Jenna squatted down in front of them.

"I like to play in the dirt, too," she said and scooped up a handful of sand. It filtered slowly through her fingers, and she thought about these children's lives. If an adult did not take care of them, they would sift through the cracks of society. Sammy might turn to drugs and gangs and the girls could become prostitutes. Jenna cringed at the thought and prayed for God to not let it happen to these children.

Her attention returned to the dirt and the girls who were staring at her. She picked up more dirt. "Sometimes I go out into my yard and dig around in the dirt to plant flowers. I pretend that I'm working so people won't laugh at this grown woman for playing in the dirt. You are lucky that people don't laugh when you make mud pies."

Smiles split across both of their faces. The biggest girl said, "We make mud pies all the time. Deborah tries to eat them." She giggled at her sister's red face.

To cover the child's embarrassment Jenna quickly inserted, "Deborah? Your name's Deborah?"

At the little girl's not, Jenna added, "That's my daughter's name, too."

With a hopeful expression, the older girl asked, "Do you another daughter named Sarah? My name is Sarah?"

"No, but I have a dear friend named Sarah," Jenna answered "How about that? Now I know two girls named Deborah and two named Sarah." She stood and brushed her hands free of dirt. "It's been fun playing in the dirt with you girls, but I must go now. Mr. McAdams is waiting to take me home."

"Will you come again?" Sarah asked.

Jenna looked into the face of each child and smiled. "I would love to."

"I hope so," Sammy said. "You made Mama happy."

"Can your Deborah come, too?" Deborah asked.

Jenna hugged all three children, starting with Deborah. She said, "She'll come. I'm sure she would love to meet you." When Charles pulled away from the curb, Jenna waved goodbye and felt a quickening in her heart. She thought she had problems. *Forgive me, Lord when I complain. There are so many people in worse shape than me.*

CHAPTER 15

Jenna packed a basket of food and gathered up a big bunch of flowers which she hoped that Edith Walker would appreciate. Since the day she met this sweet woman and her children, they have constantly been on Jenna's mind. She worked on various ways to make life easier and happier for them, and it seemed to help Edith. She managed to stay awake longer and even talked more with each visitor. Jenna was encouraged to find ways to help the whole family.

On Sunday afternoons games were played with the children. When they were outside, kids in the neighborhood began to join in the activities. Charles, Jenna, Chuck and Debbie went home many times worn out but content because they had brought joy into the lives of those children.

While riding home after an exhausting game of volleyball, Charles had kept glancing at Jenna. By the way she looked he figured she was in deep thought rather than trying to catch a nap. But he was not absolutely sure was on her mind, so he asked, "What's got your brows puckered into a frown now?" He reached over and tried to smooth out her skin. "That look causes wrinkles you know."

"Sorry. I'm not much company am I?"

"Whether we talk or not, I'd rather be with you than anyone I know."

Jenna's eyes widened and joy made the greenness shine like jewels. "That's the sweetest thing I've ever heard. I enjoy being with you, too, and I'm happy that you have connections."

"Pardon me?"

"Aren't you close friends with God?"

"Yes but so are you. I still don't understand where your statement is taking this conversation."

Jenna laughed heartily, capturing Charles attention a little too much. He ran a stop light. Fortunately there were no cars at the intersection, coming or going in any of the four directions.

But Jenna hollered, "Be careful!"

"I will if you'll quit being so captivating when I'm under the wheel. Now, my dear Jenna, tell me what's kept you so quiet until I interrupted your thought process."

"I was thinking how nice it would be for Edith and the kids if her parents would come to visit them, if only for a few minutes. Don't you think Mr. and Mrs. Reynolds would like to see their daughter by now? Perhaps they've got too much pride to make the first move. Then again they may not know where to contact Edith."

"The same thing has been on my mind, too. There could be lots of reasons why the Reynolds haven't made an effort to reconcile with their daughter. I can't imagine being separated from either of my children for more than a week and not hearing their voices. Years are incomprehensible to imagine."

Jenna looked sad. "You know, Edith's parents could be dead."

"True."

She gave him a sly look. "With all your experience at looking for missing people, it should be a snap for you to find them, if they're alive. Dead or alive, it would be good to know. Will you please do something?"

He smiled. "I wondered when you'd get around to mentioning it."

"So?"

"So, I am. I had already planned on doing it."

And he did. It didn't take Charles long to find Mrs. Reynolds. She was still living at the family home in Pennsylvania but Mr. Reynolds was dead.

During their first phone conversation Mrs. Reynolds told Charles about her husband's death. "He'd had a stroke, which made him weepy and sad at times. The doctor said his depression was due not only to his mind having been affected but because of his desire to see his daughter one more time. Right before he died he asked me to contact an investigator to find Edith, but almost immediately he began having serious problems that caused me to put everything else on the back burner. My husband died three months ago."

The catch in her voice made Charles think she was about to cry. "Would you like for me to call you sometime later after your grieving period has eased."

"Oh no," she said, "Now that I know Edith wants to see me, I can't wait any longer than necessary to get to her."

They talked a while longer, and then Charles made arrangements to pick up Mrs. Reynolds and take her back to North Carolina with him. "I'll come by your house first so we can get better acquainted. After you sleep on it and you decide you would rather fly, I'll meet you at the airport in Ashville. You can let me know of your plans tomorrow." He gave her the name of the hotel where he was staying and the phone number there.

His telephone rang at 6:00 the next morning. "Mr. McAdams did I waken you? I slept very little last night, thinking about going to Asheville. I'm anxious to see Edith and my grandchildren. I hate flying alone, so I've asked a friend to go with me. Rachel has a sister in Canter. I believe that's close to Asheville. Rachel wanted to go there, so this is a golden opportunity for her. I would like for you to come here first if you will. I want to find out more about my family before I meet them. Is it possible for you to come here?" She gave him directions to her house.

Charles was fully awake now. "I'd be glad to. I'll see you in an hour."

Mrs. Reynolds was standing in the doorway, waiting for Charles to get out of his car. She took his hand shook it with enthusiasm.

"You can't image how often I've opened this door and wished that

Edith would be standing there." Mrs. Reynolds' smile faded. "You aren't my daughter, but at least you have something to tell me about her. I'm anxious to hear everything."

Charles got back home a day before Mrs. Reynolds was due to arrive. He met her at the airport and drove her to the Wilson home. He called Jenna and told her about the reunion; she was excited for the whole family and wanted to rush right over to see them.

Charles reined in her desire to intrude. "If you can manage to wait until morning, I'll go with you."

Jenna chuckled, "Okay, if you insist."

The expected journey this morning filled Jenna with so much happiness that you would think it was her family being reunited. As she, Charles, and Debbie rode along the heavily traveled road that kept hampering their progress, they talked about Charles' first meeting with Mrs. Reynolds.

"It was a good one," Charles said. "She greeted me like a long lost brother."

Excitement lit up Debbie's face. "Has Edith's mother been to the house yet?"

Charles nodded. "She went last night, soon as she arrived in town. There was an immediate bonding. The women hugged and cried for endless minutes. The children stood off to the side and watched with wary eyes."

Charles stopped in front of the Walkers' home. They watched Sammy sweep the porch before Jenna said to Debbie, "Charles said Sammy was determined to tell his grandmother about his stealing. He was afraid she would not like him but thought she should know everything about the family from the start."

Debbie looked amazed. "He's quite a young man for a fourteen year old."

While climbing from the van, Charles explained. "Some children have to grow up fast when they're shouldered with the responsibility of caring for other family members. Tina grew up too fast. I believe she had fun doing it, though, because of Rosie's guidance. Sammy had no one to guide him."

Before they reached the steps leading up to the porch, the front door swung open. Sarah and Deborah ran out.

"Nannie Reynolds is here," they chorused together.

Sarah took Jenna's hand and added, "Come see Nannie. You'll like her."

Jenna did like the older woman, though Mrs. Reynolds acted somewhat reserved at first. She watched and listened to the strangers without saying much. But in a short time, Jenna's and Debbie's easy chatter and open friendliness reached to her and she was chatting with them like an old friend.

"I wish I hadn't been so contrary and given in to my husband. Since he was the head of the house, I had to let his decision rule. It was extremely hard, like a death when Edith left; I worried about her and cried for days. I knew I'd never see her again." Her eyes filled with tears.

Jenna understood much of what Julia went through with her husband. To live with an overbearing husband was not easy. She hugged her new friend and said, "But you're together now. Better late than never."

"If I'd known about her predicament, I'd been here earlier, no matter what Edward said or did. I should have had more guts years ago." To Edith she added, "I'll never be able to forgive myself or Edward, but I'm going to try now to make up for all the time we've lost. It's too bad that your father was so pigheaded. He missed out on the best years of his life, knowing your husband and these precious children. Charles, thank you so much for bringing us together."

He winked at Sammy but spoke as if he was directing all the praise to Jenna. "It had a lot to do with that beautiful woman standing over there. If it hadn't been for her love and concern for mankind it may not have happened."

Jenna had been standing with one arm across Sammy's shoulders and the other around Debbie's waist, listening and crying with joy. After giving them both a tight squeeze she said, "I believe I am as excited as anyone about this reunion."

With the help of her mother, Edith slides up to a sitting position. "Jenna, have you noticed that my mother dresses classy like you?"

From the sound of Edith's clear voice, Jenna knew that her condition had improved a lot since her mother's arrival. She longed to ask her many questions, but, recalling that she was there to teach Sunday school, she held back. First she looked Julia over, admiring her calf-length, flower-printed dress and said, "Your mother does have great taste in clothes and she's a beautiful woman. So are you. It's good to see color in your cheeks."

"I do feel some better," Edith said, patting the side of the bed. "Mother, come sit here while Jenna delivers the lesson. She's a good teacher."

Charles said good bye to the women and kissed Jenna's cheek before adding, "I'm going to ride back with Debbie." He handed her his keys. "I'll get my car from you later."

Debbie went outside and then popped back into the room. "The kids are in the car, anxious to get down the road. We'll be back as soon as church is over."

"Thank you, Debbie," Edith said with a grateful look. "They wake up each Sunday, way before they need to. They like going to church. Until you came along, it had been a long time since they have been. I thank God everyday for sending you people into our lives."

For the past month, Debbie, Jenna, and Charles had taken turns teaching lessons to Edith. While one stayed with her, the children went to church with one of the others.

Jenna and Charles got the women from their churches to prepare Sunday meals. Extra dishes had been put into the freezer for Sammy to heat and serve during the week.

Chuck assisted men from both churches in other areas. They did yard work and repairs to the house, inside and out. Due to a heavy caseload, Charles was unable to do manual labor, but each week he sent flowers to Edith.

With the reconstruction of the house, visits by the church people, and medical attention from a new doctor there has been a great change in Edith. Once a beautician was brought in and worked magic with shampoo, conditioner, and scissors, Edith's hair was given a healthy sheen. Excitement brought life back into the grieving widow, lighting up her eyes.

While watching and listening to Jenna teach, things she said made Edith look thoughtful. She later told Jenna that she wished that Ted could be there to enjoy all this fellowship she was having. "But, if he were alive, there would have been no need for all this attention in this way. I guess by defying my father for the man I love has been both a tragedy and a blessing."

When Jenna concluded her lesson with a message that Apostle Paul had written in one of his letters, Edith was once again blessed. The words, "Forget those things which are behind, because it is a high calling of God," made her turn and look toward her mother. They smiled at each other.

"Jenna?" Edith said in a soft voice, "Mother and I worked out our differences. I wish Father and I could have settled things before he died. It's too late for us, but there's still time for mother and the kids to get acquainted."

Julia added, "I have to go back home soon to take care of a few things, but I'm coming back to stay a while with my family. Before school starts in the fall, if Edith feels well enough to travel, I want to take them back to live with me in Pittsburgh."

"That's wonderful!" Jenna said, "For you I mean. I'll miss Edith and the children, but I know it will be the best thing for you all."

"There's one other thing," Julia added, "I love your painting. I would like to take it with us. How much are you asking for it?"

Jenna shook her head. "Nothing. Although she got it in a round about way it's a gift to Edith." With a sparkle in her eyes she added, "However, I would like to have the red-gold rhododendron. I'm proud of the way it turned out. I just hope another move won't kill it."

"It is beautiful," Edith said. "When you get ready for it, Sammy can help move it. He did it once, I'm sure he can do it again."

Jenna grinned. "Tell him he'll have help this time and it will be loaded on a truck." She kissed Edith's cheek. "I'm happy for all of you. You're looking so much better, so I'll continually to pray that God will give your health another boost. I want you up walking so your mother and I can take you shopping one time before you move away."

"Amen to that," Edith and Julia said in unison.

With that, Jenna left before tears of joy spilled over and ran down her cheeks. Once she was seated in Charles' Lincoln some tears did flow. She smiled through them and thought how grateful she was to have met the Walker family. "Thank you, Lord, for the unexpected treasures of life. Sometimes they're a blessing in disguise."

She beat Debbie home. The phone was ringing. She could not get the door unlocked fast enough. The answering machine picked up the message, "Hi, Jenna, it's..." She grabbed up the receiver, "Charles, I'm here. I just got in the house."

"Have you planned lunch yet?" he asked.

"No. Actually I was wondering what to fix."

"Don't fix anything," he said. "You and Debbie come to my house. Rosie is preparing a delicious smelling meal."

"Thanks. I'd love to," Jenna responded with much enthusiasm. "We'll be there as soon as Debbie drops off the Walker children. I heard that you had moved. Better give me directions to your new home."

She hung up the receiver at the same moment Debbie came into the kitchen. Jenna gave her a frown.

"What's the sour look for?" Debbie asked.

"Why didn't you tell me that one of the grand country club homes belonged to Charles?"

"I thought you knew. What difference does it make?"

"Because Charles invited us there for lunch. I accepted, but I don't know if we should go."

"We should and we are," Debbie said, striding back out the door.

Reluctantly Jenna followed. For a long time Charles had lived in a beautiful house in a rural area. She had no idea he was at the club now. The thought of him living in a ritzy place and visiting her "cracker box" of a home bothered Jenna. Still, he looked comfortable here, she thought and shrugged. "Oh well. Either he likes me the way I am with what little I have or he doesn't. I can't change things now."

Jenna and Debbie made the trip across town in good time. Jenna was both anxious and excited about seeing Charles in his home.

"Mom," Debbie said, pulling on her leg. 'You're driving too fast. Are you that excited to see Charles?"

"It would appear so, wouldn't it?" Jenna responded more amused than annoyed.

Within ten minutes, she turned between the brick columns marking the drive going up to his elegant home. The one story brick house with its three sectional roofs looked like three homes in one. Jenna's eyes opened wide. "When you talked about his sprawling home, I thought maybe he had added an extension to his other house," Jenna said with awe in her voice.

"Isn't it gorgeous?" Debbie asked, with an envious look on her face. "I'd love to have a house like this but without all those windows. I wouldn't want to wash then. By the time I finished all of them; it would be time to start all over."

"If you could afford a house this size, you could afford a window washer," Jenna said with a deadpan look.

Debbie giggled. "I certainly would have to have one."

Charles was standing at one of those windows, waiting for their arrival. He stepped through the patio doors when Jenna drove up. Reaching for her hand to help her out of the van, he looked lovingly into her eyes and said, "I'm so glad you're here. You, too, Debbie, but Chuck's waiting for you in the family room. He has a new video to show you. Tell Rosie we'll be in after I show Jenna the yard."

Jenna readjusted the Derby on top of her curly hair and linked arms with Charles. "This place is absolutely beautiful. I'd love to do a painting in this yard."

"Do it whenever you like."

In the center of the green carpeted grass lay a sunken garden, descending in ledges to the woods beyond. Each ledge contained orderly placed plants of chrysanthemums, gladiolas, and miniature roses. In the middle of the garden sat a white gazebo with lattice trim around the edge of the roof. Beside the gazebo and along the outside border of the garden grew a variety of bushes. Cement walkways wound around the yard.

"Do you mind if I take some pictures?" Jenna asked, pulling out a camera.

"Go right ahead," Charles answered and sat down on a cement bench to watch.

Jenna clicked different angles of the yard. She asked Charles to stand in the gazebo. Unashamed, he stepped inside and posed for the camera, or was it for Jenna? She took her time in getting the right shots. "You must have quite a gardener," she said between takes. "Every plant looks so perfect that they could be taken for artificial."

"Ray is the best I could find. He came highly recommended. He agreed to work here fulltime if he could have a small space to live on the grounds. There just happened to be a room at the back of the greenhouse that was filled with all kind of supplies and things that were of no use to him or me. He willingly cleaned it out and painted it up. Now it's an ideal place for a retiree with no family."

"How does Rosie like him?" Jenna asked, knowing how protective she is of this family.

"They get along great," Charles said, leading Jenna back toward the house. "Rosie already has him wrapped around her little finger. Ray's planted all the herbs and vegetables that she's requested. She even lets him in the kitchen to sample her new recipes. The really good thing about having Ray around is that I can go off on trips and not worry about leaving Rosie all alone."

When Jenna saw the wonderful lady standing at a window she asked, "You don't suppose she's upset with us for keeping lunch waiting?"

"I don't think so. She's just probably anxious to talk with you. She got excited when I told her you and Debbie were coming. She said, 'Thank, God. It's about time." I agreed wholeheartedly."

From their first meeting, back when she was either picking up or delivering the kids home, Jenna knew that Rosie was the ideal housekeeper for this family. She hugged the kids and gave them special treats before sending them off to bathe and get ready for bed. Although they liked to tease and pull pranks on her, they loved and respected her like. The pixie-face, white-haired woman treated Debbie the same way. She would come home talking endlessly about the delicious meals Rosie and Tina prepared. As soon as Jenna stepped inside the house today, she got a hug from Rosie.

Leading the way toward the kitchen she said, "Charles, I'm taking Jenna with me. Lunch is almost ready."

Charles stopped her for a second. "Did you invite Ray to come have lunch with us?"

"I did and he is," she answered, and resumed her conversation with Jenna.

Through the crack in the door, he could hear their lively chatter. Before long, Jenna came out with a platter of golden fried chicken.

For a fleeting moment, an elusive smile pulled at the corners of Jenna's mouth. It was a warning of her humor hovering beneath the surface. As now, it often showed up in time to catch Charles off guard. On her way to the dining table, she passed the platter under his nose and asked, "Doesn't this smell simply wonderful? Rosie reminds me of my mother. Both women would rather do all of the work than admit they need help. Once Rosie saw I was capable of looking after the chicken without letting it burn, she seemed grateful for my help."

Charles smiled and wrapped an arm across her shoulders. In her ear he whispered, "I know when I've got a good thing, and I'm not just talking about Ray and Rosie now. When the time comes, I won't let you leave either."

Jenna's heartbeat faltered. What was Charles actually saying? She was not to know the answer yet, because Chuck and Debbie entered the room at the same time as Rosie and Ray.

Chuck pulled out a chair for Debbie and said, "Rosie, I believe you've out done yourself."

"Chuck, my boy, you say that every time you sit down to eat. You don't have to flatter me to get an extra piece of chocolate cake."

He kissed her cheek. She brushed him aside, but it was evident that she loved his attention, especially when she scooped him out an extra large helping of creamed potatoes.

"She's precious," Jenna said when Rosie exited the room to get the dessert from the kitchen. "I can see why you won't let her leave."

Charles passed along a squash casserole. "We couldn't do without Rosie."

Chuck winked at Debbie. "When I get my own house, I'm taking her with me."

"It will never happen," Charles said with conviction.

Chuck spooned out some green beans and corn before saying, "I know." To the others he said, "We were blessed the day Rosie came to live with us."

"We know," Debbie said, "You and your sisters have constantly sung her praises, but I can't blame you. She always treated me like I was your sister, too. She even took me in hand when I did wrong, but it was always because of you."

"Me?" Chuck asked, trying to look surprised. "How did I influence you to be bad?"

"Well, for instance, you decided it was time I learned how to smoke. You made cigarettes out of sumac and toilet paper, and then sent me into the house to get some matches. I thought I'd gotten away with filtering from the supply at the fireplace in the den until Rosie showed up. She had followed me down to the pond to see what I was going to do with the matches. She sent me, you, and Lynn to bed without any supper."

Chuck laughed. "Oh yeah. I remember. To be without a piece of Rosie's chocolate cake was the worst part of the punishment."

"All of you kids were a pain for Rosie at some time or another," Charles said, trying to look serious but failed when a big grin burst forth. He then told several stories of which related to their ideas for solving great mysteries. "They could come up with some hilarious problems and solutions." When he told the one about Tina seeing a monster in the pond and had Chuck diving into the waters to find its nesting place, I thought Rosie would have a fit. She didn't want her boy to be caught in a situation where he might drown."

Jenna's eyes were huge when she asked, "Was there a monster?"

"Not really," Charles answered. "Tina has always been creative with crafts. She came up with a rubber two-headed beast. By rigging up a line hooked to the valve, from a distance, she could pull the plug and make it sink when Chuck got too close. Soon as Chuck dove into the water, Lynn would distract him from the area of the monster to give Tina time enough to retrieve it. Chuck kept coming up for air and going back down. He was determined to see where the thing was hiding. It was Rosie who finally let the cat out of the bag."

Rosie was back at the table, dishing out portions of cake during this tale. When everyone looked at her as if she was a snitch, she defended herself for giving away Tina's mystery. "I thought my boy was going to drown."

Story after story had them all laughing so hard that they had to give up trying to eat. Charles controlled his laughter enough so that he could listen to the sound of Jenna's voice. Her laughter was light and bubbly and her eyes sparkled like the overhead chandelier.

Debbie was the first able to speak; she directed her statement to Ray. "I wasn't involved in that episode of The McAdams Mysteries, but I had fun taking part in some other ones. They had some of the best adventures. Tina should write a book about them."

The phone rang. Rosie got up to answer it. "Charles, Kenneth wants you. He sounds nervous." She backed into the kitchen where she stopped when Charles said, "You're sure this time it's not false labor? Kenneth, try to stay calm. We'll meet you at the hospital."

He dropped the receiver back into place and said, "The baby's on the way. Rosie, make sure everything's turned off." He grabbed Jenna's hand. "Come on, folks, we've a short time to get to the hospital." To Ray he added, "Would you please call our pastor and tell him Lynn's about ready to have her baby."

Jenna pulled on her hand, trying to get Charles to release it. "You don't want me to go."

Charles looked disappointed. "Don't you want to?"

"Of course I do, but this is a family event. I'm afraid Kenneth may think I'm horning in. Lynn's special to me, but I haven't been around Kenneth a lot."

"Jenna, trust me, he won't mind. I doubt that he'll know or even care who's there."

By the time Charles got Jenna and Rosie into the Lincoln, Chuck and Debbie were ready to drive off.

"Meet you there," Chuck shouted and waved. He gunned the convertible to life and headed down the drive.

Jenna kept darting glances at Charles. He was rubbing the scar. "You're so serious-looking," she said. "Are you worried about Lynn and the baby?"

"I am. After she had such a difficult delivery with Kelly, I'm concerned that this one may be just as bad."

Jenna bowed her head and held a conference with God in silence. She prayed for Lynn, the baby, the doctor, and the family.

Not much conversation went on between the three in the car during the rest of the way to the hospital. It left Charles free to concentrate on the heavy traffic.

At the hospital, he shoved through the doors, pushing them open wide and ushered the ladies down the hall to the maternity ward. From a distance, they saw Kenneth pacing up and down the hall. He kept pacing even after they stopped near him. While still moving he said, "I'm so glad you're all here. My sister's in labor at the Forsyth Hospital in Winston Salem. My parents are there with her." He looked at Jenna and asked, "Why did they have to go into delivery at the same time?"

"I'm not a detective," she answered, "All I can say is that Mother Nature knows best. All babies come when God says so."

Before Kenneth had a chance to pick up his pace again Charles asked, "How's Lynn? Is the baby's head down? Lord, I hope it's not going to be another breach birth." He turned to Jenna and said, "Kelly started to come out feet first. The doctor managed to get her turned in time. I don't want Lynn going through that again."

Jenna had not been at the hospital when Kelly was born, but Debbie told her about the difficult delivery later that night. She made it a point to be Lynn's first visitor the next morning.

Chuck grinned at Kelly and said, "I suppose that's why the kid never looks where she's going. She steps in where angels fear to tread."

Kelly frowned and asked, "What does that mean?"

"You walk up to strangers, men and women, and start conversations. I believe if anyone of them would say, 'Come with me and I'll buy you some candy or ice cream,' you'd go right off with them."

"I was taught to be friendly."

"Friendly yes but chummy like pals no," Kenneth said, "at least not until you know them better." He turned toward Charles and answered him. "Lynn's not having a breach birth. Everything's fine, so the nurse says."

Jenna took Charles by the arm. "Lynn's in good hands here. Come and sit down with me."

To Jenna and Rosie, Kenneth said, "I know you two will take care of Charles, but more importantly, Lynn will be comforted to know that her two mother figures are here."

The tall, brown-headed man with the bluest eyes Jenna had ever seen touched Jenna's heart. She stood and hugged Kenneth. "That was nice of you. Tell Lynn if she needs an extra hand to squeeze as the pains hit, I'll come in and give her mine."

"Thanks, but since she's practically broken my wrist you better stay out here."

Charles picked up Kelly and turned her to face Jenna and Debbie. "Ladies, as you all ready know, this king fish rules our homes."

"Papaw, I'm no fish," Kelly said, tweaking Charles' nose. "I'm a girl. Daddy said I was going to get a little brother."

"Do you want a brother?" Jenna asked.

Kelly leaned her head sideways, seeming to consider the question. After a second or two she said, "If he's a good boy, it will be all right."

"What do you consider a good boy?" Chuck asked.

"Someone who does what I tell him. Will you be a good boy and get me a soda?"

Kenneth eyed his daughter and said, "Be careful, young lady. Uncle Chuck has your number." To Charles he asked, "Will you take care of Kelly and keep her out of trouble? I plan on being with Lynn during the delivery this time."

"Don't pass out like you did last time," Chuck teased. To Jenna he added, "This man looks tough, but he's real sensitive."

"I remember what happened last time," Debbie said. "With the way he looked I thought he was the one having the baby."

With a flushed face, Kenneth admitted, "It did get to me when Kelly was born, but I think I'll handle it better this time."

"You'll do fine because you know what to expect," Charles said. "Don't worry about this little lady. She'll be fine."

While Charles sat there with Kelly on his lap, Jenna took some pictures of them. She wanted to help keep the atmosphere light for Charles, so she suggested different poses. Some were sedate and serious-looking while others were crazy and funny.

"Mom, are you getting ready for another painting?" Debbie asked. Turning to Charles she added, "Mom takes tons of pictures of the subject she's about to transfer to canvass. Don't be surprised if you see your face looking back at you from somebody's wall."

Jenna gave a playful smile and said, "I thought I'd make a mug book. Should something else get stolen, I'll have a file to view for a possible thief."

Charles frowned. "In that case you better have more than my ugly mug in it." He looked upset with Jenna's remark so she said, "I have oodles of mugs, take Chuck's for instance," and snapped a couple pictures of him.

"Have you decided what painting you're taking to The Safford House?" Chuck asked. John Paul asked me the other night if I knew when you were bringing it. I told him about the one that was stolen but assured him you'd be there soon with something wonderful for him to hang in his gallery."

"Thanks, Chuck, for smoothing over the reason for my delay." She did not want to tell anyone, not even Debbie, about the painting she planned to take to John Paul. She packed away her camera and said, "I've been considering a couple of paintings packed away in storage. I've got a pretty good idea what I'm going to show him."

Jenna was tempted to pass up this time with Charles in order to go home and make some sketches for a new painting. When his head turned her way and those beautiful dark eyes caught her attention, she settled back to wait with him. The desire to please this man fought with a passion to produce a work of art. She decided that one more day away from the easel won't make that much difference.

These on again, off again, desires to please Charles or to paint can be hazardous to my career and my social life, she thought. She knew she needed to make a decision to which was the most important or learn to balance them without hurting her relationship with the man she now loved.

Why can't I enjoy Charles' company as much as possible and work in some time for solitude, too? Since he had to make frequent business trips out of town, why could she not learn to use those times for painting, and then be prepared to spend as much time as possible with him when he came home. How hard can that be?

Separating the two when she was married to Stuart had been difficult. That was because he seldom went out of town on a separate trip from her. Also she never took his feelings into consideration. She just went out and painted or worked with her plants. Before Stuart pulled his stunt, she never questioned why he quit intruding on her quiet times. For many years, nothing mattered when she was secluded with her easel and paints; they were such a big part of her day-to-day existence. It was not until Stuart went looking for companionship elsewhere that she realized they had a problem. Something had changed. It took his death for her to come to an understanding about their failing marriage. A lot of the problem had been her fault.

While sitting here with some of her favorite people she came to a firm decision. If God blessed her with another husband she would not mess it up by deserting him for hours at a time. Before attempting to be alone at all, even fifteen minute, she would discuss it with her man first and be sensible about the length of time she would be away. She did not want another failed marriage because she let work come first. If the man in question should be Charles she would not want him to let work come first and neglect her. They would definitely need to discuss this possible problem before she ever committed to marriage again.

Sitting now surrounded by Chuck, Debbie, Kelly and Charles, the word solitude took on new and ominous connotations. Over the past few weeks it grew steadily, as though it were a living entity, getting bigger and more dominant. The entity took on a new identity called loneliness, and Jenna hated the thought of living with it. She shivered at the idea.

Charles put an arm around Jenna and drew her close. "Are you cold?" he asked.

She shook her head and huddled closer. "No. I'm okay."

A nurse entered the waiting room, and everyone jumped up.

"Do I have a baby brother?" Kelly asked.

"Not yet, honey. I'm here to give you all an update, though. We're on our way to the delivery room. The little fellow seems anxious to get out into this big world. Lynn's doing great. Kenneth's a little gray, but he's hanging in there. It won't be long now," she said and rushed back down the hall.

"We'll soon have another member in our family," Charles said, hugging Jenna tightly. "Maybe one of these days soon our family will expand even more."

When Kenneth came into the waiting room in his hospital gown and with his shoes and head covered with a tissue-like material, Jenna knew that Lynn's delivery had gone better than the last time. Kenneth's happy and proud look confirmed it. The grayness the nurse mentioned could not be seen. He looked ecstatic and took Kelly into his arms and beamed at the others.

"My son has arrived! Little Nathan is napping. Lynn is tired and on the verge of going to sleep, too. But first she wants to see her daddy."

Before going to see his daughter, Charles patted Kenneth on the back and pumped his arm as thought he was trying to get water from an old-time outdoor watering system. "Congratulations, son," Charles said. "Can Jenna go with me?"

"Sure. But the nurse said you should only stay a minute." To the others he said, "I hope you understand that she's not ready for visitors tonight."

"Don't worry, Kenneth," Rosie said, "I understand why I shouldn't go in right now." She saw Jenna's surprised expression and added, "I get carried away when one of my babies is in the hospital. I cry too much. I'll see her when she can handle my tears. But, Kenneth, can we get a little peek at Nathan?"

"I'll go see," Kenneth answered and left the room. In a matter of minutes he returned and led them to the nursery window. "While you're oohing and aahing over the prettiest baby in the nursery, I'm going to call and see how my sister is doing."

Behind the large pane of glass stood a nurse handing to Charles the baby wrapped in a blue blanket. He turned and with the bundle tucked in the crook of his arm moved closer to the window.

Nathan kept on sleeping. Delicate lashes fanned his peach-colored skin. Strands of brown hair stuck out from around the edges of his green cap. Comments, oohs, and aahs erupted from the little group on the other side of the window.

Jenna pulled out her camera and began taking pictures of Charles and his new grandson. She snapped three shots of them before taking pictures of the group at the window. "Charles, you stay here as long as they'll let you. I'm going out to join the troop."

Watching Charles kiss and smile at the baby, Jenna thought they both looked so adorable. Jenna wanted more than anything to take the lovable man in her arms. Her love for Charles has grown more since she first acknowledged the way she felt about him. Her chest swelled with love and pride, threatening to cut off each breath. She lowered the camera and stared at the nursery scene.

An unusual expression must have filled her face because Charles looked puzzled.

"Jenna," he mouthed. "Are you okay?"

She nodded and gave him the thumbs up sign.

CHAPTER 16

"Wake up, Jenna," Charles whispered.

She straightened up in the car seat. "Where am I?"

"In my car."

She looked toward the back seat. "Where's Rosie?"

"She rode home with Chuck and Debbie. Remember?"

Jenna looked embarrassed but Charles could not see the redness of her face in the dark. "I'm so sorry that I fell asleep, and it was not from boredom as it used to be with Stuart and his friends. It was because I was so comfortable. Still that's no excuse."

He squeezed her hand. "Don't think anymore about it. I accept it as a compliment that you trust me enough to know you're in good hands."

"I do trust you in every way," she said softly.

He kissed her hand, turned into her driveway and turned off the switch. "Well, you're home safely," he said, and rubbed her cheek with the barest of touches. When he got out of the car to go around and open her door, she looked from him to her cottage. Her haven and shelter from the storms.

All of a sudden the house was not as small as it used to seem. Now it appeared too big. With Debbie away at work or out with Chuck, the quietness left her feeling lonely and lost many times. Jenna knew there would be even more lonesome days ahead when Debbie went back to college.

During the past couple days; she considered spending time doing more constructive things. When she was not at meetings or working, she could paint from early morning until lunch time and then clean the yard or house until late evening. She could even beg for extra work at the office. She just dreaded the thought of living the rest of her life by herself. Even though Stuart was terrible to her with his abusive tongue she could rely on another body being around the house at times. It was good and bad. Jenna shook her head. She was becoming a basket case to even consider Stuart's presence as being good, especially when she expected the next words out of his mouth would be something damaging to her ego.

When Charles opened the car door on her side and held out his hand to her, she continued to sit there and stare at him for a minute. When she was sure that the man standing guard over her was not Stuart, she reached out to Charles and let him assist her up to the porch.

While she unlocked the door, a wave of despair and self-pity swept through her. She flung herself at Charles. He instinctively wrapped his arms around her, surprise evident in his voice when he asked, "What's wrong, Jenna?"

She smiled, but it was a sad look. "Oh, I was just thinking how lucky you are to have such a great family."

Charles placed a finger under her chin and raised her face up. "I consider you part of my family, too," he said quietly. "For years you've been like a mother to my children."

"But I'm not a relative," she said softly.

"We can remedy that," he said in an equally soft voice. "I love you."

Jenna moved back, trying to free herself from Charles. "Don't say that," she said, shaking her head. "You don't mean it. You're only dishing out more of the McAdams charm, and I don't need it."

"Listen to me, Jenna," he said reaching out to draw her back into his arms. "I do love you. You may have doubts about me being faithful because of Stuart. I understand them to a point, but I'm not Stuart. I'm nothing like him. I can't image any man with a beautiful, loving and caring woman in his life would ever think of turning to another woman."

"You don't know me really," Jenna said. "I have bad dreams and talk in my sleep. Evidently I roll and toss a lot because nearly every morning my bed clothes are in a ball."

He chuckled and said, "That's because of not feeling secure. I believe that one of these days you'll feel confident enough in yourself and with me that you'll be able to sleep through the night without any nightmares." He kissed her forehead and added, "About yourself now, you are an exciting woman, fun to be with, and a great listener. You've never appeared bored by ramblings about my mischievous children, and yours, too for that matter."

"That's what I'm talking about. See, you have a wonderful family to make your days on earth happy."

"Did you not hear me include your daughter with my mischief makers? What's yours is mine and vice versa, so far, where children are concerned."

"True," she said and chuckled.

"Jenna, since we've been seeing each other, granted it's been a short time, but it seems longer. My life hasn't been the least bit dull or lifeless. I hope it will stay that way. You must believe me; I would never intentionally put you through any grief again."

Jenna opened her mouth to tell Charles she believed him, but he stopped her. "Don't say anything now." He pulled her close in his arms and rested his chin on her head. "I'm going to Florida for a few days. While I'm away, think about all this love bottled up inside me. I want to let it spill over onto you. I want us to share the rest of our lives together. Honestly, I am not pouring on the charm. This comes from my heart."

Jenna heard sincerity in his voice and believed what he said he truly felt. When she tried to tell him this he would not let her speak. "I'm going to Florida to wrap up another case. When I return on Friday, my sweet Jenna, we are going to a place where we can get in a corner to eat and talk without being interrupted. I don't care how many people are here and how much food is on the table, we are not going to let anyone delay our discussion. I want to talk about your feelings and our future."

"Okay," she murmured.

He gave her a kiss and left. On his way home he detoured and went by the hospital to see his daughter and grandson before leaving town.

Just in case she was asleep, he stuck his head around the door and whispered, "Lynn, are you awake?"

"Daddy!" she exclaimed. "Come in." She propped up in the hospital bed with a smile of pure joy.

To Charles she looked like a child herself as she cradled Nathan and nuzzled his face. "Can you handle something else cuddly and lovable?" he asked.

"What?" she asked her eyes bright with interest.

He pushed the door wide revealing a big brown teddy bear that he was hiding. "I'll swap this for Nathan."

"No swapping. I want both." Laying the bear close to her side she added, "This is great, Daddy. I know it will be a while, but I can't wait to see Nathan snuggle up to this bear in his own bed."

"Kenneth will be glad when you both are at home," Charles said, making himself comfortable at the foot of her bed. "You've bagged yourself a good man."

"I know. Kenneth is a great husband and father." She smiled tenderly at Charles. "You are also a great father and would make a wonderful husband if given the chance."

He did not comment but asked instead, "Have you heard anything about Kenneth's sister? Has she had her baby?"

Lynn frowned. "Oh yes. She had no more gotten to the hospital than out popped Little Robert. She's had four babies and each one's been a breeze."

"But she can't love them anymore than you love yours," Charles said, "just like I've always loved mine."

"We all know it, too. Since you're here so late tonight, I gather you've got important business to take care of for McAdams and Son early in the morning or you're about to leave on a long trip tonight."

Charles pinched her big toe. "I'm leaving for Florida in about thirty minutes. I wouldn't be going out of town right now for any other reason than business. I've got a new grandson needing his old granddad's attention."

Lynn put Nathan in the bassinette beside her bed and reached for her daddy's hand. "I know you love every member of your family, but I believe you also have feelings for someone else. Am I right?"

He grinned. "You could say that."

"You haven't said much about your relationship with Jenna. How's it going?"

Charles squeezed her hand and then did a thorough examination of her finger nails before finally mumbling, "It's going."

Lynn jerked her hand from his clasp, thumped her pillow, and flopped down. With a heavy sigh she said, "It didn't work, did it? And after all our careful planning…I don't understand why not. You two are suited for each other."

With a suspicious gleam, Charles eyed his youngest child. "What didn't work?" he asked softly.

Lynn gulped. "Nothing in particular. I was just thinking out loud."

"You said something significant, though. What's been going on? Have you and Chuck been matchmaking?"

Lynn opened her mouth and closed it again with a snap. She sighed, looked adoringly at her daddy for a long moment, and then confessed. "It was primarily Deb and I. Chuck helped some."

When Charles rolled his eyes and looked upward she said, "We thought, and still think that you and Jenna are perfect for each other." She looked a bit contrite before apologizing. "I'm sorry if we messed up your life in any way."

Charles sighed. "You didn't. I fell in love all by myself."

"Hallelujah! Whether you want to admit it or not, I know you've wanted to marry again. You're not the kind of man to live alone. You need someone to cherish and adore."

"You're right, little matchmaker. I do and not just to anyone. It has to be Jenna or no one."

"Well, get on with it, Dad," Lynn advised. "Here you have the woman practically falling into your lap. Granted, we kids helped put her there, but what's the problem?"

Charles ran a hand over his hair. "I don't know how she feels about me. I don't know if she will trust me not to leave her when she needs me most. She built a protective wall around herself when Stuart nearly destroyed her with his abuse and then with his affair. I imagine she's afraid the next man in her life will be bad for her, too."

"I see what you mean, but I believe you still have to try to convince her otherwise."

"I intend to, but..." He stood and began pacing the floor. "I could see how defensive she was the first time we went out. I decided to be Mr. Macho and try to break down her wall. Instead, my wall tumbled and left me vulnerable to love. When I told Jenna tonight that I love her, it may have been too early."

Lynn leaned forward with her eyes wide open. "What did she say when you told her?"

Charles stopped his pacing, shook his head, and said, "Not a lot. She accused me of pouring on the McAdams charm."

"You do use it a lot when it's not necessary." Lynn fell back on the pile of pillows behind her. "Did you try to make Jenna see that you were serious?"

Charles looked like a defeated man and spoke sharply, "Of course I did. I meant what I said."

Lynn drew back. "You don't have to take your frustration out on me."

He gave her an apologetic look. "I'm sorry, honey, but I'm anxious about this. She's the only woman, other than your mother, that I've ever loved. I'm afraid Jenna doesn't take me seriously."

"Well, that's what you get for flirting and being such a great charmer to every woman you meet."

"Not everyone," he defended, "just with those whom I need their help."

"How do you think Jenna feels about you? Surely you've gotten some reaction from her by now."

Charles walked over to the opposite wall. While staring at a photograph of the hospital, he said, "I think her feelings go beyond friendship. She might even love me, but I don't believe she will ever admit it for fear of being hurt again."

With a show of impatience, Lynn asked, "Don't you think the thing to have done was to have made an outright proposal to see where it got you? Daddy, are we going to have to do that, too?"

"No you're not!" Charles answered with a snap in his voice. "But it will have to wait until next week." He raked a shaky hand through his hair and spoke in a softer tone. "I'll miss Jenna like crazy. I don't like being far from her for one minute. I want us to spend the rest of our lives together. The thought of her turning me down is nearly driving me crazy."

"I'm sure everything will work out the way we want it to," Lynn assured him. "I've asked God to make it happen."

Charles' lips twisted sideways. "Maybe God will grant your request for no other reason than to get you out of his hair. I don't know why I was blessed with such nosy, interfering, and bossy children."

"Because God loves you and knows what's best for you."

Charles nodded. "I know He does," he said and leaned over to kiss her on the forehead. Without another word he turned and left the room.

Friday came too soon for Jenna. She had not quite finished her project. She stood in her workroom looking with worry at the clock on the wall. All week the hands had flown around the dial. While trying to beat the clock, she worked furiously on her painting. Each time she took a break, her thoughts were centered on Charles. She could hardly wait to see him. She had so much to tell him.

It was early morning now and her painting was still not completely done. It needed some touch up work before she would be satisfied with it. She was getting there, though. Dressed in jeans and an old paint-stained shirt, she sat down once more to add a few details. She added a little more color to the girls' hair and gave a tweak of the brush to the ends of a few leaves.

An hour later, she stretched backward to ease the tension in her back and shoulders. To be absolutely convinced that nothing else should be added, she gave the painting one last examination, viewing it from every angle. A rush of excitement filled her. "It's done," she said in a breathless sounding voice. "I can't wait for John Paul to see it. I believe it's the best thing I've ever done." Leaning forward, she signed her name and then wrote "Divine Intervention".

She also wanted Charles to see it. *I hope he will love it as much as I do.*

He called her yesterday afternoon and said that he was just crossing the border of Florida. "I can't wait to see you, Jenna."

"I want to see you as soon as possible. I have something to show you," she said, and almost told him about the painting but held back. She felt there was more he wanted to say and did not want to interrupt him. When he did speak he sounded like someone who was afraid of the outcome to a confrontation. "About our last meeting…have you thought about anything that I said?"

The sound of his voice woke up the butterflies in her stomach. She wished he was pulling into the driveway now so she could show him the painting and get his opinion. On the other hand she did not know if their meeting would be a good one. His voice sounded too reserved, not like someone in love. Was he having regrets about declaring his feelings for her? Or could something else be wrong? Perhaps Charles was just concerned about her feelings for him. That's it, she declared. I better put him at ease.

"I've thought of hardly anything else. I can't wait to see you."

Charles must have heard the sob she tried to cover. "Are you crying?"

"Yes. I have a tendency to weep when I'm happy as well as when I'm sad."

She had cried over the loss of her marriage, but Charles brought joy to her life. The tears she had shed after Charles professed his love were a mixture then of sadness and happiness. His words had left her speechless and weepy. She believed that his feelings for her were sincere, and she also felt deep down in her heart that it was love. But was it the forever kind?

Jenna believed she was in most of his thoughts just he was in hers. His next words confirmed it.

"I can't get you out of my head. I talk about you to anyone who will listen, mainly God. I go to sleep telling Him how much you mean to me and I wake up thanking Him for giving me another chance to see you.

I do care more for you than I would have ever thought possible. Jenna, take good care of yourself. It would kill me if something bad happened to you."

"Drive carefully, Charles. We'll soon be together."

With one of the biggest smiles that ever stretched across Jenna's face she went to get cleaned up. Dressed in a dark gold-colored shirtwaist dress with purple and yellow flowers, Jenna fastened her hair up into a French twist. She topped the simple hairdo with a tan straw hat, trimmed with a band and a bow in the same material as the dress.

Excitement bubbled within, but Jenna quenched the flow of enthusiasm from going down into her legs. She could not afford to be careless and stepped along the path with extreme caution to protect the painting in her hands.

All morning her emotions had swung back and forth like a pendulum. They moved from nerve wrecking anxiety to a rip-roaring frenzy. The expectancy of Charles' arrival and his reaction to what she planned to tell him caused a feeling of turmoil to wreak havoc in her stomach.

Two facts remained constant with Jenna Wilson: she loved Charles McAdams with all of her heart, and she missed him like crazy. But neither of those facts were topics on which she based her nervousness. No, the subject at hand was whether or not John Paul Montague would like her painting well enough to put in his gallery.

The morning after Charles said he loved her, Jenna headed for her workroom with a spring in her steps. She had a lot to do in a short time. It was crucial that she get the occupants in this scene just right. Whether she continued to paint anymore portraits depended on the outcome of this particular piece of work.

She wondered how Charles would react when he saw it. He should like it, she thought, because she felt it was the best she had ever done, and he was my inspiration. Charles may not realize that he influences my work, but after he sees Divine Intervention he should know how important he is to me.

After leaving The Stafford House, the drive went slowly due to heavy traffic. Jenna glanced at her watch every little bit. Pointed hands inched around the dial toward five o'clock. Charles was supposed to be at her house by six. By the looks of the traffic Jenna would not be there to greet him. It worried her that Charles may think that she did not want to see him as badly as she claimed.

She knew if he thought that he would be hurt, so she tried to drive faster. But not being able to move but half-a-car length at a time, her speed was hampered. Jenna drummed impatiently on the steering wheel. After a minute or two she slapped the wheel and begged, "Come on cars, move it!"

While sitting still, her mind went back to her meeting with John Paul. She arrived at the restaurant/gallery and got her painting into his hands without incident. The meeting went great, better than she dared to hope, but not at first. His long, thin face stayed focused on the painting for what seemed like an eternity to Jenna. The only movement she detected was a slight rising of his eyebrows.

He's going to reject it, she thought. It's not good enough to hang in his gallery.

She prepared herself for the biggest disappointment in her painting career but prayed for God's help anyway. *Please intervene God. Make him accept it.*

John Paul carefully propped the painting on an easel. He turned toward Jenna with a look of genuine delight. His next words nearly made her flip. "I love it. Forgive me, Jenna, for being so slow with my reaction, but I was so overwhelmed I couldn't speak."

"You honestly like it?" she asked, her eyebrows nearly up to her hairline. "I was so afraid that you were disappointed with it."

"No, my dear. It's very good. Aren't you pleased with it?"

Her head bobbed. "I think it's the best thing I've ever dome. I thought of bringing another painting, but something happened to it. That's a long story. From the beginning of this one I've felt good about it. Before I ever started making sketches I prayed over it, asking God's blessings. With each phase of the preparation and then the actual painting, I felt in my heart that Divine Intervention would be exceptional."

The traffic began to move and Jenna came back to her surroundings, but John Paul's last words swam in her head. "I have a feeling this won't be here very long. You had better come up with another painting pretty soon."

To say she walked on cloud nine described Jenna's reaction in a mild way. When she left the gallery, she fairly danced in the parking lot as she made her way back to the van. To a couple coming toward her and grinning at her reactions, she asked, "Can you tell I'm happy? I'm so very happy. One of my paintings is hanging in the gallery. When you go upstairs, look for the one signed by Jenna Wilson."

She finally got into her van and drove off. When the traffic began to slow her progress on the highway, it also slowed her excitement, but her heartbeats were rapid for another reason. She was not going to be home when Charles arrived.

I better get Debbie to leave him a note or stay at home until he arrives. I hope Charles won't be upset.

At the next exit she turned off and pulled into a rest area. Instead of making the call right away, she went to the rest room. The hamburger she had eaten earlier must have been bad. Her stomach pain was unbearable.

In haste she dropped her pocketbook on the floor when she sat down. Drawn nearly double she saw a hand stretch forth from the next stall. Before she could react, her pocketbook was pulled to the other side out or her reach.

"Hey!" Jenna shouted. "Put that back over here."

The only response she heard was the sound of the outer door slamming shut. When Jenna finally got her clothes in order, she went out to an empty room. She ran outside the building and saw her van racing out of the parking lot and onto the highway. Not another car or person was in sight. What now?

All the security guards seemed to have vanished. How was she going to get help? The thief had taken her identification, all her money, her cell phone, and the jacket inside the van. She needed it now to ward off the chilly air. To stop some of her shaking, she wrapped her arms around her body and held tightly to each arm. She did not know if she shook now from the cool air or anger.

She stomped her foot and wrung her hands. How stupid of me to carelessly drop my pocketbook where someone could get it, she thought. Maybe I don't have the sense to come in out of the rain. The thought reminded her of Stuart and her stomach knotted with pain again, not from the bad meat she had eaten but from her loss of more property.

The longer she stood there with her hands curled into fists at her sides, the angrier she got. She paced the entranceway, glancing at the phone every little bit, willing it to ring. She ran over and poked her finger into the refund hole. Not one coin lay in the slot.

Emotions slammed against her mind in a brutal attack. She wanted someone to show up, but then again she was afraid that someone would. Last week, a television news reporter said that a woman was raped at a rest area. The location slipped her mind. It may have been this one, she thought, and without a friend or a gun for protection, it could happen to me.

The outer doors open. Girls came in giggling and running to the restroom. Jenna wanted to approach them for help, but they ignored her and kept chattering to each other. With her eyes wide open and her hands shaking, she kept watch for someone who looked sympathetic and possibly helpful.

Back at her house, people there kept watching the front door, hoping she would come through it at any minute.

The grandfather clock struck seven times. Charles frowned with each bong. Chuck kept giving Debbie anxious looks as she twisted the table napkins into knots.

"Something terrible must have happened to Mom," she said. "It's unusual for her not to telephone when she's going to be delayed, and she's not answering her cell phone."

Chuck's brows drew together, looking like a blond streak across his tanned face. "She may be in serious trouble," he whispered to his father.

Debbie realized the men were worried, too. Before she exploded and began crying, she tried to rein in her emotions to convince them and herself that everything would be all right. "Mom knows how to look after herself when she's on the road. She drives like the van's her weapon and doesn't feel intimidated by other drivers. We'll hear from her soon."

Chuck responded with "If you say so."

"I do," she said and bopped him on the arm.

"Ouch. I'm going to have you up for abuse."

With a serious look Debbie said, "Just be thankful that I didn't abuse you with my tongue by calling you baby or wimpy."

With an apologetic look he said, "Me and my big mouth. I'm sorry."

"I know and I shouldn't have said what I did." She looked from Chuck to Charles and said, "I want you to know that I really appreciate you both for staying with me. Mom will be even more appreciative when she hears about it. To know that you are concerned about her well being and not degrading her will make a world of difference. If Dad was here he'd be saying things like, 'It deserves her right for running off and not leaving a note as to where she was going.' Or 'She's such a dumb broad she's probably lost.' That would be completely off the mark. Just because she has trouble with math doesn't mean she can't follow directions. She's a whiz with recipes, games, and trips. You can tell her one time how to get to a store or warehouse and she'll go straight to it. She's not lost. Something has happened to delay her or she would have been here when you arrived, Charles. I know for a fact that she's was looking forward to your homecoming."

Chuck snickered. "There was one time when she got lost."

Debbie looked puzzled.

"Don't you remember the mystery game we played with her called Who Murdered the Preacher?"

Debbie gave a dawning look. "Oh, yeah, the one that Tina's friends staged for us in Winston-Salem. You had simple directions to get to the hotel where the staged performance took place but gave Mom a completely different route to its location. After about fifteen minutes she gave up the goose chase and pulled into a service station. 'I have a feeling that Chuck doesn't want us to get there,' she said, 'but I'm going to get better directions from a local.' In a matter of minutes we were pulling into the parking lot of the Lawrence Joel Coliseum where the crime was to be solved."

Chuck gave a mischievous grin and said, "When you two came in, I thought Jenna was going to kill me, and then with a sly look she said, 'Thought you'd pull a fast one over me didn't you? Okay, Smarty Pants, since you don't seem to have all the clues, I'm going to get them.' She tossed a confident smile and walked off."

Charles asked, "Who solved the case?"

"Jenna did of course," Chuck answered. "I don't know for sure, but I believe she bribed one of the team members to help her."

Debbie gasped. "Chuck McAdams you know better than that. Mom always played fair. She was just smarter than we were."

Charles' smile looked forced when he joined Chuck at the kitchen table. "I hope Jenna isn't lost, hurt or in trouble of any kind now."

Debbie served the guys a cup of coffee, but neither one drank more than a swallow. They were more interested in the hands on the clock that crept around the dial. Debbie could not sit still; she paced from the side door to the front door. By 8:00 p.m. she was fit to be tied. Her hands went up in the air. "I don't know what to do. If only I knew where to reach Mom I would call her. Charles, how long was it before you were notified of Francine's accident?"

He frowned. "Within the hour," he said and pulled out his cell phone. "Chuck, you call the hospital, I'll call the police station."

Chuck shook his head at his father and mouthed, "Nothing", so Charles pressured the officer on duty to help him. "I know it's not been twenty-four hours, but something has happened to Jenna or she would have called her daughter." In a milder tone he added, "As a special favor, I'd appreciate if you would send out a couple men to look for her. You will? Thanks, Sergeant Martin. I owe you one."

An hour later, two policemen that Charles knew arrived at Jenna's door. One of them was carrying a large tan pocketbook.

"It looks like Mom's," Debbie said, reaching a hand toward it. She shook so much she could hardly open it without spilling the contents. The first thing she saw was the compact she had given to Jenna for Christmas. The next thing was a picture of her and Jenna on an amusement park ride. Another picture showed Tina, Chuck, Lynn, and Debbie, making faces at the camera. "It's hers all right," she whispered.

Officer Hawkins then said, "I need you to come with me for identification."

"Why? What's happened?" Debbie asked, and grabbed hold of Chuck's hand.

"A blue van belonging to one Jenna Wilson wrecked near Asheville. I'm sorry to tell you, but the only person in the van is dead."

Debbie swayed and clutched Chuck's shirt.

"Hang on, honey," he said. "You don't have to go alone. Dad and I are going with you."

The three marched like zombies into the morgue. Wedged between the men, Debbie could not fall.

"In Jesus name please don't let it be mother," she prayed aloud.

"Amen," both men echoed.

Their prayers were answered.

"Darryl, can't you see the woman's blond?" Charles asked the policeman. "Didn't you look at the picture of Jenna's driver's license? She's redheaded."

"Some women change the color of their hair as often as they change clothes," the officer responded.

Charles nodded. "You're right." He expelled a relieved sigh. "I'm thankful though that it's not our Jenna."

While Debbie was hugging Chuck, Charles stared down at the woman on the slab. "Chuck, who does this look like?"

Chuck took another look and then asked, "Isn't that Josh Harrington's wife?"

"It is." To the officer Charles explained who the woman was and gave some information about her husband. I would like to go with you to see Mr. Harrington.

They left the morgue, relieved that it was not Jenna in there. But where was she?

Back at the house Charles said, "We've still got to find Jenna. Chuck, you go south and I'll head north. Debbie you man the phone. We'll call you every fifteen minutes."

Before they split up they all went into the house to check for phone messages.

The recorder was empty.

CHAPTER 17

Jenna came to the conclusion that she was stranded, and her heart began to beat fast. Within seconds it felt as if it might fly right out of her chest. She had no way to travel, no money to call home, and she was hungry. She had not eaten since breakfast. She was in quite a predicament.

People began coming through the doors. Jenna rushed to meet them. They pushed right past her, not giving her a second look. Everyone acted like she was invisible or contagious.

Tension built up stronger as one after another shunned her, but she was determined to get help. She kept approaching the women. "Hi, my name is Jenna Wilson," she began…I'm sorry to bother you, but could you lend me a quarter? I need…"

No one listened to her. If they did not walk by without speaking, they made rude comments. One woman asked, "Did your pimp forget to pick you up?"

Another one asked, "Why don't you make a deal with one of those men over there? You could get twenty-five bucks in a heartbeat."

Their remarks made Jenna more wary about approaching men for help, especially the gray haired man with a long beard standing by the door. He looked at her with such a penetrating gaze that Jenna felt like locking herself in one of the bathroom stalls. Her heart beat so hard she thought she was having a heart attack. She avoided further eye contact and strode to a vacant corner seat in the lounge area. There she hunched over and tried to make herself smaller.

She silently prayed. *Father in Heaven, I beg of you to get me out of this place. If it's your will, Lord, please let me know that you're with me. The Bible says you won't forsake me when I need you. God, I need you like I've never needed you before.*

Some of last Sunday's sermon came to mind. The preacher had said that if you trust God, he is willing to provide. Jenna trusted God. Now. When she first found out about Stuart and Sheila, she did not trust anybody, not even God. About two months ago she regained a trust in Him. She believed that he would never let her down. Even though Jenna believed that God would never desert her, right now she could not see a way out of this predicament.

A shadow fell over the spot in front of Jenna. She looked up to see the bearded man standing there. Her eyes flew open wide. All she could think was: *What's he going to do to me?*

But she was quickly put at ease by the calming sound of his voice and his words when he said, "Don't be afraid of me, missy. I'm here to help you."

She could not believe that this man, a total stranger wanted to help her when no one else bothered to give her a word of encouragement. What did he expect in return?

Jenna did not respond in words but stared into his silvery blue eyes. The longer she looked, the more they fascinated her. A soft glow in them sent out waves of calmness and filled her with peace. A gentle lift of his lips caused his whole face to fill with radiance.

With temptation riding on her shoulder, Jenna felt like throwing caution to the wind and asking for a lift home, but she held back. Instead, she asked, "What kind of help can you give me?"

"You want to get home, right?" At her nod he added, "I can help you get there."

He looked kind and spoke with a gentle yet firm voice. Tension completely eased from Jenna's body. "I need to call someone to come get me," she said, and explained about her pocketbook and van being stolen. "Would you lend me a quarter for the pay phone?"

"I've already called the highway patrol and reported that you have a problem and need help. Someone should be here to take care of you shortly."

Jenna smiled, lighting up her eyes. "Thank you so much," she said, offering her hand. When he did not shake her hand but turned and started across the room she called out, "Sir, wait."

With a slight turn of his head he said, "Yes?"

She walked toward him saying, "My name is Jenna Wilson, what's yours?"

"Knowing my name is unimportant," he said, and left with Jenna staring at him with a puzzled expression. She stepped forward to follow him but at that moment a bunch of teenagers came in, blocking her way. When they raced into the rest rooms, Jenna finally looked out the door. She could no longer see the old man. He was gone.

She shook her head, thinking, He has not been here at all. It was all a dream. I still don't have a way home.

Her slender thread of hope broke and filled her with despair, again. Jenna tried to pray but her words seemed to go no higher than the top of her head. Anger welled up within her. If she could get her hands on the woman who stole her pocketbook, she would make her wish that she had never looked at it much less stolen it.

Sometime later Jenna was trying to ease out of her cramped position where she had sat hunched over too long. Her back was in pain now. Just what she needed: more problems and no medication.

Still staring at the floor, Jenna saw a pair of shiny black shoes step into her line of vision and stop. She followed a path from the shoes up and over a muscular body covered in a neat uniform to a friendly face. His appearance made Jenna's heart leap with excitement, but she quenched the feeling.

After the last encounter she refused to get excited over seeing another possible way of getting home. She figured this man was an illusion, part of a dream. Even when the officer called her by name she refused to respond.

"You are Jenna Wilson aren't you?" he asked.

At her nod he showed her his identification. "Don't be afraid of me. I'm here to take you home."

He looked like all the other highway patrolmen that she saw cruising the county roads. But it really did not mean much until she realized he was well known in this area. Some of the people passing in and out of the building called him by name. Maybe she could trust him. *God, please help me to make a connection where I'll feel like this man is real and safe.*

Trooper Redman offered to help her to stand. She latched onto his hand and eased into a standing position. With a look of amazement she asked, "You are really here for me, to take me home?"

"Yes, mam. A man called and described you in detail." His eyes twinkled when he added, "He said I'd have no trouble finding the beautiful redhead with the face of an angel."

Again the room began to fill with people coming and going. Some spoke to the officer while others looked at them with open curiosity.

Go, Jenna, she urged herself. *Ignore the inquisitive people and walk away with dignity.*

She willed her legs to carry her forward. When the car door swung shut behind her, they began to move. The car and its movement felt real, not part of another dream. From the backseat, she leaned forward and gave the patrolman her address. "Did you see an elderly man with a long gray beard out front when you came in?"

"Yes," the officer answered. "He told me he was waiting to make sure someone came for you."

Jenna's face filled with awe. "That was nice of him."

Trooper Redman asked questions relating to her theft until they stopped in front of her house. It looked like her place, but was it actually there. Should she get out of the car? Would her feet touch the ground or would her body have an ethereal quality about it? She was still unsure that this was not a dream. With the officer holding her door open and smiling down at her she had no choice but to get out of the car.

"As soon as I get all the facts pertaining to your theft, I'll contact you," he said, getting back into the patrol car.

She knocked on his window. "Excuse me, sir. Did the man at the rest stop give you his name?"

"Oh, I nearly forgot," he said, pulling a piece of paper from his shirt pocket. Maybe it's in this note he said to give you."

He had no more than backed out into the road when the front door of the house burst open and Debbie came running out. "Mama!" Her hug was so tight that Jenna had to squirm to get free so she could breathe.

Charles stepped forward. "Darling, I've never been so glad to see you."

Jenna stood rooted to the spot, looking from one person to the other. Charles called her darling, and now with tears in his eyes Chuck was hugging her.

Her eyes were filled with questions. The main one was: *What's happened here that's thrown them into such a tizzy?*

"Mom, say something," Debbie said. "We've been worried to death about you?"

"Why have you been so worried? I had some problems. It was an unbelievable experience. When Chuck laid an arm across her shoulders she asked, "Are you real or am I dreaming?"

"Before you arrived, it was a nightmare," he answered. "I can assure you this is no dream. Don't I feel real? You feel real to me." He turned to Debbie and asked, "Wouldn't you say she's not a ghost?"

"I was afraid if Mom ever came back home she would be here as a ghost," Debbie responded and hugged Jenna again. "I'm so happy that you're alive and walking around down here."

Shaking her head, Jenna said, "You won't believe what I've been through. I can hardly believe it. Let's go inside, and I'll tell you all about it."

Seated on the couch, she proceeded to tell them about her visit to the cemetery and then her stop at the rest area where her pocketbook and van were stolen. "I can tell you one thing, I was so angry. If I could have gotten my hands on the woman that snatched my pocketbook she wouldn't be alive now to steal another one."

Debbie looked at Charles. He cleared his throat and said, "She won't be able to steal anything ever again."

Jenna frowned. "What do you mean?"

"She's dead. We thought it was you. We've been through a trying ordeal, too."

"Dead? Me? Why?"

Charles wrapped his arms around her and spoke in a strained voice. "Sergeant Brown of the local police department brought your pocketbook here. It was found in your crashed van, along with a dead woman. We didn't know that the van had been stolen, so we naturally assumed that the body was yours. I can't tell you how I felt. I thought I would never have another opportunity to convince you that I love you."

Jenna took his face in her hands and kissed him. "I'm sorry for your grief, but it wasn't my fault."

"No one's blaming you," Chuck said, "but going to identify the body, thinking it was you, was probably the worst thing I've ever done. I've been to the morgue numerous times to see if the corpse was someone on our missing persons list. Today was a totally different experience."

"Mom, please tell us everything," Debbie said.

"When I came out of the restroom, I realized that I was completely alone. There was not even a car in sight, and the guard must have gone home for supper." Her stomach growled. "I was so hungry myself that I'd have given my shoes for a pack of nabs from the snack machine. I then forgot about being hungry when I recalled a news report last week about women being raped at rest areas. I was afraid that the next man who came in would attack me."

"Oh, Mom, I wish I'd been with you."

Jenna chuckled and said, "So you could have worried along with me. From then on, every man that came in made me feel anxious, that was until this one man showed me some kindness. He was different from anyone I'd ever seen. He was the exception. There was something strange about him, too. He was there one moment, gone the next. I thought he and his offer of help to get me home were all part of a dream.

A while after he disappeared, a highway patrolman showed up. He called me by name and said he would take me home. I thought he was part of my dream, too, until you guys came out of the house."

"Believe me, Jenna, you are living in reality," Charles said, "even the moment I felt sorry for the dead woman was real. And like you, I got very angry at her when we learned what she had done to you."

"How did you know? Why didn't you come get me?"

"I had just gotten off the phone with Sergeant Brown who had spoken with the woman's husband and learned what had happened to you when the patrol car pulled into the driveway."

"Who was the woman?" Jenna asked.

"Casey Harrington, wife of Josh Harrington, a local bum," Chuck answered. "He makes his living sponging off people. He'll do anything for a buck."

Jenna nodded. "I know the couple."

"How?" Debbie asked in amazement.

"Josh brought Casey to the doctor's office several times for follow up visits after her foot surgery. Each time, Josh would ask someone in the office about washing windows or our cars. I felt sorry for them and let him wash my van one time."

"Don't let him do anything for money again," Debbie said, "He's the reason his wife's dead and you were stranded."

Jenna looked puzzled. "What are you talking about?"

"They were nearing the entrance to the cemetery when you pulled out. As they followed you they discussed getting back at you for not believing him when he said he knew where your painting was. What was that all about?" Debbie asked.

"He wanted a large sum of money for information," Jenna answered, brushing that part of the conversation aside. "That's another story."

"That incident evidently made him mad," Charles said, "but he had no idea Casey had gotten as angry as she did until she came running out of the rest area with your pocketbook. She gave Josh some of your money and told him to go to the store for some bread and wine and she would go on home in your van."

"But she didn't make it," Jenna said in a soft voice.

"No," Charles answered. "She ran off the road and hit a tree."

Tears filled Jenna's eyes. "Poor woman. What a way to die." She wiped her tears and looked around for the piece of paper the officer had given to her.

"What are you looking for?" Debbie asked.

At Jenna's foot lay the wadded piece of notepaper. She opened it and smoothed out the wrinkles as best she could. "The old man who helped get me home left this with the patrolman."

Debbie went to look over her shoulder. "What does it say?"

"I hope it contains his name and address so I can send him a thank-you card, but...listen to this. 'The true reward for kindness lies not in the thanks you get but in the memory it leaves in your mind.' Isn't that beautiful? There's no name. I guess I'll never know who he is."

"I believe he's your guarding angel," Charles said. "Let's thank God for getting you home."

CHAPTER 18

Jenna and Debbie were having breakfast when a man in a brown uniform arrived. "A registered letter for Mrs. Jenna Wilson," he said and offered a paper for her to sign.

To Jenna's surprise it bore the name: The Stafford House. She ripped open the envelope, hoping it was good news. One glance at the type written message revealed an answer to her prayer. Someone wanted her painting and enclosed was a check for an exorbitant sum.

She read aloud the note. "Divine Intervention drew many favorable comments. I know several people who want to buy it. You can see by the check that this one particular customer is most anxious to have it. Please let me know if you accept the sale. It's signed, John Paul."

"That's wonderful," Debbie said.

"Can you believe it?" Jenna said, making an expansive gesture with both arms. "You know what this means? I can repay Charles and not have the burden of his loan hanging over my head.

"Slow down, Mom," Debbie said. "What painting are you talking about?"

"The one I took to The Stafford House the day of my robbery."

"Oh yes. With my concern for your safety, I forgot to ask which painting you took for John Paul to see."

"I completed a new painting, Divine Intervention. It wasn't quite dry, but I wanted John Paul to see it right away. And I was too impatient to wait until you got off work so you could go with me." She held up the check. "For this reason I'm glad I went, even if I had to face some trials. John Paul was pleased with it. I gather that someone else likes it a lot, judging by this letter and check. Isn't it wonderful?"

"It might be as wonderful to me if I knew more about the picture," Debbie answered.

"I have Charles dressed in jeans and a knit shirt, sitting in his yard, surrounded by a mass of flowering bushes. In his arms is little Nathan; Kelly is leaning against his leg, looking at the baby. To the side sits a wheelbarrow, a rake, and a pair of gloves. The look on Charles' face seems to say, 'This is divine. Thank you, Lord, for intervening and giving me a break from work.' I think it's the best painting I've ever done."

Debbie smiled. "It sounds wonderful. I want to see it. Maybe you should wait awhile before you commit to selling it. Does Charles know about it?"

Jenna shook her head and sighed. "I haven't had the opportunity to tell him. I wish you hadn't said to wait. I know what I want to do with the money. I suppose I should tell John Paul to hold off on selling it for the moment."

"Good idea," Debbie said. "You don't have to make a split second decision. Someone else might be willing to pay a lot more for it." She watched the interesting expressions flicker across her mother's face. First there was disappointment, then surprise, and finally relief.

"You're right," Jenna acknowledged. "I would like for you, Charles, and Chuck to see it. It's not as if I have to pay back his loan this very moment. After I call John Paul, I suppose I should tell Charles about the painting."

Debbie laid a hand on her mother's arm. "Let me make the calls." Her eyes flickered with mischievous delight. "Let the painting be a complete surprise for Charles. I'll see if he and Chuck can meet us at The Stafford House, if so, you can let them ease up to it as we walk around." Debbie clapped her hands and added, "I do love pulling surprises."

Jenna laughed and said, "I know."

Debbie's expression grew serious. "I won't this evening to be a special occasion in your honor; the painting of course but for having you home safe and sound. After your ordeal at the rest area, I want to make every occasion a special event."

With a watery-eyed look, Jenna inhaled and started to speak but Debbie continued, "I'm going to call the McAdams men. If they agree to have dinner with us, I'll call The Stafford House and make a reservation."

Jenna went to put the check in her desk drawer, leaving Debbie alone to make her calls. A few minutes later Debbie came dancing into the den. "They will be here at six o'clock. I hope you don't mind, but I talked to John Paul, too. He answered the phone. I told him you weren't ready to accept the check yet, that you wanted some friends to see the painting first. He said that he wouldn't let it go until you gave him the word."

"Thank you. I'm afraid if I had spoken to him I probably would have told him to close the deal."

Debbie took her dishes to the sink, saying, "Mom, you worry too much. I've got to go. It's almost work time. If you must dwell on something, let it be about tonight. Consider what you're going to wear, who you'll be with, and what's in store for Charles."

Before going into the restaurant, Debbie said she wanted to see the gallery first, so they all went upstairs. Jenna spotted her painting sitting on an easel where it was accessible to the eye as soon as you walked through the door. She lagged behind the others, pretending a great interest in other paintings. Out of the corner of her eye, she saw the trio stop in front of hers. She then turned to see their reaction. A strange silence surrounded them.

Chuck spoke first. "Dad, it's you and the kids."

Without seeming to move a muscle he answered, "I see, and we didn't even pose for the picture."

His calm response bothered Jenna. She thought he would have sounded more enthusiastic. She hoped he would anyway. She edged up a little closer to the group, hoping to hear something positive from Charles.

But it was Chuck who turned toward her and said, "Good job, Jenna." To Charles he said, "Dad that would look great over the mantle in our Living Room."

Charles still did not comment.

Jenna wished he would show some expression. *Maybe I should have asked him before doing the painting, the thought. He's probably upset because I didn't. What should I do about it now? Should I remove it?*

Charles finally took his eyes from the painting and acknowledged Jenna. He motioned for her to come closer. She slowly moved forward and he took her by the hand. "I had no idea you were going to do a painting with me in it. It's wonderful," he said, kissing her cheek. "I guess all those pictures you took in the garden and at the hospital really did have something to do with this."

At her nod he added, "I thought Debbie was making a joke when she said some day I might see my face staring back at me. It didn't register with me that I would actually be one of your subjects."

Jenna gave Charles a smile designed to weaken his self-control turn his knees to jelly. It must have worked, because he sat down on the nearest bench and looked from her to the painting, back and forth several times. The tenderness in his eyes was all Jenna needed to make her go over and sit down beside him. She loved the look of wonder and awe in his expression and wished she could pull out some paint supplies or a camera and capture that look.

No one existed but the two of them until Chuck cleared his throat and Debbie spoke.

"Mom, the painting is great; it's better than Peaceful Existence or anything else you've done." She gave Jenna a big hug and then turned to Charles. "Would you believe that the painting is already sold?"

"Sold?" The abrupt and sharply spoken word caused Charles' companions to stare at him when he rose to his feet. Jenna could see the muscles of his jaw clenching. When he spoke again his tone was gruff. "Who bought it?"

"A customer I guess," Jenna answered in a soft voice.

"This morning, Mom received a registered letter and a check from John Paul," Debbie explained. "She immediately made plans for the money."

"It was a gift from God," Jenna said, "to repay your loan."

Charles looked upset. "Repay me? What's the rush, Jenna? Are you trying to break all ties with me and get me out of your life?"

Jenna shook her head. "No. I don't want you out of my life. I would feel better, though, if I didn't owe you the money. I don't like having big debts." Her look challenged him to make something bad out of her wanting to be debt free.

Crosscurrents swirled around them.

Jenna laid a hand on Charles' arm. "Please try to understand how important this is for me."

"I do," he finally said. "Wait here a minute. I'll be right back." He returned shortly without giving them an explanation for his hasty exit. He just took Jenna's hand and started toward the stairs. Over his shoulder he told Chuck they were leaving. "You and Debbie go ahead and eat. Jenna and I will eat later. Right now we've got something to discuss."

Once they were seated in his car, Charles asked, "Your house or mine?"

"Mine," Jenna answered. If she did not like the way he acted she could throw him out. If they were at his place it would be a long walk home because, again, she was without her pocketbook and a vehicle.

Both Jenna and Charles were quiet all the way to her house. She did not know whether to apologize for the painting, to ask him what was wrong, or to keep her mouth shut. She knew that once she opened it a million questions would pour out.

When there were in sight of her cottage, Jenna sighed with relief. Charles gave her a quick look but said nothing. She hoped they would talk without a lot of tension and strain. She wanted him in a good mood when she told him she loved him. She hoped and prayed that Charles believed her. "God, please take control."

By the time he walked around the car to help her out, his smile made him look more approachable. His expression had softened when he took her arm with a tender touch.

She left him standing in the middle of the den and went to check the answering machine. With Charles watching her every move she felt as graceful as a klutz. She could not look his way when she stumbled over the throw rug in front of a chair. She knew he would be laughing or trying to hide a snicker so she refused to look at him until she checked the telephone. She then turned to face him and presented a twisted smile.

"Okay," she said, "go ahead and get it over with."

"Get what over with?" he asked with an innocent look.

"Laugh at my clumsiness."

He grinned and said, "As tempting as it is, I'm not going to laugh at you." He pulled his hands from his pants pockets, took hold of her shoulders, and looked lovingly into her eyes.

Jenna smiled sweetly, loving the way his brown eyes turned to dark pools of chocolate when he was emotionally involved.

Without another word, they went into each other's arms. He cuddled her head against his chest. Jenna knew without a shadow of a doubt what she was about to say was the right thing. Of course her heart pounded fast and almost as hard as when she got stranded at the rest area. The rhythm was almost as intense as the night she caught Stuart in bed with Sheila. This time, though, the pounding came from happiness. She stood on tiptoe and kissed the scar on his neck.

He leaned back and asked, "Why did you do that?"

"Because it reminds me that we all have scars. Some will fade as I suspect this will do in time, but others stay with us forever. If you can love me with the scars left from Stuart's abuse and infidelity, I can certainly love you with yours made by a stranger."

He took her face in his hands and asked, "Jenna, you're sure?"

"I'm sure."

When he opened his mouth to speak, she said, "Let me finish. I want to talk. Few people at the rest area would let me complete a sentence, much less let me explain my predicament. I'm determined to say what's on my mind now."

"Okay," Charles said. "Let's sit down first."

She turned to face him on the couch. "I know I seem like an air head to some people. When I focus hard on projects, I tune out everything around me. I forget appointments and time. I thought with Stuart being an artist he would have understood and accepted my behavior. At times he pretended to, but it was all for show."

"He really didn't know how to appreciate you. Then again, it may have been because he wasn't the dedicated artist you are."

Jenna nodded and said, "You could be right on both counts. I'll never know his real reason for the way he treated me, but I've learned something about myself: that it's wrong to let one thing take over your life to the exclusion of everything else, especially people. I'm not saying it won't ever happen again. I'm saying that I see what happened to some extent that it's probably what made Stuart seek someone else for company."

"He didn't have to do that. He should have talked to you, worked something out. He was just a plain fool."

Jenna cupped his hand and raised it to her cheek. "Thanks for saying that, but I hope and pray that I'll have my priorities in order from now on. Do you think you could help set me straight when I slip?"

"Darling, if you marry me, I will help set you on the straight and narrow road to anywhere you want to go. Truthfully, you don't need help from any mortal man. There's absolutely nothing I would change about you, even if I could. I love you as you are. Please say you'll marry me." His lips brushed hers.

"Do you promise to pick me up when I stumble?"

"I'll not only pick you up, but I'll carry you anywhere you want to go. I hope you know that the work situation goes both ways. I told you before how I've worked around the clock on cases. I know now that the importance of solving some of them was not as imperative as I thought at the time. If you will remind me that I have capable employees to help carry the load, I'll try not to get bogged down with work."

Jenna snuggled close in his arms. "I believe I can help you with that."

He nuzzled her ear. "There's nothing we can't handle together as long as we love each other and seek God's help in directing our lives day by day. Now, are you going to marry me?"

"Yes!"

"When?"

"Is September too soon?" she asked.

"That's a month away. Tomorrow would suit me better."

"I don't think so," Jenna responded, trying to look stern but failing. "There are so many things to do first. We have to get the license, a place to have the ceremony; something to wear…the list goes on."

"My darling, Jenna, you can wear that beautiful green dress you wore the first time we went to The Stafford House. Any of the other outfits you own will work or go buy something new. As I told Chuck, you would look good in a feed sack."

Jenna jerked up straight and said happily, "That's what I'll wear, a flowered feed sack." She flipped her hair over one shoulder and began separating it into three parts. "I'll even plait my hair and go barefooted. What do you think?"

"Perfect. I'll get some bibbed overalls and a pair of brogans. We'll do it up right with a hoedown."

They laughed and then Jenna's expression sobered. "Where did you disappear to at the gallery? Did it have something to do with my painting?"

Charles nodded and his smile grew wide. He looked like a kid with a cone of chocolate ice cream. "I love that painting. You made me look like a loving and caring grandpa. I am one of course, but you did wonders with me and the kids."

Jenna hugged him. "Thank you. I feel it's the best thing I've ever done."

His thumb rubbed the back of her neck. "Then why do you want to sell it?"

"You know. I don't want to feel obligated to you."

Charles gave her a smug look. "You don't have to, now or ever. Since you're going to be my wife you won't have to pay me back. I can take care of all your needs."

Jenna's eyes lit up. She grasped the meaning of the dream she had after their first date. Charles had asked God to let him be the one to help carry her burdens. *It will soon be a reality,* she thought and rubbed the hairs standing up on her arm.

"Jenna, my love," Charles' voice broke through her musings.

"Hmm?"

"Neither will you have to think about your painting being in the hands of a stranger. You won't have to part with Divine Intervention again."

Her eyes opened about as wide as her mouth. "Did you...tell me...where is it?"

"It's still at the gallery. I'll pick it up later. I gave John Paul a bigger check than the one he sent you, but I agreed to leave the painting there until after the art show he's having for the October Fest. Is that okay with you?"

"Okay? Maybe it will draw some commissions for other paintings. It's wonderful! I'm delighted. Thrilled. Overwhelmed. Ecstatic. Excited. Shall I go on?"

"Not at this particular moment. If you don't mind I'd prefer to hold you and think about our future." While wrapping his arms around her he said to himself, *I love to see Jenna gloriously happy. Thank you, God, for bringing her to me. I wonder if I should thank the kids for their part in bringing us together.*

Jenna looked up into Charles' face. "I know I talk a lot, especially when I'm happy. I wanted my red-gold rhododendron to win first place by the beautification society, if it had I'd been thrilled, but I wouldn't have been this excited. I love being near you and would be happy if you'd hold me forever." Jenna offered a silent prayer: *I want to always make this man happy. Thank you, God, for sending Charles into my life. Perhaps I should thank the kids for their part in matchmaking.*

"Lynn?" Debbie said quietly into the receiver of her cell phone. "Get your wedding dress ready. Chuck and I came into the house just in time to hear Mom accept Charles' proposal.

"Don't you think an outdoor wedding at your father's house would be super? It would be The place for God to bless their marriage before family and friends."